IRL: IN REAL LIFE

AN AFTER OSCAR NOVEL

LUCY LENNOX

MOLLY MADDOX

Cover Art by: Cate Ashwood at Cate Ashwood Designs

Cover Photo: Eric Battershell Eric Battershell Photography

Beta Reading by: Leslie Copeland at LesCourt Author Services

Editing by: Sandra at One Love Editing

ACKNOWLEDGEMENTS

We'd like to thank the following:

Leslie Copeland, Sloane Kennedy, Shay Haude, and Chad Williams for invaluable beta feedback.

Diana Peterfreund for the cosplay help.

Cate Ashwood for fast, talented design work.

Eric Battershell and Johnny Kane for a stunning cover photo.

Sandra Dee for speedy, thorough editing.

Our husbands for their general aptitude in all things geek and gamey. Gamery. Whatever. You've spent decades in the gaming chair for a reason, and we applaud you for your diligence.

Our parents for raising us to be readers and for bragging about us to all their friends. And, finally, our Other Sister. Yes, there's a third sister, and our friends always ask "do you mean the author sister or the other one?" Sorry, Jen. If it's any consolation, you're more than The Other Sister to us. If the pressure to write "like your sisters" ever becomes too much, just let us know. We'll put you in charge of the sex scenes since you're the only one of us who took anatomy.

Lucy's Dedication:
For Molly.
I would have never taken the leap had it not been for one sunny day spent with you in the pool talking about writing to the id. You told me to write with the door closed, be indulgent, write what I wanted to read.
So I did.

Molly's Dedication:
For Lucy.
I know it's weird to dedicate this book to you since you co-wrote it and all, but this series wouldn't exist without you and I've loved every minute working on it together! See, I told you that one day you'd appreciate the fact that I tried to mimic you in all ways growing up, white Gap t-shirt and all.

1

CONOR

I'd never sent a dick pic before.

Correction, I'd never *intentionally* sent one. I did accidentally one time send my best friend a pic of my inner thigh with a *tiny* slice of cock shaft in the corner, but that was because I didn't realize the camera was open on my phone while I was quickly changing for my after-school job at Taco Bell. It had happened over ten years ago, but the asshat still brought it up whenever it was convenient.

It was frequently convenient.

But this time was intentional. Or, as intentional as you can be when you've had four Sex on the Beaches... Sexes on the Beach... hmm... too many *somethings* and are horny and hard in a hotel room hundreds of miles from home with nothing else better to do.

An hour earlier, as I'd been in the hotel bar drinking my nerves away about an upcoming business presentation, I'd gotten hit on by the bartender. The man was cute but young. A little on the skinny side, but he had a gorgeous smile. Every time he'd smiled in my direction, I'd felt my face ignite and had to look away. Unfortunately, I also had to throw back the rest of my drink and ask for another to quell my nerves. When the bill eventually came, so did his phone number.

After paying my tab and pocketing the number with an embarrassed nod, I'd run away. And spent the next forty-five minutes stroking myself to fantasies of sex with a stranger and trying to talk myself into doing something crazy for once. *Hmm.*

Click.

There. Anonymous dick pic. Sent.

I felt a thrill of nervous excitement. I'd actually done it. Actually hit Send. I let out an adrenaline-fueled laugh in the empty hotel room at my unusual boldness and grinned at the image on my phone. That wasn't just a dick. It was a fabulous phallus. Tall and proud. Robust, really. Good light, healthy coloring... As long as I didn't go back to that hotel bar all week and see the guy in person again, I was golden. I'd done it. I'd come to New York and gone a little wild.

Then the second thoughts started crowding in.

I should not have had that much to drink. I've never sent a dick pic before, much less to a stranger.

212-555-0160: *And how much was that?*

I blinked at my phone. Had I texted my thoughts...? Ah, yup. Seemed I had. My thoughts had gone right through my fingers and into the text message screen. Fuck.

Should I respond? Why the hell not? It's not like I was going to see him again unless I went back to that bar.

I began typing.

Conor: *Dude, don't you remember? I was nervous about tomorrow's big presentation? You're the one who served them to me.*

There were a few beats of nothing before the response came.

212-555-0160: *Did I? I don't think so.*

I did a double take at the screen. He had though. The bartender had been the only one working. And he'd been the one to slide his phone number across the bar on a sticky note.

Before I had a chance to argue with him, he texted again.

212-555-0160: *I'm still at work, but I certainly appreciate the eye candy you sent.*

My head was fuddled from the alcohol. Of course he was still at work. I'd left him down there only an hour before, too chickenshit to take him up on his wink and offer of a late-night visit to my room.

Conor: *I changed my mind. Come to my hotel room.*

I blinked, surprised at how easily I'd sent that invitation. Then a slow panic began to boil in my stomach. What if he actually took me up on it? Shit, I'd never had an anonymous one-night stand. It wasn't my style. And as much as I'd used the excuse of being a little tipsy to send the dick pic, I was sober enough to know that sex with a stranger was definitely outside of my comfort zone.

212-555-0160: *Hm, now that's a compelling offer, sexy, but I don't know you. And it's late.*

So weird. That hadn't been a problem only an hour before. Even though my overwhelming feeling was relief he wouldn't be knocking on my door anytime soon, I still felt like whining. Just messaging someone a dick pic had gotten me all hot and bothered.

Conor: *But I want to get off.*

That didn't sound pathetic. Did it?

Conor: *You don't have to know me. Hell, you don't even have to come to my room. Just tell me something sexy.*

A part of my brain couldn't believe the words coming out of my fingers. But sending the photo had made me feel bold—demanding in a way I'd never felt comfortable being when I was face-to-face with a man.

Conor: *Tell me what you'd do to me if you were here.*

My cheeks burned with a blush, and my breathing came faster. I watched the screen, but there was nothing. I felt an odd sense of disappointment coil in my chest.

Conor: *Please?*

I added the please out of... good manners. And not at all because I wanted to prod him into responding. It would be mortifying to put myself out there so thoroughly only to be rejected.

There was a pause. I held my breath, waiting.

212-555-0160: *How badly do you want it?*

I shuddered, my cock jumping at the words. I stared at the phone and heard a slight whimper from somewhere nearby.

Conor: *So fucking badly.*

Another pause and I found myself whispering *please please please* under my breath. Suddenly there was nothing more that I wanted than this. To hear what this man would do to me if he were here, standing at the end of the bed, me splayed naked in front of him.

212-555-0160: *How many drinks did you have?*

Why was he asking me that again?

Conor: *Four? I think?*

212-555-0160: *Drink a glass of water and go to sleep. You said you have an important day ahead.*

The bottom fell out of my stomach. Rejected.

Conor: *My last drink was over an hour ago. I'm sober.*

212-555-0160: *That's not what you said earlier.*

Shit. He was right. But that had just been an excuse for sending the dick pic.

Conor: *Sober enough for sexting.*

212-555-0160: *Baby, if I'm going to tell you what to do, I want you 100% focused on me and my instructions. No confusion or second guessing in the morning.*

I let out a groan. God, the thought of him telling me what to do made me even harder. The tip of my cock glistened with precum. While a part of me appreciated that he didn't want to take advantage of me, suddenly I wanted nothing more. It made me feel a little cheeky.

Conor: *Maybe I'll just take matters into my own hands then, and go to bed.*

I smirked at my response.
His answer was immediate.

212-555-0160: *No.*

My eyes flared wide, my balls tightening. Before I could formulate a response, three dots appeared on the screen.

212-555-0160: *In three hours you should be sober. If you're still interested then, you may contact me and ask me politely if I will help you out with your little problem.*

I barked out a laugh.

Conor: *Demanding, aren't you?*

212-555-0160: *Yes. You'd do best to keep that in mind if you decide to text me again. Good night.*

I stared at my phone. My cock still throbbed in my hand. I tightened my fingers, sliding my fist down, the sexy bartender's words swimming in my head. I stroked again, harder, wondering if I'd have the balls to reach out to him in three hours. Knowing I probably wouldn't.

I arched my back against the bed, picturing the sexy bartender kneeling over me, telling me what to do. How to hold myself. How hard to stroke. How fast.

I could feel my climax coiling inside me, my body vibrating with the need for release.

Right as I was about to tip over the edge, my phone dinged, startling me.

212-555-0160: *Oh, and no touching yourself. If you come tonight, it will be at my discretion.*

My jaw dropped. The gall of this man! Before I even realized it, though, my body complied, fingers instantly releasing myself as though I'd been caught doing something I shouldn't. My cock strained, so close to coming. All it would take is another stroke, maybe two. But I couldn't move. My hand remained still. My breath came fast, my entire body flushed, my balls tight and aching.

Just do it, I told myself. *Come and pass out and be done with this.* I had an important presentation in the morning; the last thing I needed was to stay up all night sexting a stranger.

Except my body refused to listen.

"Fuck," I groaned. I rolled onto my stomach, shoving my face into my pillow and groaning in frustration. I may or may not have humped the mattress once before forcing myself to lie still. Then I reached for my phone and set my alarm.

THREE HOURS later I was awake, hard, and entirely sober. I sat on the bed, cradling my phone in my hands, staring at the screen. I'd typed out a dozen different messages and deleted them all. I kept second-guessing myself. I wanted to sound interested but not desperate. Sexy but not pathetic. Maybe sophisticated, like this was something I'd done a million times before.

My phone buzzed. It was from him.

212-555-0160: *You going to press send or just keep typing and deleting?*

I glanced up sharply, scanning the hotel room for hidden cameras.

Conor: *How did you know?*

212-555-0160: *I've watched the three dots appearing and disappearing from my screen for the last half hour.*

So much for coming across as sophisticated and worldly.

Conor: *Oh.*

212-555-0160: *Sobriety have you second guessing?*

Conor: *No.*

If anything, it was the opposite of that. I wanted it too much but didn't know how to tell him that.

212-555-0160: *Why the hesitation?*

I squirmed. But then I figured why not be honest? It's not like I had to see this guy again. I was already planning to avoid the hotel bar for the rest of my trip.

Conor: *Would it surprise you to learn I've never done this before?*

212-555-0160: *You've never sexted before?*

I felt my face flush.

Conor: *Well, no, not really. But I meant I've never... uh... had someone tell me what to do.*

212-555-0160: *Ah. I see. Does it interest you?*

I stared down at my throbbing cock. Really I should just send him another dick pic—it would be all the evidence he'd need. But the confidence I'd felt before with the fortification of a few drinks was gone, and sobriety had made me revert to my usual timidity.

I closed my eyes. *Take the risk*, I told myself. It wasn't even that much of a risk—I'd never even given the bartender my name. This would just be anonymous sexting. A onetime thing—a way to blow off sexual frustration and try something new.

I blew out a breath.

Conor: *Yes.*

212-555-0160: *Yes what?*

I blushed as I typed out my answer.

Conor: *Yes, giving up control does interest me.*

212-555-0160: *How far do you want to take this? Because if you truly want to give me control right now, the appropriate response is Yes, Sir.*

I cringed. Already I'd screwed up.

Conor: *Oh, right. Ok. Sorry.*

There was a long pause where he said nothing, and I wondered if he'd changed his mind or I'd said something wrong. I skimmed back over the last few exchanges and realized my error.

Conor: *I mean, yes, Sir.*

212-555-0160: *Better. Are you naked?*

The question made me dizzy as even more blood rushed south. I glanced down at myself. I'd shucked off my jeans and underwear earlier but still wore my shirt.

Conor: *Mostly.*

212-555-0160: *Take everything off and get on the bed. Do it now.*

My dick stood up straight and eager like the proudest soldier in the battalion. I guess someone liked being bossed around.

Conor: *Yes, Sir.*

Sending the text caused the muscles in my abdomen to flex with desire. My fingers flew over the buttons of my shirt as I yanked it off and tossed it into the corner. I lay in the center of the king-sized bed like an offering.

Conor: *Done.*

212-555-0160: *Prove it.*

Oh god. Precum slithered out of my tip and down the underside of my cock. I squeezed my eyes closed and took a calming breath before holding the phone on my chest and opening the camera app. The shot managed to get my sternum down to my navel, my ridiculously interested cock, and the hairy muscles of my thighs before ending on my bare feet. The first pic I took had the corner of my discarded underwear in it. Not sexy. So I flicked them off the bed and tried again.

Better.

I sent it over.

212-555-0160: *Stroke your cock. Imagine it's my hand tightening around you.*

More whimpering noises from somewhere. Someone in this hotel room sure was desperate.

I was about to type out *yes sir* when I had another idea.

Conor: *Send me a pic of your hand so I know what I'm supposed to be imagining.*

212-555-0160: *I don't think you understand who gets to make the rules here.*

I cringed, wondering if I'd broken some sort of unwritten rule. It wasn't like I had a lot of experience with this. I didn't like the idea of disappointing him and was about to type out an apology when he texted again.

212-555-0160: *But since this is new to you, I will accommodate you.*

A picture flashed on my screen. It was of the stranger's hand, resting on something solid and wooden, probably the bar. I'd never spent much time imagining another man's hand, I'd just never considered it to be the sexiest part of a man's body. But this man's hands... I couldn't believe I hadn't noticed them earlier down at the bar. They were glorious. With long fingers that looked lean and strong and a wide palm that narrowed to a bare wrist dusted with dark hair. His shirt was rolled up, the white edge of one cuff just visible at the edge, the muscles of his forearm straining underneath.

My mouth went dry, my own fingers trembling in anticipation as I typed out, *Thank you.* I felt a thrill in my chest as I added the word *Sir.*

I set my phone next to me and grasped my dick, closing my eyes as I imagined the bartender's hand tightening around my length. His thumb drawing circles around the precum-slicked slit.

212-555-0160: *How does that feel?*

Conor: *Amazing.*

212-555-0160: *Show me. Send me a picture.*

I snapped a photo of my hand grasping my dick. It wasn't until it was sending that I realized my toes were curled in the shot. Oh well. It felt fucking amazing. I kept stroking up and down, enjoying the feel of my tight hand and the cool sheets against my back.

212-555-0160: *You have a gorgeous cock. If I were there I'm afraid I wouldn't be able to keep my mouth off it.*

I groaned, imagining the wash of his breath against the length of my shaft. His tongue tracing the ridge of my head. The wet heat of his mouth enveloping me.

212-555-0160: *Would you like that?*

God I wanted nothing more. I was getting close, my jaw clenched and muscles tight with the need for release. It was torture to release my cock in order to type a response.

Conor: *Yes, Sir.*

212-555-0160: *Good. Now on your knees, hands on your thighs.*

I stared at the message. Part of me felt like ignoring it. My hand felt awfully good just like this. I didn't want to stop stroking myself. Except I was already responding. Already moving.

Conor: *Where?*

212-555-0160: *On the bed is fine.*

I let out a trembling breath, shifting into position.

Conor: *Yes, sir.*

212-555-0160: *Lean forward, your face on the mattress. Ass in the air. Lick your finger.*

I shuddered. I knew where this was going and suddenly felt oddly vulnerable. Kneeling like this on the bed, my ass exposed.

212-555-0160: *Do it now.*

Mother of god.

Conor: *Yes, Sir.*

Every time I typed the words a thrill jolted through me.

212-555-0160: *What's your name?*

The question threw me. It was so unexpected that I'd automatically started giving him my real name when I caught myself. What was I thinking? I'd already sent the man a dick pic; no way I was giving him my real name. I could see the headlines now: "Idiot Conor Newell Texts Compromising Photo to Hotel Barkeep."

I was taking too long to answer. My eye caught the label on my Samsonite suitcase.

Conor: *Sam.*

212-555-0160: *I'll pretend you didn't just lie to me.*

I cringed, wondering if he was disappointed in me. The thought left a bad taste in my mouth. I wanted to apologize, which made me even more confused. He was a stranger. This was an anonymous one-night stand—emphasis on the anonymous aspect. So why did I care what he thought about me?

Before I could untangle my thoughts and figure out how to respond, he texted again.

212-555-0160: *Touch your hole with your wet finger. NotSam.*

My heart thundered in my chest as I reached my hand toward my ass and did what he asked. How the fuck did that skinny bastard have the ability to light my every damned nerve ending on fire?

The minute I pressed my finger against the sensitive skin at my entrance, I dropped the phone and went for it. One hand stroked my dick while the other teased my hole. It wasn't anything different than I did at home in the dark, but knowing *he* knew it was happening made it hotter than hell.

212-555-0160: *Are you imagining it's me behind you, NotSam? My cock pushing against your entrance? Sliding into your ass? Is that what you want right now?*

It was too much. The thought of the stranger's hands on my hips, his long fingers pressing into my flesh as he held me in place and fucked me sent me spiraling. Ignoring the phone in favor of chasing this feeling, I pumped harder, imagining it was his hand circling my cock, squeezing tight as he drove me over the edge. With my face pressed against the mattress, I shouted out my release, warm fluid shooting up across the bedding and all over my hand. I fucked myself with my finger until all the aftershocks had ended.

I collapsed onto my side, gasping for air, my body spent.

Before I could stop myself, I took a photo of my cum-soaked hand and chest and sent it before reaching for the tissues.

Conor: *OMG. That was amazing.*

There was a long pause. Long enough that I wondered if he'd gotten bored and wandered away. I started to regret sending him the picture of my climax, but then three dots appeared on the screen.

212-555-0160: *You ever come again without my permission, and I'll redden your ass.*

The mental image of his promise caused my spent cock to twitch. Then I realized the implication of his text: that what we'd done might happen again. That there might be a next time. I smiled at the thought that I'd pleased him enough to want more. Even though I knew it wasn't going to happen.

Conor: *Yes Sir.*

I felt my eyelids growing heavy, the late evening and flush of orgasm cocooning around me and dragging me toward sleep. My phone buzzed and it took effort to pry my eyes open.

212-555-0160: *How did you like your first experience of being told what to do?*

I smiled, feeling sleepy and warm and safe.

Conor: *I liked it very much. Thank you.*

212-555-0160: *Good. You will text in the morning to check in and tell me how you're doing. Before and after your presentation.*

I blinked, sure I couldn't have read that right. He'd remembered I had a presentation in the morning and he wanted to hear from me again? Was it possible he actually cared about me? That this wasn't just a one-night stand for him?

My mind raced, my heart pounding as I tried to figure out how I felt about that. Was I interested in him? Did I want more? Then the second half of his text came through and my thoughts came to a screeching halt.

212-555-0160: *Giving up control can be an intense experience and not everyone handles it well the next day.*

Oh, right. That was part of it. I shook my head, blushing at the thought that the stranger had actually been interested in more from me.

Conor: *I'll be okay.*

212-555-0160: *It wasn't a request, NotSam.*

My chest squeezed at his words.

Conor: *Yes sir.*

212-555-0160: *Good. You did well and deserve some rest. Get some sleep and good luck with your presentation tomorrow.*

My phone buzzed, and a new image popped up on the bright

screen. There, in its thick, stiff, and multi-inched glory, was the hottest dick pic of all.

My own cock made a valiant effort to stand up and cheer for the unexpected visual gift, but exhaustion won over, and I drifted to sleep.

It didn't occur to me until the next morning when I was appreciating the late-night photo again, that the stranger's dick wasn't surrounded by the denim jeans the hotel bar employee had been wearing. It was surrounded by fine black suit pants and the tails of a white, button-down oxford shirt. And in the corner of the frame was a glimpse of rich, burled mahogany wood like the kind you'd see in an executive's office. The shirtsleeves were rolled up to the elbow, exposing the tanned, muscular forearms of a completely different man than the skinny bartender.

Horror washed over me as I realized the implications of this discovery.

Who the fuck had I been texting?

2

WELLS

For the millionth time, I caught myself reading through the unexpected sexy texts from earlier in the night and forced myself to put my phone facedown on the desk. My forty-second-floor corner office was dark and still this late at night. The lights of the city twinkled outside both walls of windows, but inside was lit only by the soft glow of two side table lamps. I'd turned off all the other lights when "Sam" had stopped responding. I'd assumed he'd dropped the phone to chase his orgasm, and the thought of him jacking that pretty dick and fingerfucking his own ass had been enough to get me hard as nails.

I'd flicked off most of the lights and taken my own cock out, snapping a quick pic as a quid pro quo for the guy who had me so unexpectedly turned on.

Even though I didn't know what his face looked like, I knew what the tight buds of his nipples looked like, the soft curve of his belly under a trail of dark hair, the ruddy, swollen cock slick and shiny from precum at the tip. I imagined running my tongue over all of it.

I thought of him kneeling on the bed, his ass up, his face pressed against the mattress as he looked back at me. I imagined teasing him with my cock, running the head of it around the edge of his entrance. Pushing against it softly, slowly.

I wondered what he would sound like as I started easing my way inside him. Would he gasp? Whimper? Bite his lip?

Would he maybe press back against me, hungry for more?

Just that thought had me shuddering, heat flushing through me, gathering at the base of my cock. I clenched my teeth, throwing my head back. Wanting to roar with pleasure. Wishing I were in that hotel room, pouring myself into my sexy stranger's ass.

My fingers tightened, as if it was his cock I was squeezing rather than my own. I growled out a "Fuck," as warm fluid spilled over my knuckles, down across the back of my hand, and onto my suit pants. Then I sat there panting, staring at the evidence of my pleasure. Surprised at how fast I'd come.

I glanced at the door and cursed under my breath. It wasn't even locked. And while I was certainly the only one still at the office this late at night, it wasn't like me to forget something so basic. Usually I exercised much better control over myself, especially when it came to sex.

But the stranger's text had taken me by surprise and caught me off guard. I'd spent the last several days preparing for a critical meeting scheduled for the following morning, and I was exhausted and stretched thin. Plus it had been an abnormally long time since I'd had any sort of sexual encounter.

Normally I'd take a break and spend a few hours exorcising my sexual frustration, but I'd parted ways with my regular sex partner several months before and had yet to find someone to take his place. And it wasn't like I was the type to pick up a stranger from a club and take him home. I was a man with certain preferences when it came to my lovers: I liked them obedient—willing to cede control to me at times. I didn't require full-on BDSM; I wasn't into a total power exchange or whips and chains, though if that was something they liked, I was always willing to give it a try.

But I was a man who liked to be in charge. I liked to take care of my partners. To provide for them. To know they were safe. And with that came a possessiveness over my partners that could too often be mistaken for emotional attachment. Even though I was up-front with every man I entered into a sexual relationship with that it would never lead to more, invariably they began making demands of me.

Demands I couldn't fulfill.

That had been the problem with my last partner: he'd wanted more.

He'd wanted something I couldn't give him: promises. Commitment. Emotion. Even, eventually, love.

The moment I'd realized he wanted more, I'd ended it. In the past, finding a replacement lover had never been difficult. This time, though, nothing had felt right. No one appealed to me. So I'd buried myself in work—in a world where emotions didn't come into play and where I exercised complete control.

That's why my response to the stranger's text had been so surprising. I'd been reckless. Not adhering to my usual need for total control. I didn't know the man's name. Where he was from.

He could have been a rival—a corporate raider tasked with taking me and my business down. I cursed under my breath. Sending him a dick pic had been impulsive and stupid and wholly unlike me. With a testy flick of my wrist, I snapped several tissues from the box on my desk and wiped the evidence of my pleasure from my hands. I then yanked my zipper closed and forced my focus back on work.

Before the random text, I'd been reviewing a background file on the woman I was slated to meet with in the morning. She'd invented a new type of biomedical 3-D printer that used hydrogel and biological material to create critical large human blood vessel prostheses, and my company was aggressively negotiating the purchase of the technology.

There were two components to the process: the printer adaptation itself and the medical materials used as the "ink." Through a clever bit of maneuvering, we'd acquired the rights to the latter the month before. Now I intended to use that as leverage to buy the patents to the former.

Until recently, Dr. Elizabeth Newell, the engineer who'd perfected the mechanics of the printer, had been unwilling to even discuss selling the technology to us. I'd made a reasonable offer and she'd refused. She still hadn't accepted that now that Grange BioMed owned the rights to the "ink," either she sold us the printer technology or her invention was useless.

It put my company in an excellent bargaining position. She had no choice but to sell, and at a price well below its value. Usually, once a deal reached this point where all the pieces were in place, I stepped aside and let the lawyers take over. But Dr. Newell had been insistent I remain involved. Perhaps she still hoped to win me over with a personal connection. If so, she hadn't done her research. There was a reason my nickname was Glacial Grange.

I got what I wanted. And I didn't make warm fuzzy friends while doing it. For me, emotions didn't enter the equation.

Speaking of getting what I wanted... my eyes drifted back to my phone. I unlocked it and the screen glowed with the photo of NotSam's cock, his hand wet with his release. I wondered if he was already asleep, tucked under the generic white hotel comforter. I felt hungry, for some reason. Unsatisfied.

Not sexually—my body still tingled with the afterglow of my earlier orgasm. But there was still something missing somehow. I zoomed in on the picture, scouring the image for details. The dark trail of hair that snuck down his abdomen to his crotch. The curve of his hip and swell of well-muscled thighs. I noticed a trace of scars across his knuckles and wondered if he'd gotten into fights as a kid.

Heat flared in my chest at the thought of him as a young teen, facing off against a wall of bullies. I ground my teeth, anger seething as my inner desire to protect roared to the surface.

And tonight, I thought to myself. He'd asked a total stranger to his room for sex. That was the kind of thing that could have gotten him sick or hurt or robbed. Before I could stop myself, I found myself typing a message to him, asking him what he was thinking. If he understood how reckless he'd been and admonishing him to take better care of himself.

Thankfully I realized what I was doing and stopped myself before I pressed Send. I stared at the words I'd typed, stunned, before quickly erasing them.

I shook my head, scoffing. Why the hell did I care if someone took advantage of this guy? I didn't. He was a stranger and an adult. Not my responsibility. I forced myself to put the phone down.

I tried returning to work, but thoughts of the anonymous texter kept interrupting until finally I gave up and moved to the sofa to catch a few hours of sleep before the sun rose. I'd spent plenty of nights on the oversized leather piece, and my assistant, Deb, had stashed a pillow and thick blanket in one of the armoire cabinets in the corner of the office for nights like these.

It seemed like I'd barely closed my eyes when I woke to a knock on the office door. "Yeah?" I called out, sitting up and running a hand down my face.

Deb poked her head in. "I figured you'd slept here. Just wanted to let you know it's almost seven. I've ordered you some breakfast. Should be here in twenty. It'll give you enough time to shower and change. There's a clean suit in the closet."

I glanced at her fresh, young face and gave her a smile. "Thanks. Don't know what I'd do without you."

"Starve and go naked at the very least," she said with a wink. "I'll bring you coffee when it's ready."

The moment she closed the door, I rushed to the desk for my phone. I checked my texts before anything else and felt a stab of disappointment. Nothing from NotSam. But had I really expected anything? He'd been drunk. Sure, I'd made sure he was sober when he came, but still, it was easier to be bold in the safe darkness of night. With the sunrise often came regret.

I frowned. I didn't like the thought of him feeling guilt over what we'd done. I thought about texting, checking in. Making sure he was okay. I reasoned it was what I'd do with anyone I slept with. Especially someone I pushed out of their comfort zone like I had with him.

I hadn't realized how long I stood there debating the point until a calendar reminder about the morning's meeting buzzed my phone. I needed to stop thinking about the stranger and focus on work. I made my way to the private bathroom hidden by a discreet panel in one of the interior walls.

I showered quickly, successfully avoiding any thoughts of the stranger until I was standing in front of the sink with a towel wrapped around my waist, getting ready to shave. My cell buzzed with an incoming text and I immediately reached for it, smiling at the familiar name on the screen.

NotSam: *I... I don't really know what to say. I thought you were the bartender from the hotel. I'm so sorry. I don't usually do things like that.*

Ah, so that explained it. My grin grew as I read the words again.

Wells: *How did you realize I wasn't your bartender?*

NotSam: *Your photo. You were wearing a suit.*

My stranger was smart and perceptive. I liked learning that about him.

Wells: *Indeed I was. Were you disappointed?*

The three moving dots flashed on the screen for longer than it should have taken to respond. I found myself frowning. I hadn't expected it to be a difficult question to answer. Finally, the words appeared.

NotSam: *No. It was hot as hell.*

My heart rate kicked up. My throbbing cock starting to thicken.

Wells: *Are you prepared for your presentation today?*

NotSam: *You remembered?*

I smiled. Of course I had. Everything about him had been impossible to forget.

Wells: *I did.*

NotSam: *I'm really nervous. There was supposed to be someone going with me but I just got a text that he'll be late which means I have to do it alone and... I'm just a little overwhelmed. Shouldn't have had the mocha latte at Starbucks. Now I'm jittery too.*

The words surprised me. That he would be so open, so vulnerable, with someone he barely knew. The desire to protect him flared to life in my chest again. I wanted to make it better for him.

Wells: *Where are you?*

NotSam: *Lobby men's room of the building where the presentation is. My hands are shaking, and I feel like I'm going to throw up. The last time I was in New York, I was ten and my church choir visited St. Patricks Cathedral. I ate a hot dog from a street vendor and puked on the ferry. What if I do it again?*

I snorted, but my heart went out to the guy. He needed to get out of his head. I glanced at the time on the screen and saw I still had twenty minutes until my own meeting. What I should have done was wished him luck, put the phone down, and concentrated on shaving and getting ready. But then his next text came through.

NotSam: *God, why did I even send that? You don't care. Sorry. I ramble when I'm nervous.*

I responded without thinking.

Wells: *I do care.*

And I realized it was true. But I didn't want to linger on the thought, so I quickly added:

Wells: *Listen to me. Go into a stall and lock the door.*

While I waited for him to do what I'd asked, I ran my thumb around the head of my cock, letting my fingers dance across the stiffening flesh.

NotSam: *Okay?*

Wells: *Close the toilet seat and sit down. I want you to unzip your pants.*

I imagined him hesitating. I guessed the delay in his response was him trying to decide whether to comply or ask what I had planned for him. I grinned, waiting to see which he'd choose.

NotSam: *Now what?*

My cock jumped at his compliance. It appeared he was a people pleaser, something that made me like him even more. My head exploded with thoughts of all the things I wanted to tell him to do. All the ways I could ask him to touch himself... touch *me*. I wished I knew what he looked like so I could imagine his face flushed with the desire to please me.

Wells: *Stroke your cock. Block everything out of your head except for me. Do what I say.*

I closed my fingers around my own cock as I waited for his response.

NotSam: *Fuck, someone just came in.*

Wells: *Don't stop. Ignore them.*

NotSam: *They can hear me breathing. Fuck.*

I smiled, picturing his discomfort. Knowing that he wouldn't stop because he wouldn't want to disappoint me.

Wells: *Let them hear you. Only listen to me. You feel good NotSam?*

NotSam: *Fuck.*

It wasn't enough. I needed more. I wanted to be in that bathroom with him, standing over him, watching as he pleasured himself for me.

Wells: *Send me a photo. I want to see what my words do to you. Show me your hard cock. Are you leaking for me?*

NotSam: *Stop. I can't keep quiet. Please.*

Despite his protest, a photo flashed on the screen. The sight of him had me throbbing. His erection was ruddy with veins prominent in the light of the bathroom. His balls were drawn up tight, and I could just catch a glimpse of royal blue cotton underwear shoved behind his sac. Sure enough, there was sticky wetness shining on his tip.

God, I wanted to taste it.

Wells: *Remember the rule from last night. No coming until I say so.*

His response was immediate and immensely satisfying.

NotSam: *Please can I come?*

I waited for a beat.

NotSam: *I'm close. So close.*

Wells: *How long until your presentation?*

NotSam: *Presentation?*

I grinned. Clearly my plan to distract him had been effective. Before I could give him permission to come, however, the office phone in my bathroom buzzed. It was Deb. I considered ignoring it, but she would just come knock on the door if I did.

"What is it?" I barked.

"Sorry, I... ah, just wanted to give you a heads-up that security called up to confirm credentials a few minutes ago. Mr. Newell should be here any minute."

My finger hovered over the disconnect to dismiss her, but then her words registered.

"Mr. Newell. I thought it was Dr. Newell?"

"It seems she's sent her son in her place. His name is Conor."

This was an unexpected change. I despised being taken by surprise. Dr. Newell had been the one to insist I be involved in the negotiations. And now she'd decided to bow out? It felt like a ploy. It wasn't going to work.

"Once you seat him in the conference room, wait ten minutes before buzzing me please," I told her.

She hesitated. She knew how important punctuality was to me. But she didn't question the order. "Yes, sir, Mr. Grange," she said before disconnecting.

My cell phone buzzed. I'd missed three texts from NotSam, all of them begging to please come. Another one popped on the screen.

NotSam: *I'm going to be late to my meeting. Please can I come? Please?*

Poor guy—I hadn't intended to make him wait so long. And yet he had anyway.

For me.

My own erection roared back to life at the thought.

Wells: *Come for me, beautiful. Send me a picture afterward so I can see how much you enjoyed yourself.*

I stroked myself, imagining this man somewhere in the city nutting in the stall of a public bathroom while trying desperately not to be heard by people coming and going outside the flimsy door.

A photo appeared on my screen. His cock was thick and glistening, cum still dripping from the tip, trailing over his fingers. I couldn't stop myself from picturing those fingers trailing along my own flesh. Cupping my balls, grasping my cock. Sliding along my flesh.

Never had a fantasy as mundane as a simple hand job gotten me so wound up. It was too much. The thought of my pleasure spilling across his knuckles sent me over the edge, and I ground my teeth to muffle the sound of my orgasm as it shuddered through me.

Afterward, I grasped the edge of the counter, my legs unsteady as I tried to bring my breathing back under control. My phone buzzed with another message.

NotSam: *Thank you.*

I stared at the words, surprised how warm they made me feel. I glanced back at the picture he'd sent, noticing part of his navy blue necktie could be seen from where he'd pushed it aside with his dress shirt. There were little silver Daleks in a repeat pattern across it.

My sexy stranger was a *Dr. Who* geek. Why did that make me smile?

Wells: *You've got this.*

I waited a beat to see if he'd respond. But of course he'd be rushing to his presentation. I had my own meeting to worry about. I caught sight of myself in the mirror and noticed a stupid grin lingering around the corners of my mouth. I might not have minded so much if I hadn't also noticed the thick wash of stubble coating my jaw and chin. I glanced at the time. I had a little over ten minutes before I needed to be ready. I could either shave or do some last-minute research on Dr. Elizabeth Newell's son.

I scowled at my reflection. I'd let myself get distracted by my anonymous texter at the expense of work. It wasn't like me. I ran a brush through my hair, cursing the fact it had already dried enough that the natural wave refused to be tamed, and yanked on my suit pants.

As I buttoned my shirt and put on my tie, I conducted a quick Google search on Conor Newell. I'd vaguely remembered from my biographical research that was the name of Elizabeth Newell's only child, but I didn't recall him being related to her biomedical research.

When the image of the younger Newell came up on my computer screen, I noted how attractive the man was, in a lithe, quiet sort of way. But what was more interesting to me was the career information listed for him.

Conor Newell owned a game store. As in, board games and puzzles.

What the hell was he doing representing an advanced biomedical printer to a group of experts? Were we being played? But that was impossible. We were Dr. Newell's only option. The technology was worthless with the patents to the biomedical ink we already controlled.

When Deb buzzed a moment later to let me know the gamer dude had been waiting a full ten minutes, I stood and straightened my suit.

I never appreciated my peers referring to me as Glacial Grange, but today was one of the days I'd be hard-pressed to deny the truth of the moniker. This kid was going to feel my extreme displeasure at his mother's decision to send in the second string on this one.

3

CONOR

I stood in the men's room stall with sticky ejaculate on my fingers wondering what in the fuck I'd just done. Had I really allowed some random stranger to *sext* me to completion on my way to one of the most important presentations of my life?

My hands shook as I wiped them off with toilet paper and readjusted my clothing. I had to admit I felt a little less harried than before. When I'd entered the imposing skyscraper lobby with its giant glass atrium and serious security counter, I'd been nervous as hell and jacked up on too much caffeine. My attorney friend, James, had just texted me to inform me he'd been held up with another client and would be late to the meeting. The news had left me terrified of having to hold my own against a room full of corporate execs and big-city attorneys.

At least now I felt...

Nope, still nervous as hell. But I couldn't help noticing the tiny smile on my face as I washed my hands in the basin. Hell, I'd had more action in the past twelve hours than I'd had in the previous six months back home in Asheville.

After drying my hands on a couple of paper towels, I smoothed down my good-luck tie and buttoned my suit coat. I could do this. I *would* do this. My mom's entire future was riding on how well I did in this meeting.

No pressure, jackass.

I cleared my throat and reached for the door handle. When I entered the corridor leading back to the elevators, I tried not to notice the high-powered corporate types rushing here and there around me. Everyone looked so professional and put together. I felt like a bumpkin by comparison. Sure, I'd owned my own business for several years, but I'd never had the kind of job where so much money was on the line. And it wasn't just money. My mother's health depended on what happened today.

If I couldn't convince these executives to buy this biomedical printing technology at top dollar, all of my mother's treatment plans might as well be written in disappearing ink.

As I left the vaulted atrium to enter one of the high-speed mirrored elevators, I cleared my throat for what seemed the millionth time. The air in this building was stuffy. I missed the fresh, clean air of the Wolf Branch trail behind my mother's house. The sound of trickling water from the winter-slowed French Broad River wandering past the Blue Ridge Parkway not far away. If I closed my eyes, I could almost replace the ding of each floor whizzing by with the *shirr*ing sound of the dried leaves still clinging to some of the trees deep in the Nantahala Forest.

"Sir?"

I snapped my eyes open to see two women looking at me expectantly.

"Isn't this the floor you wanted?"

"Yeah, yes. Sorry." I flashed an apologetic smile before jumping through the closing doors just in time. When I looked up, three men in suits stood in an elegant lobby staring at me. Even the young female receptionist blinked at me from her spot behind a sleek, brushed metal... launchpad. Well, more likely it was a desk, but there were curves and monitors, buttons and switches. Her headset looked like something that would be on the newest iteration of *Star Trek*.

"May I help you?" she asked with the precise raise of a perfectly plucked eyebrow.

"I'm uh..." I looked back over my shoulder at the executives as I passed them. "I'm, um, here to see..."

That Asshole. That's what I'd been about to say because that's how we always referred to him at home. Never by name. My mother refused to allow anyone to even speak it in her presence. He was always just *That Asshole.*

And of course now, when I needed to actually remember his name, I totally blanked.

Oh god.

The receptionist stared at me, waiting for me to speak. Which made my brain seize up even more.

"The... the head guy," I stammered. "The big guy. Not tall, I mean... in charge. Well, maybe he's also... never mind. I think his name is..." I felt my face heat and my pits begin to sweat. "His name... is..."

Slim Shady? No.

Asshole, Asshole, Asshole! my brain chanted.

My stomach dropped, and I felt my throat dry up.

I'd seen a photograph of the CEO and wondered if describing him would help.

"Tall, dark, and handsome?" I squeaked. "Little intimidating? Scowly, but in an *ohmygod* kind of way?"

Shut up. Shut up.

Before I had the chance to describe the tiny mole below the edge of the man's lip, the barest hint of a laugh line appeared next to one of the receptionist's eyes.

"Might it be Mr. Grange himself?"

Wellington Archibald Grange the Third. The scariest motherfucker to ever be considered a corporate raider.

The man my mother despised with every ounce of her disease-riddled body. The man who wanted to gobble up my mother's life's work like it was a generic box of bran cereal and shit out a shoddy version of it to sick people in need at a staggering upcharge.

"That's the one," I said, straightening up and trying to put on a brave face. "Conor Newell here to see Wells Grange, please."

THE MINUTE I stepped into the fancy conference room, I began to fidget. I couldn't help it. I was nervous as hell, and the sight of the expertly polished wooden table surrounded by fancy leather chairs just made me feel even more out of my element. My friend James was supposed to be here with me. Despite being the geekiest gamer in my late-night chat group and a super-fun cosplayer at all the cons, he was an uptight corporate attorney in real life. This was his world, not mine. And, it wasn't like I could be angry with him since he wasn't charging me.

But still. It meant I was on my own. What if I somehow fucked it up?

My stomach twisted and I swallowed, trying to ease the panic threatening to overwhelm me. Taking a deep breath, I walked around the far side of the large table to take advantage of the view.

We were dozens of stories above the city, and I wondered how many people would be terrified just being able to see how high up they were. Probably a lot. Maybe it was even part of the reason they used this room—to intimidate people.

Well, it wouldn't work on me. I loved being high up. I summited peaks, rock climbed, and rode every zipline I could. I'd even bungee jumped from a bridge near the Grand Canyon one time. Heights weren't a problem for me, but this fucking suit and tie were making me feel caged.

I was used to graphic tees and worn jeans. Chuck Taylors instead of shiny, tight wingtips. I leaned my forehead against the glass and looked straight down, putting my hands behind my back and imagining the beginning of a giant bungee jump into the city below.

I practiced slowing down my breathing, but halfway through the inhale, my phone buzzed in my pocket.

Sexy Stranger: *I'm sure your phone is silenced during your presentation, but I wanted you to have a message waiting for you afterward to let you know you did great. And even if you didn't, it will still be okay.*

My heart swelled and my entire body suddenly relaxed.

Conor: *It hasn't started yet, but thank you. That's the nicest thing anyone's said to me in a while.*

There was a brief pause before a response popped up.

Sexy Stranger: *I hope that's not true. Tell you what, regardless of how it goes, save some alone time for me tonight. I can either help celebrate or forget.*

The relaxation he'd brought me disappeared in a puff of sexy smoke.

Don't fuck this up. I typed out a message.

Conor: *I would really like that. I never asked—what's your name?*

There was a slight delay, and I glanced up as I heard footsteps approaching the open conference room door. I'd just started to slide my phone back into my pocket when it buzzed with his reply. I skimmed it, my body instantly heating at the words.

Sexy Stranger: *Hmm... I think learning my name might need to be a reward. Perhaps we can think of a way for you to earn it tonight?*

I dropped my phone onto the table and practically fell into a chair to hide my sudden erection just as a man entered the conference room. At the sound of my awkward movement, he looked up from his own phone. We locked eyes. The slight smile that had been hovering around his lips disappeared and was quickly replaced by the cold and distant expression he was known for. The one that had graced the pages of the *Wall Street Journal* and *Forbes* magazines.

Wells Grange. *That Asshole.*

The man who wanted to practically steal my mother's life's work and use it to line his already fat pockets.

The man whose face, despite my better judgment, was a regular visitor of my hottest dreams. Because the reality was that, asshole or not, Wells Grange was gorgeous. Today even more so than usual, in a way that caused my pants to tighten more than they already had.

In every photograph I'd ever seen of him, he appeared perfect and polished, his cheeks freshly shaven and hair smoothly combed so that his features seemed molded from steel rather than flesh. But this morning his jaw bore a dark shadow of stubble and the soft waves in his hair refused to lie flat. It made him look a little rugged, despite the suit and tie.

It made him look human.

But that wasn't what caused my nerves to flare. No, my stomach began twisting because of his eyes. Normally cold and calculating, this morning they bore the traces of something that was hard to describe.

Hunger. That's what it was. The man was hungry for something. He burned for it. I swallowed thickly. For the barest moment, I wanted it to be me he desired so fiercely. I nearly laughed out loud at the thought. At the absurdity of it.

Wells Grange was the enemy. He was That Asshole. The only thing he was hungry for was power and money, and my mother's invention would give him both. He didn't want me, he wanted my mother's patents. He wanted to win.

And suddenly I understood how this man had become so successful. Looking into those eyes, I didn't understand how anyone could resist succumbing to that hunger.

If Wells Grange wanted to devour me, there wasn't a damn thing I'd be able to do to stop him.

4

WELLS

Well... he was cute. If you liked men awkward and fumbling. Which wasn't normally my type.

I slipped my phone in my pocket and strode around the large table to extend my hand to the man in the chair. I waited for him to stand. He didn't. I frowned. Surely he knew how rude it was to deliberately sit when someone entered the room for a meeting.

He was odd. And he looked so uncomfortable I wondered if that was even his own suit.

"Wells Grange," I said in the deeper, commanding tone I saved for negotiations. "You must be Dr. Newell."

I knew he wasn't, of course. I simply wanted to make a point. I leaned forward, taking advantage of our relative positions to crowd his space.

"N-no, sir. I mean, no. That's my mother. My mother is the doctor. Not a medical doctor, mind you. She's..." He seemed to realize his mouth had run away with him, and he quickly snapped it shut before taking a breath through his nose and letting it out. His eyes flashed to my mouth before closing for the briefest second.

He held out a hand and said in a much steadier voice. "Conor

Newell. I'm Dr. Elizabeth Newell's son. My mother should have sent you an email to inform you of the change."

As our hands met, I noticed his had the slightest tremor running through it. Normally, the aggressive negotiator in me would silently declare victory at such a tell, but this time for some reason my victory didn't feel as satisfying. I actually found myself on the verge of reassuring him. *What the hell?*

I pulled my hand back quickly and shoved it in my pocket. "Well, I hope you're as well versed on her patented tech as she is. Let's get started."

I leaned forward to press the pager button on the phone in the middle of the table. "Deb, please have the rest of the team join us." As we waited for the others to file in, I turned and made my way back to the opposite side of the table to give myself a chance to shake off the unusual reaction to this kid. After sitting, I glanced back over at him as if to size him up for some kind of, what? Sports team recruitment?

He was probably a couple of inches shorter than I was but still at least five ten. His hair was shaggier than most of the corporate types I was used to. The thick dark brown mane was shot through with streaks of lighter brown as if he spent plenty of time in the sun. How could that be if the man owned a game shop? If I hadn't seen the photo of him online, I'd have pictured Dr. Newell's only child as some pale, sickly type bent over a folding table under fluorescent lights with a motley crew of social castoffs dressed in dirty superhero T-shirts.

Conor looked up at me in time to catch me studying him. His eyebrows raised in question, drawing attention to his hazel eyes. I couldn't deny the man was good-looking. Anyone would find him so. Healthy, fit...

His questioning look turned worried. He glanced down self-consciously, as though assuming he had something on his tie that had caused me to stare at him. He smoothed down the tie in question, and that's when I saw it.

Navy tie, tiny pattern of silver Daleks.

It was unmistakable.

Fuck me.

I stared at it.

No possible way.

Snippets from last night's texts flashed through my mind. *Hotel room, important presentation in the morning...*

"Where did you get that tie?" I asked in a gruff-sounding voice. As if learning the origin of the offending garment would make a difference. I ground my back teeth together to keep from shooting myriad questions at him like bullets.

"Um..." he said, glancing down as if to remind him of which tie he wore. "DragonCon? But like... a long time ago. My dad got it for me. And he's been gone a while."

Just then, Deb arrived along with one of my senior vice presidents and several folks from legal and our research and development department. They nodded toward me as they filed in and took their places at the table, but I ignored them. I couldn't stop staring at Conor's tie, imagining the dark happy trail on the other side of the dress shirt, the mesmerizing cock that lay hidden beneath the zipper of his suit pants.

I narrowed my eyes at him. "What hotel are you staying at?"

The question caught both of us off guard and must have surprised Deb as well because she coughed and spoke up before Conor could answer. "I arranged a Central Park suite at the Four Seasons as usual, sir."

I glanced over at her and noticed the furrow in her brows. She was no doubt wondering what the hell had gotten into me. I was wondering the same thing.

I cleared my throat again and tried to regain the upper hand. This deal was a billion times more important than some sexy texts and a wrong-number dick pic.

"Let's get started, shall we?" I nodded to my senior VP to take over the meeting.

As he introduced the others in the room, I slipped my phone out of my pocket. I was pretty certain Conor and NotSam were the same guy, but there was one way to know for sure. I typed up a text and hit Send.

Wells: *I'd like to have a nice dinner sent to your room tonight.*

Conor's phone vibrated in his pocket, making him jump.

Son of a bitch. I was right. They *were* the same person. What were the fucking chances?

He fumbled for his phone. "Sorry, I couldn't turn it off in case it's my mother," he explained quickly. "She, ah... I'll just..." He peered down at the screen and took in the message with a small smile. His ears turned bright pink before he quickly shoved the phone back in his pocket.

So responsive. I wanted to take one of those pink earlobes into my mouth and suck until the blush spread across his entire body.

"Was it your mother?" I asked. "Is everything all right at home?"

His eyes widened. If possible, his ears burned even hotter. "Oh. Yes. Thank you. Where was I?"

Liar. I wanted to laugh. The little minx.

"You were introducing yourself," I told him. The blush spread to his cheeks. It took every ounce of control not to grin at the sight of it.

"Oh. Right. Me. I was... I mean I *am*... me. I mean, obviously, I'm me." He laughed nervously and fumbled with something in his pocket, finally pulling it out only to lose hold of it. A small plastic Yoda figurine bounced across the table.

I leaned forward to grab it, noticing it wasn't a figurine after all but a USB key. I quirked an eyebrow at him.

"Uh, my presentation? I mean, the data. My data. Well, Mom's data. Dr. Newell's, that is. A slide deck. You know, PowerPoint?"

I handed it back to him with a smirk and tried fruitlessly not to notice how soft his skin was when his fingertips brushed mine. "Yes, Mr. Newell. I know PowerPoint."

"Right," he murmured. "Thanks. It's... yeah. I'll just... save it. For later."

He let out an obvious sigh of relief when one of the research techs took over and began asking questions about the most recent viability study. I watched Conor closely as he answered, trying to reconcile the eager flirt from my texts with the man standing in front of me.

Of course I had to consider the possibility that the "accidental" dick pic the night before hadn't been an accident at all, but some sort of attempt at creating blackmail material or at gaining the upper hand in negotiations. If so, the strategy would backfire spectacularly. I didn't take kindly to people who played dirty in business. I might have had a reputation in my professional life of being a hard-ass, but I was always ethical. I never lied or cheated.

Watching Conor, it was difficult to imagine he was capable of lying or any kind of cheating. He just seemed so earnest. So open. So... innocent. Though perhaps innocent wasn't the right word after the photos he'd sent me last night. Except he'd admitted it was something he'd never done before. I shifted in my seat, wondering what else he'd never done.

Wondering what else I could introduce him to.

My hands itched to reach for my phone. I wanted to text him something naughty so I could watch his face catch fire again. But I couldn't do that to the poor guy. Not right now. He was still nervous, that much was obvious. He'd gotten off to a rocky start and still hadn't quite recovered. It was clear that he was well versed on the technology but wasn't an expert. He was trying, though, and I found myself internally rooting for the man, especially since I knew from his earlier texts how important this presentation was for him.

I squeezed my eyes closed for a quick moment. Since when had I rooted for the opposition? I snorted at the thought, the sound loud enough to interrupt Conor's long rambling answer about the uptake mechanism. He fell silent, eyes darting toward me in surprise. His gaze held mine for a second, maybe two, before dropping toward my mouth and then immediately away.

"Um, did you have a question?" There was a softness to his voice, nerves making him slightly breathless. I liked it. Imagined it was how he might sound if I crowded close against him.

I felt my pants tighten and pulled my chair closer to the table to hide the evidence of my sudden erection. I didn't like how easily he could affect me. It made me feel off balance. Because of that, my response was perhaps harsher than it needed to me. "No," I said crisply.

Alarm flashed in his eyes, followed by worry. He thought I was displeased by him. And all I could think about was just how well my anonymous texter had pleased me earlier that morning. How eager he'd been to do what I'd asked. How many times he'd begged to come because I'd told him he couldn't find release without my permission.

I couldn't stomach the idea of that eagerness being quashed. I shifted in my seat. "I thought your answer was quite elucidating. Please, go on."

He stared at me a moment. He wasn't the only one. Every pair of eyes in the conference room found their way toward me, even if for the briefest second. My comment had been entirely out of character. I ignored them.

"Okay. Um. Thanks. I mean, right. Okay. So okay. Next I wanted to talk about the biomaterial uptake mechanism's reaction time to data input as it relates to material temperature." He clicked for the next slide in his presentation. A photo of slick, red venous material being fed into the uptake mechanism filled the screen.

The blood drained from Conor's face. "Oh god." He closed his eyes and looked away. His hand reached for the back of the nearest chair and he gripped onto it to steady himself. He took several deep breaths. "The uh..." He gestured toward the screen without looking at it. "Um... stuff..."

I couldn't believe it. The kid was squeamish.

Toward the other end of the table, two of the R & D techs traded a glance and a soft snicker. My inner desire to protect raged. I scowled at them, but they somehow failed to get the seriousness of my silent message. One of them leaned to the other and whispered something under his breath. The other one laughed.

That was it. I stood. Fast enough that my chair kicked out behind me, rolling almost all the way to the wall of windows. I pointed at the two techs. "Out."

Deb jumped to her feet. It was clear she had no idea what was going on or why I was acting the way I was, but she stepped in to smooth things over. That's what she did, what she was good at. "Right, I believe what Mr. Grange means is that we received a message that you two are needed in the lab downstairs."

My nostrils flared. I wanted to fire the two on the spot. Deb cut me a look to say she was handling this and, while I may be wound up now, I would thank her later. I glared at her.

Conor stood frozen, practically trembling from a combination of nerves, squeamishness, and my unexpected outburst. Dammit.

"Everyone out," I barked. "And someone get that damn picture off the screen," I added. One of the other techs lunged for the video controls.

Deb clenched her jaw. She was not pleased with me. "An excellent idea—now would be the perfect time for a break. We have coffee and refreshments in the conference room next door." She led the others from the room.

Conor started to follow but had to steady himself with a hand on the wall. "Not you," I told him.

He froze.

"Sit," I ordered.

He sat.

I stared at him, having no idea what to say next. I'd been acting on instinct, on my gut desire to protect him, but clearly I hadn't thought this through. I went to the credenza against the far wall and retrieved an ice-cold bottle of water. I loosened the cap and set it in front of him. "Drink."

He gulped the water hungrily, and I tried not to stare at the column of his throat and the sharp edge of his Adam's apple bobbing as he swallowed. I wanted to trace a finger down that throat.

I started to pace away from him, wanting to put distance between us, but then stopped myself. I was being ridiculous. I was a master of control. I didn't need distance to keep from reaching for him. As if to prove the point to myself, I stepped closer to Conor, intentionally crowding his space.

"Thank you," he said, wiping his mouth with the back of his hand when he was done. Only then did he seem to realize how close I was. He let out a shaky breath and rolled his chair away slightly.

"You okay?" I leaned my hip against the table, closing the distance again.

He fiddled with the cap to the water bottle, flipping it over his fingers. "Yeah. I don't normally do this." He crossed one knee over the other, using the movement to push himself away again.

I wasn't sure if he was referring to getting woozy or to presenting this kind of scientific demonstration. It didn't really matter. I shifted from one foot to the other, erasing the gap. "Would you like to reschedule for a time when your mom can—"

"No," he blurted, shaking his head. "I'm okay. I can do this." He tried to move his chair again. But something was in the way.

He glanced down at where my foot blocked the wheel, then looked quickly up at me. His eyes met mine and there was something vulnerable in them, but yearning too.

Well, well. Could it be that Conor Newell was interested in me in real life?

I wanted to lean forward and place my hands on the armrests, trapping him. I wanted to hover over him, force his head to tilt back. I wanted to claim his mouth with my own.

As if he could sense the direction of my thoughts, his eyes dropped to my lips, then dragged back up to my eyes.

I wondered if he could see how attracted to him I was, how wrong-footed I suddenly felt.

My hands itched to touch him. Seeing him up close, I realized his hazel eyes were streaked with honey gold. There was an empty piercing hole in one of his ears, a missed spot of unshaven whiskers at the very edge of his jaw. I clenched my fingers around the edge of the table to keep from reaching for him.

"Have dinner with me tonight."

I wanted to bite the words back as soon as they were out of my mouth. What the hell was I thinking? Had I really just asked the guy I was negotiating a deal with out on a date? Was I seriously going to risk a multimillion-dollar deal for, what? One night with a gamer geek?

Conor's eyes widened in surprise. Before he had a chance to reply, I laughed and pushed away from the table, putting distance between us.

So much for my ability to control myself.

"With my team, I mean," I said. "We have reservations at Segreto for seven. Deb will arrange a car to pick you up from your hotel."

Out of the corner of my eye, I saw him reach into his pocket for his phone while he considered my invitation.

"I was planning to eat at my hotel," he said, hesitantly.

I wasn't used to being turned down. In business or in bed. But that wasn't why I wanted him to say yes so badly.

He intrigued me. I wanted him to come to dinner so I could spend more time with him in real life instead of over the phone.

That alone should have had warning bells sounding in my head. And maybe they were, but I ignored them. I knew how to apply pressure to get what I wanted. "It's our custom to get to know our potential business partners over a nice dinner, Mr. Newell. We're talking about a deal worth a lot of money."

Conor nodded and stood. Suddenly, we were face-to-face, barely more than a foot of space between us. I expected him to flinch or shrivel back. Instead he straightened his back. "Yes, fine," he bit out. "I'll be ready." He held my eyes a moment longer and then turned on his heel and left the room. I stared after him, wondering what had just happened. Had my little sexy gamer geek just stood up to me?

I grinned, now looking forward to tonight more than ever.

5

CONOR

The moment I stepped out of the conference room, I practically collapsed into a trembling mess on the floor. Deb, Wells Grange's assistant, was standing by the receptionist's desk and must have seen how unsteady I was because she instantly appeared at my side.

"Everything okay, Mr. Newell?" she asked, placing a hand under my elbow.

I nodded, still unable to form words. What had just happened in there? Had Wells actually been coming on to me?

Had I been coming on to him?

And had I really just stood up to him?

I shuddered. Half in relief at being free of the man's intense gaze and half in memory of how that intense gaze had made me feel. Like I was the most delectable dish on the menu and he was a man who hadn't eaten in months.

She cut a glance toward the conference room and lowered her voice. "I know Mr. Grange can come across harsh, but he really is a nice man underneath the bluster."

I snorted. *That Asshole*? Unlikely. "If that man is nice under the bluster, you must define bluster as a thick hard shell of dense kryptonite wrapped around a hundred and eighty pounds or so of jack-assery. And, by the way, I'm Superman. So that shit is extra harsh."

And since the man in question was a healthy, trim specimen, that didn't leave much room inside for "nice." Not that I noticed his figure because I certainly did not.

She pressed her lips together, trying to smother a smile. But she couldn't keep the spark of amusement from her eyes. She cleared her throat and ushered me toward a pair of chairs tucked into an alcove. "You did a good job in there."

I shot her a sideways glance. "You are a very smooth liar."

"And I get paid well for it."

"You must. I imagine you sleeping on piles of hundred-dollar bills falling out of your mattress."

"Pfft. I sleep on silk, sweetheart. And the bills are safely tucked inside my brokerage account."

I laughed as I collapsed into one of the ornate chairs. But then the horror of the last few minutes swept over me again. I'd almost thrown up on myself. And half of the R & D team of Grange BioMed. In front of Wells Grange himself. Who may, or may not, have wanted to eat me alive. In both a good and bad way.

I shuddered again at the thought and dropped my head into my hands. This was a disaster. "My mom was supposed to have taken that slide out of the presentation. I must have loaded the wrong file on my USB drive."

"If she's anything like my mom, maybe she was testing your internal fortitude."

I looked up at her with a smile. "One of those, huh?"

"Oh yeah. She once sent me to ballet class with only my tap shoes. When I asked her about it afterward, she said I should have taken it as an opportunity to learn how to tread lightly."

I couldn't hold back another laugh. "Cruel bitch," I said. "You poor thing."

She chuckled and nodded. "Don't worry. I got her back. That Sunday I 'accidentally' wore my tap shoes to church. It turned out, I never did master the treading lightly thing."

"Please tell me you're from the South. Because I swear to god if that was in one of those 'women should be silent in the church' churches, I'm going to praise Jesus and pass the collection plate."

She raised both hands to the sky. "Amen, Brother Newell. Natchez, Mississippi, born and raised. Went to State. And people wonder why I'm such a bulldog."

"Southern girls are ruthless. Never say never to a cheerleader or sorority sister. I learned my lesson at a young age," I teased.

"You have a sister?"

"I wish. Only child. You?"

"Four sisters, Conor. And all of them meaner than spit. Why do you think I had to get the heck out of there? I'd be married with three kids and a monogrammed SUV right now if it weren't for a one-night-stand-turned-into-long-weekend in the Hamptons. When that unfortunate event went south, I happened upon a really nice businessman who took pity on me and offered me an entry-level job at his company so I didn't have to go crawling back home to Mama."

I had a feeling I knew who she was talking about. I didn't want to hear anything nice about Wells Grange.

"Hmpfh."

Her laugh was so sudden, it made me jump. "He stripped off his kryptonite and jackassery long enough to bring me here and get me started as an errand-runner. He hooked me up with two other young women in human resources who had a spare futon in Queens."

"Not possible," I grumbled. "The man is the first successful proto-type of cryonic suspension while still living."

Deb rolled her eyes. "Scientists. I swear to god, the jokes around this place. I should have applied to work at *The Daily Show* recording studio. The comedy has got to be way better there." She winked at me. "Feeling better?"

I nodded and gave her what I hoped was a grateful smile. She'd helped me gather my wits and regain my equilibrium. "Thanks, Deb."

The smile on her face softened as she locked eyes with me. "You can do this, Conor. You each have what the other wants. Don't forget that."

It took me a split second to remember she was referring to the deal. I had the printer, and he had the cash.

As if it was that simple.

I mumbled another thanks. Before heading back to the conference room for another torture session, I ducked into the men's room. The moment I slid the lock on the stall door, I heaved a sigh of relief. I appreciated Deb taking the time to make me feel at ease and pump up my self-confidence, but I needed a minute to myself.

My phone was like a living thing inside my pocket; I couldn't help but pull it out and reread the message from my sexy stranger.

He wanted to have food sent to my room? What kind of person did that? And was it even smart to tell him where I was staying?

After stopping and starting typing several times, and hoping he wasn't noticing those three traitorous dots on his screen, I gave up. The reality was, I didn't know what to do. I'd agreed to dinner with Wells and his team, but I was already tired and knew that by the end of the day I'd be exhausted.

Everything about this morning had been overwhelming: the gleaming office tower, the fancy conference room, the high-powered executives. Wells Grange himself. He had to be one of the most intense individuals I'd ever met. Power radiated from the man like he was born to it. I wondered if he'd ever had a moment of insecurity. He seemed so confident, so sure of himself, so absolutely aware of the dominance he exuded over everything in his orbit.

Including me. I shivered, thinking about standing up to him for the briefest moment in the conference room. The confusion in his eyes. It had been a heady moment. Terrifying, but exhilarating.

I wondered for a moment what it would be like to take Wells out of his element and put him in mine. To switch our positions. I imagined him upstairs in my shop, in the old loft I'd converted into a massive game room. There were over a half dozen large tables made from reclaimed wood, several of them covered with miniatures for various war games. Three of the walls were lined with floor-to-ceiling windows, the fourth dominated by a row of bookshelves stuffed with every game imaginable, all of them available to be checked out and played.

Saturday nights the loft hummed with energy, every table covered with game pieces and surrounded by people laughing and arguing and debating and storytelling. I rotated among them, answering questions, adjudicating disputes, offering tips and suggestions. That was my world. That was my forty-second-floor conference room equivalent.

But if I had Wells Grange to myself in my shop, I wouldn't take him to the loft. I'd take him to the back nook where I had an old chessboard set up. It had been handed down through my family, the pieces carved by my great-great-grandfather out of an ancient piece of bogwood he'd dug up from his fields back in Ireland. The pieces were worn smooth from generations of hands sliding over them, moving them from square to square.

Chess was an equalizer. Anyone could learn to play it well. It was also a game of strategy. Planning. Patience.

I imagined Wells Grange would make an excellent chess player.

Good enough to beat me? I smiled to myself. That would be interesting to find out. I was sure Wells probably thought so. He'd probably start with Queen's Pawn opener, a cocky grin twitching the corner of his lips, assuming he'd already won. Then I'd counter with King's Indian Defense. That's when he would know who he was up against.

That's when he would realize I didn't intimidate so easily. I may not be as powerful, or arrogant, or polished as Wells, but I had my own strengths. I knew how to read players in order to learn what cards they held in their hand. I knew how to listen to determine their strategies and goals. And I knew how to wait patiently, making my own plans, so that I could ultimately make a play for the win at the end.

Wells Grange would end up with my mother's printer patents—of that there was no debate. The issue was under what terms and conditions. And the real question was how much he would pay for them.

Essentially, Wells and I were playing a kind of game. My objective was to collect as many resources as possible in the process. Thinking of the negotiations in this way made me feel more confident, like we were in my world now instead of his. Of course, playing his game meant going to dinner with him and his team, I realized. Which meant declining the sexy stranger's offer of dinner in my room.

With a resigned sigh, I typed up a response to my sexy stranger's invite. Then I slipped the phone back into my pocket, washed my hands, and started back to the conference room thinking about the next move to make with Wells Grange.

Just because he'd eventually put me in check, didn't mean I couldn't make him run the board and lose a few pieces in the process.

6

WELLS

I was having trouble concentrating on the business task of acquiring this fucking piece of equipment that could earn my company into the billions of dollars.

All because of a little gamer geek I'd gotten off the night before.

And again this morning.

And hopefully again tonight.

I ground my teeth as my cock stirred, causing my pants to grow uncomfortably tight. I was not the kind of person who put this much thought into the men I had sex with. And I hadn't even had actual sex with this guy. So what the hell was my problem?

Focus.

"Deb!" I barked. It took her longer than it should have to appear in the conference room door, and I scowled. "Did you make those reservations?"

She crossed her arms, undaunted by my stormy demeanor. "Do you have any idea how impossible it is to get last-minute reservations for eight people at Segreto?" she asked. "They've been booked up since before they opened."

I waved a hand. "I trust you can find a way. You're a miracle worker; that's why you're my assistant."

She rolled her eyes. She was one of the few people in my life who refused to be intimidated by me, and she got away with it because she was damn good at her job. "Yes, sir. Anything else?"

I opened my mouth, then hesitated. I'd been about to ask her if she'd seen Conor leave the conference room. If he'd seemed okay. But that would be absurd. Instead, I tapped my fingers against the polished table for a moment, thinking. Finally I told her, "Find out what you can about Conor Newell's businesses."

Deb seemed surprised by the request. "Sir?"

Her expression indicated she suspected my interest might be personal. She was wrong. This was completely business related. "Leverage, Deb," I reminded her. "Always know more about your opponent than they know about you."

She lifted her eyebrows in mock innocence. "So does that mean you'd like me to open a file on Conor Newell's personal situation as well? Request one of our PIs do a deeper dive into his life?"

When I hesitated, she smirked, adding, "Leverage, Mr. Grange."

I scowled at her. "Five minutes and I want everyone back in here. I'm tired of wasting time."

She waited until she'd left the conference room to laugh. But I could still hear her. If she wasn't so good at her job, I'd have fired her ages ago. The problem was she was damn perceptive, a trait that had served me very well in the past during a few dicey, high-stakes negotiations.

I just didn't like when she turned her power of perception on me. I made a note to bump up her annual bonus. She deserved it for having to put up with me on a daily basis.

While she gathered the others, I took my seat at the table and pulled out my phone. I frowned. Nothing from NotSam. Something uncomfortable tightened in my chest.

I opened the text app, just to make sure. Still nothing. Then three little dots appeared on the screen. I grinned, anticipation blooming. I imagined him somewhere nearby, hovering over his phone, typing out a message to his stranger.

To me.

The thought gave me pause, and for the briefest moment I wondered if I should tell him I was the man he'd been texting. I wondered if it was wrong to keep my identity from him.

But what if I told him and he stopped texting me, or worse, accused me of some kind of corporate espionage? Or what if this was some kind of intentional scheme on Conor's part to manipulate me? Did I want him to know he'd been found out?

As much as I didn't think he was the type to do something so underhanded and malicious, I couldn't rule it out. For now, I thought it was best to continue the subterfuge.

And if I was being honest with myself, I was enjoying it. What harm could a little text flirting be in the grand scheme of things?

The three dots disappeared from the screen. No message appeared. I waited. Nothing. Was he regretting having accepted my dinner invitation this evening? I frowned. I didn't like how that made me feel.

With a grunt I flipped over to the browser and called up the article I'd read earlier about Conor Newell. I scoured the page with fresh eyes. This time I was reading it with the knowledge Conor was my NotSam. He lived in Asheville, NC, which was just as well, I supposed. It wasn't like I was in the market for a relationship. And if, after the negotiations for the technology were completed, I revealed I was the man he'd been sexting and we wound up in bed together for a night of celebration, well then... so much the better, right?

My jaw ticked. What else could I discover about him before the meeting resumed? There was an article in his dinky hometown paper written on the fourth anniversary of his game shop opening. It seemed Broad River Board Games was a popular addition to the downtown Asheville scene. The article went on and on about how charming it was and how it attracted visitors from all over the region.

Conor had graduated from Western Carolina University where his mom held tenure. Majored in Business Entrepreneurship which had included an exchange trip to Peru for a semester. Before that, he'd graduated from the local public schools in Asheville and had been the founder of a Dungeons and Dragons club there.

Complete geek. It was kind of adorable, and it made me realize even more how out of his depth he was in the meeting. He hadn't been joking when he'd said he had reason to be nervous.

There was no mention of his father in the article, and all I knew about Dr. Newell's late husband from other research was that he'd been older and died a few years back from natural causes. He'd also been a professor in the science department at WCU before his death. I wondered what Conor's life had been like as an only child of two older, academic parents.

My phone buzzed with a text and I immediately swiped to my messages.

NotSam: *I have dinner plans, but... can we... I mean, can I text you after?*

I felt my cheeks stretch. I liked the idea of having dinner with him knowing that as soon as he left me he would be racing back to his hotel to be with his anonymous lover.

Wells: *I think I may be able to arrange that. I have my own plans this evening but I'll text you when I'm free.*

He sent me back a smiley face emoji that made me snort out loud.

Unfortunately, it was at that moment that I realized that I was no longer alone. I glanced up. A tall, good-looking man stood in the doorway to the conference room. He was a little older than I was, wore a thousand-dollar suit, and had clearly caught the ridiculous grin on my face from texting with NotSam.

We locked eyes, and for a split second all traces of amusement disappeared and his eyes narrowed as if sizing me up and finding me somehow lacking.

He stepped forward, extending a hand. "Mr. Grange, I'm James Allen, attorney for Dr. Newell and a friend of Conor's."

I couldn't help but eye him up and down. Typical Manhattan corporate attorney. The man dripped money, from his haircut to his wingtips to the Tom Ford briefcase he carried. How in the world had the Newell family from nowhere, North Carolina, managed to hire this guy?

I stood and took his hand. "Welcome. You're late."

He glanced around the empty conference room as if to silently say, *Am I?*

I scowled, inwardly cursing Deb for not getting everyone back in here sooner. Before I could explain we were taking a short break, I heard a soft squeal from the lobby. Next thing I knew, Conor came rushing into the room.

And straight into James Allen's arms.

I inhaled sharply at the sight of the two men embracing.

"James!" Conor gushed, ending the hug and grabbing the other man's upper arms. "Thank god. Everything okay?"

"Just a minor annoyance," the attorney said. "It will be fine. How did the presentation go?"

Conor laughed and the sound of it did strange things to my insides. "I didn't vomit, so I'm putting it in the win column."

James chuckled. He looked at Conor with a familiar affection that had me wondering how the two knew each other. Clearly this was not a typical attorney–client relationship. Especially given the grin that brightened Conor's eyes in a way I hadn't seen all morning. Despite the uptick in my heart rate, I found myself grinding my teeth in irritation.

The lawyer turned his attention to me, his expression turning frosty. "I trust Mr. Grange didn't try to take advantage of you without your attorney present?"

Conor's eyes slid to mine before darting away, the slightest blush tinging the tips of his ears. "No, he uh... well, I mean... We have a date tonight. Dinner I mean. Hell, not a *date*, but dinner. That isn't a date. Because sometimes dinner can be a date but not always. Like here. Tonight. The whole team will be there. You should come." He then turned to me. "James is invited, right?"

I looked at the way Conor kept his arm wrapped around one of James's, like he was holding on to the slightly older man as if he were a lifeline. I wanted to tell him no fucking way. But the way Conor looked at me, his chin tilted slightly down and his eyes wide and hopeful...

No one could say no to that.

"Of course," I bit out.

Conor grinned widely, and for the first time I noticed the crinkle of laugh lines near the corners of his eyes. He looked like a man who laughed often. Just not around me.

Which was fine. I didn't need him to laugh, I just needed to get this fucking meeting back underway so I could put an end to the damn lovefest in front of me.

"Deb!" I called. She appeared in an instant. "Get everyone back in here. And add one more to the reservation for dinner tonight."

She gave me that look that meant she didn't appreciate my tone of voice. Then her eyes slid to Conor and James with their linked arms, and her expression morphed into one of understanding. What she thought she understood, I didn't know.

"No problem," she said before ducking out of the room to gather the team.

I turned to James. "Now that you're finally here, we can get started with the negotiations," I said in a clipped tone. "Have a seat."

Conor's smile dropped in an instant, and the loss of it was like a frigid wind blowing up my pants leg. I was an ass. But I was an ass ready to spend millions of dollars, and it was time to make it happen.

James shot me a look that was more calculated than surprised. There was something familiar about the way he looked at me, as if he somehow knew me. I wondered if we'd met before somewhere, if for some reason I should know him. But had that been the case, I would have remembered. James was the kind of man who stood out—tall, handsome, and charming with a sharp jaw, salt-and-pepper hair, and a smooth smile full of perfectly straight, gleaming white teeth.

He was the kind of man I would have given a second, and perhaps even a third, look at in the past. Now I just found his presence annoying, a feeling that only intensified when James cupped Conor's elbow and led him toward one of the chairs.

"Don't worry," he murmured in a gentle voice, taking the seat next to him and rolling it closer. "I'm here now, I'll take over. You can relax."

The look of gratitude and relief that crossed Conor's face set my chest on fire.

As the rest of the team began filtering in, Conor leaned over the arm of his chair, his face inches from James as they huddled, discussing something I couldn't hear over the grinding of my teeth. James laughed and Conor's grin deepened. I'd had enough.

I slipped my phone from my pocket and called up my text convo with NotSam. I typed out a quick message and hit Send before I could think better of it.

> **Wells:** *I've been thinking about you and how gorgeous your cock looks when it's glistening with precum, desperate to be stroked. Don't drink too much at dinner. You'll need your stamina for what I have planned for you tonight.*

Conor practically leaped out of his chair at the new message alert. He apologized to James before scrambling in his pocket. The minute he saw the message, his eyes widened and his cheeks ignited. I now knew what he would be imagining all afternoon, and it wouldn't be James Allen.

I grinned to myself and cleared my throat. "Now that we're here, let's begin the negotiations, shall we?"

7

CONOR

Walking out of that steel and glass tower was what I imagined walking out of a short stint in prison must feel like. I could finally take a deep breath and remind myself who I really was.

Listening to James and the other attorneys drone on and on had exhausted me more than I'd let on. Maybe it was the stress of being out of my comfort zone or the worry that the deal would somehow not close in time to help my mother much, but now that I was out in the crisp winter air, I felt invigorated.

I was also, blessedly, alone again. James had raced off to meet his live-in boyfriend, Richard, for an after-work thing at the office, and I knew from long hours talking to James that Richard wasn't one to excuse tardiness easily. It was just as well. I had a sexy stranger on the other end of my phone who I was itching to talk to about my day.

Conor: *I'm free!*

It only took a few moments before a reply popped up.

Sexy Stranger: *Don't sell yourself short, kid. You've got to be worth at least twenty bucks.*

I wondered if my ridiculous grin stood out among the serious business people crowding the sidewalks beside me.

Conor: *Tell me something funny. I could use a laugh.*

Sexy Stranger: *Did your presentation go that badly then?*

Conor: *Not really. Just all serious and boring. Oh and awkward as hell at one point for which I have you to blame. Your text earlier made me hard. I had to take great pains to hide it.*

Sexy Stranger: *Were you thinking of me and my plans for you tonight? Is that why you were hard?*

I felt my cock stirring again and picked up my pace, hoping to keep myself in check at least long enough to get back to the hotel.

Conor: *Yes.*

Sexy Stranger: *Good. That's what I like to hear.*

Warmth spread through my chest at the idea of having pleased him.

Conor: *I was glad to be done with everything so I could finally text.*

Sexy Stranger: *You back in your hotel room?*

I looked around at the bustling crowds. I'd elected to skip the taxi in favor of stretching my legs.

Conor: *No. Walking there now though. Keep me company?*

Sexy Stranger: *Why do I feel like I should be regurgitating a naughty limerick right now like a trained jester of some kind?*

I snorted softly while trying to picture my mystery man in colorful striped tights and a cap with bells on it.

Conor: *I can see you in the get-up.*

Sexy Stranger: *And how, pray tell, do I look?*

Conor: *I'd do ya.*

Sexy Stranger: *You're an odd one. Have a clown kink I'm unaware of?*

Conor: *Nah, but apparently I have a submissive kink of some kind.*

There was a delay, and I began to feel my stomach twist with nerves. Maybe I'd gone too far. Or misread the situation. When I saw the three dots, I sucked in a breath and held it.

Sexy Stranger: *And how do you feel about that?*

Conor: *You sound like a psychologist.*

Sexy Stranger: *Answer the question.*

Conor: *Okay, now you sound like an attorney.*

Sexy Stranger: *NotSam, I need to know how you're feeling about what we did.*

His concern made my chest warm under my uncomfortable business suit.

Conor: *Excited. Turned on. Hopeful for more. There, are you happy?*

Sexy Stranger: *Indeed.*

Conor: *And you? What's your kink besides bossing people around?*

I'd meant it to sound flirty but wondered if it had come out sarcastic and biting instead. I pursed my lips and tried not to run into anyone while I stared at my phone, waiting for an answer.

Sexy Stranger: *Pleasing my partner in bed. Taking care of them after.*

I froze midstep. The person behind me cursed angrily before brushing past me, his shoulder knocking mine. I reread the text several times, my pants growing tight. If that was his kink, sign me up.

I took a shaky breath and resumed my walk.

Conor: *Cuddling?*

Sexy Stranger: *Not normally, no.*

My stomach dropped. *Not normally* meant *sometimes yes*, but that it was the exception rather than the rule. I frowned, something uncomfortable twisting my insides. It felt almost like... jealousy. I wondered what it took to be that exception.

What I would have to do for it to be me.

The thought that it might never be me struck me harder than I expected. Which was ridiculous since we were anonymous sext buddies only. Not like we'd ever meet in person and actually be in a position to cuddle. And why did I even care about some stranger's opinions on sex and relationships? I didn't.

Conor: *I see. Love 'em and leave 'em, huh?*

Sexy Stranger: *No love. Just sex. And you? Are you the cuddling type, NotSam?*

I chose not to linger on the first half of his response, preferring to focus on the second part instead. I took a minute to think through my answer before typing. Did I want to play a role, or did I want to be the real me with this guy? The idea of trying to be someone he wanted made me feel as exhausted as the long day of meetings had.

Fuck it, if he didn't like the real me, he could stop responding.

I really hoped he didn't stop responding.

Conor: *Cuddle whore here. Founding member of the cuddle club, in fact. You should consider joining; we give out free spoons.*

Sexy Stranger: *And do you prefer the big or little one?*

Conor: *I'm 5' 10". While I'd love to be the little spoon all the time, it depends on who I'm with.*

Sexy Stranger: *Ah. A middle spoon?*

I looked up to realize I'd walked several buildings past my hotel entrance. I chuckled to myself and turned around, almost taking out a young woman with my bulky messenger bag.

"Sorry," I murmured.

"Less texting, more looking, yeah?" she barked. "Idiot."

I forced myself to pay attention until I was safely through the glass vestibule and into the marbled lobby.

Conor: *Almost got beaten up by a business woman on the street. This city is insanely aggressive.*

Sexy Stranger: *Are you alright? Rush hour isn't for tourists.*

Conor: *I'm fine. Sidewalks were packed, but I wanted the fresh air. Wait, did you just call me a tourist?*

Sexy Stranger: *Does the shoe fit and is it causing blisters yet?*

I stopped at the elevator and took stock of my feet. Now that he'd mentioned it, I did feel an uncomfortable pinch on my right heel.

Conor: *Does it make you feel powerful to be right all the time?*

Sexy Stranger: *It does indeed.*

Conor: *You have a smug smirk on your face right now, don't you?*

Sexy Stranger: *Are you in your room yet?*

My dick thickened, and I quickly moved my messenger bag around front to hide it from any interested parties among the people waiting for the elevator. When the doors slid open, I stutter-stepped into the corner of the mirrored box and continued to hold my bag in front.

"Thirty-third floor please," I murmured to the older gentleman nearest the buttons.

Conor: *Almost there.*

Suddenly my screen filled with a vivid color photo of muscular, curved thighs covered in just the right amount of dark hair. Nestled at the top of the gorgeous thighs was god's gift to genital lovers every-where: full balls and a long, hard cock with that mesmerizing hand stroking it.

Conor: *Dear god. Hold me.*

Sexy Stranger: *I'm busy holding something else right now. Get in your room and get naked on the bed. You have ten seconds.*

My heart hammered in my chest, and I glanced up to see what floor we were passing. Some kind of elevator deity must have been giving me cell service despite being inside the flying box.

The doors slid open on the twenty-ninth floor and no one moved. "Anyone? Twenty-nine?" I asked in a rush. "No?"

I laser-eyeballed the older gentleman in hopes by will alone I could make him press the door closed button. No such luck.

After a thousand years, the doors finally slid closed and shot us up to my floor where I practically created a vacuum with the way I bolted out of the elevator so fast. I fumbled my room key and then dropped my phone before getting my shit together and racing through the door. I got my clothes off in less than three seconds and long-jumped for the bed, bouncing up and down again before settling on my back and opening the camera on my phone.

My dick was tall and proud as I snapped a pic and sent it across the city to parts unknown.

Conor: *Aye-aye, Cap'n. One-eyed salute at the ready.*

I lay there excited and hopeful, looking forward to the sexty play-time ahead.

There was no response.

I stared at the phone for seconds, then minutes. Finally, after a full twenty minutes, my erection long deflated, I gave up. Surely, he wasn't punishing me for taking longer than ten seconds?

Was he?

My heart fell. I hated disappointing people in general, but I sure as hell hated disappointing him. For some reason it stung more than it should have. His lack of even a message telling me something had come up was the nail in the coffin.

I eventually got up and pulled on workout clothes to take out my frustration in the hotel gym. There was no need to locate my earbuds since I'd be damned if I was bringing my traitorous phone with me.

8

WELLS

Just as I was about to lead Conor to another intense orgasm over text, my phone died.

"Fuck!" I clicked every button I could to see if it had just gone to sleep on me. It never died this early in the day, regardless of how much I used it.

And then I remembered I'd forgotten to plug it in the night before when I'd slammed it facedown on my desk.

Fuck.

I stood up from my office sofa half-naked and pulled up my suit pants to redress before crossing to the desk and plugging my phone in. Before it powered back up, there was a knock on my door.

After tucking in and checking myself over to make sure I was completely put together again, I unlocked the office door and swung it open.

Deb handed me a coffee and a business card.

"James Allen left his card for you. Said he had to get to another appointment but he'd see you at dinner this evening."

I took the coffee from her but not the card. "Keep it. I don't need it."

After a split second of wondering about the attorney who'd spent the afternoon charming the pants off Conor, I changed my mind.

"On second thought," I said, reaching out, "I'll take it. Thanks. Any luck on the reservations?"

Her face lit up with a satisfied grin. "Of course. I'm now new best friends with Arccadio at the host stand. You'll have to thank him from me when he seats you. Also you owe him $500 cash. By the way, he recommends the pumpkin risotto special tonight. If I thought you cared about me at all, I'd beg you to bring me takeout after the dinner meeting."

I thought about what I'd much prefer doing after the dinner, and it had nothing to do with risotto or Deb.

"Lucky for me, I don't care about you at all," I said in a dry voice. "You're on your own for dinner."

She rolled her eyes again and turned to go. "Lean Cuisine for one again. Maybe I'll heat up two and let Pebbles have some this time," she muttered as she walked away.

She and I both knew her tiny purse dog lived higher on the hog than frozen meals, and for that matter, so did she. What she didn't know was that I was fully aware of her long-term relationship with the head chef at Corton. If there was a more well-fed woman at Grange, I was unaware of her.

I turned back to my phone in hopes of seeing a very naked Conor Newell on my screen, but before I got there, Dr. Yvonne Krauss, the lead research and design scientist on the 3-D printer deal, popped her head in my office.

"Have a sec?"

I turned to face her with a forced smile. "Only. What do you need?"

"I've written up my thoughts on the viability of going to market with Dr. Newell's technology today and emailed them to you. From the scientific side, my team is confident in moving ahead as planned."

I was pleased to hear it, although not surprised. Dr. Newell had been perfecting her technology through years of work and testing with all of the appropriate peer-review papers to back up her success.

"Thank you. Any concerns you'd like me to raise along the way?"

She took a minute to think. "We're still confirming production cost details with the consultants, but it looks like everything is as we expected. No surprises."

She continued on for a few minutes, expressing her excitement for the future of Grange with this completed technology in our hands, until I finally had to cut her off.

"Sorry, Yvonne, I don't mean to clip this conversation short, but I need to swing by my place before dinner tonight. I hope you're joining us at Segreto."

"Yes, of course. I'll see you there at seven."

As soon as I closed my office door behind her and scrambled to my phone, I was rewarded with a photo of Conor that was now almost twenty-five minutes old.

I debated whether or not to apologize for leaving him hanging all this time. But of course I knew the answer.

Wells: *My phone died and then I was regrettably detained at work.*

There was no response.

I wanted to kick the leg of my desk, but I had neither the time nor the patience to replace scuffed shoes.

Dammit. I pulled my coat off the back of my chair and buzzed Deb.

"Have the car sent around. I'm heading home."

The text didn't come until I was tossing the keys into the bowl in the foyer of my apartment. The wall of windows overlooking Central Park drew me to them the way they always did, the dark treetops of the park far below setting off the sparkling lights of the city all around them. I could look down into the wide expanse of green and imagine it was the dense forest of the Catskills where I'd spent summers growing up hiking and fishing.

I pulled out my phone and read the message.

NotSam: *Are you mad at me?*

My chest felt like it was going to implode. My fingers itched to type the words, *No, baby. Of course not.* But of course I didn't. Instead, I blinked at the screen, unaccustomed to such thoughts. I cleared my throat and pulled myself together.

Wells: *Should I be?*

NotSam: *I just thought... nvm.*

I moved to the plush leather sofa in front of the fireplace in the living room and sank into it.

Wells: *Not mad. Disappointed I missed getting you off. I shouldn't have left you like that. However, I assume you didn't come without my permission.*

NotSam: *Of course not.*

NotSam: *I mean... No, sir.*

I closed my eyes and palmed my cock through my suit pants. There wasn't time for me to do what I wanted to do with him before I had to shower and dress for dinner.

Wells: *Good. I'll make it up to you later tonight.*

NotSam: *I'll text you when I get back to my room?*

He was so earnest and sweet. Part of me wanted to wreck him, but part of me wanted to wrap the kid up in a cashmere blanket and set him in front of a warm fire.

I took a minute to picture him there in my penthouse with me. Perhaps stretched out naked on the plush cream carpet of my hallway floor, whimpering and begging for me to take him before we even had a chance to make it to the bedroom. His eyes would be wide, pleading like they'd been earlier in the conference room. Perhaps he'd even take his bottom lip between his teeth, scraping across the sensitive flesh. Inviting me to do the same.

I groaned.

Wells: *You're going to be the death of me, NotSam.*

I glanced at the words I'd typed in surprise. While the sentiment was true, there was no need to let him know just how much he was affecting me. That knowledge would give him power, and I preferred to be the one in control.

Control I desperately needed to reassert unless I wanted to blow this entire project.

I deleted what I'd written and typed something else.

Wells: *No. I'll text you when I'm ready for you.*

I tossed the phone on the coffee table and rubbed my face with my palms. What the fuck was I doing? If it was just sex I wanted, there were other ways to go about it. Smarter ways. I thought about the last person I'd had a sexual arrangement with and wondered if I should simply reach out to him and tell him to meet me here later tonight.

But then the way we'd ended things flashed through my mind. Ugly and emotional. Tangled in bullshit feelings and expectations. On his end, of course. Not mine.

No, thank you.

Maybe I could flip through other previous sex partners and find someone for later... I sighed and stood up, pulling my tie loose as I headed back to my bedroom.

The problem was I didn't want someone else.

I wanted Conor Newell. And that was a very big problem indeed.

ONCE WE WERE SEATED at the trendy Italian fusion restaurant in Hell's Kitchen, my wallet several large bills lighter than before, I couldn't help but stare across the table at Conor.

We'd shaken hands when he'd arrived, and it had taken all my self-control to let his go after the appropriate interval. The tips of his hair had still been wet from a shower, and he'd smelled of a high-end fragrance. It had taken me a moment to remember the Four Seasons probably used Bulgari bath products. No way was Conor the kind of guy who normally smelled like that. More than likely, his normal scent was supermarket deodorant combined with Dial soap. Maybe Axe body spray for special occasions or something equally nightmarish.

But I was completely sure he could carry it off like nobody's business, and, if given the chance, I'd suck it into my nostrils like a tweaker snorting a mountain of blow.

I forced myself to focus on the menu in front of me. What the hell was agnello arrostito? I tried recalling the semester of Italian my mother had forced me to take at Penn.

No dice. I guessed I was having the risotto after all.

"Um..." Conor mumbled into his own menu. "Do you think they have an English version of this?"

I glanced up at him, prepared to suggest the risotto, but James answered before I could. "I speak Italian, *tesoro*. What are you in the mood for?"

I knew enough from his tone to figure "tesoro" was a term of endearment. I wondered idly what "pretentious asshole" was in Italian.

Conor smiled sweetly and murmured back and forth with James, who leaned in awfully close in order to hear what Conor asked. They chuckled over some of the descriptions until finally making a decision.

Thank god. I'd been about to take out my text app and order Conor back to his hotel room just so I could put some distance between him and the older attorney. I took a deep breath. I needed to relax or else this was going to be a very long dinner.

Once the server had taken our orders and menus, I lifted my wineglass in a toast. "To new partnerships and smooth negotiations," I said, smiling at Conor.

"To saving lives and helping others," James cut in with a judgmental glint in his eye. At least that's the way it appeared to me. I wondered what the man's problem was, and if it was with the deal in general or me specifically?

"Of course," I added smoothly. "To the future of vessel prosthetics and continued research as well. And to Dr. Elizabeth Newell without whose hard work and dedication, none of this would have been possible."

Conor's face flushed, and he gave a slight nod of appreciation in my direction. Despite having spent the day in the office together with the same team around the restaurant table, he still seemed uncomfortable and nervous.

When the young waiter serving the wine leaned in to refill my water glass, I whispered to him to make sure to keep Conor's water glass full as well. I wanted him plenty sober for our texting later that evening.

"Of course," he murmured back with a flirty smile. "And I promise to take care of you too, sir."

I nodded my thanks and glanced over to Conor, only to catch him glaring at the young server over my shoulder.

Interesting.

Instead of acknowledging it, I turned to the senior R & D tech who happened to be sitting on my right. "Nigel, did you have any other questions or issues we need to go over before moving forward?"

It was a bullshit question. I'd already heard from him the same way I had from Yvonne. Everyone on the Grange team was thrilled with the information and happy to complete the acquisition. Thankfully, Nigel took the opportunity to gush about it rather than questioning me.

"Of course. Isn't this exciting? I've spoken to Karen in operations and she..." He droned on about next steps once the terms of the agreement had been settled, and I had to admit to tuning him out a bit. One and a half ears were on Conor and James's conversation with Yvonne about hiking parts of the Appalachian Trail.

"Mr. Grange has experience hiking the AT, don't you, Wells?" Yvonne asked.

I noticed Conor's eyes widen in surprise. "Really?" he asked.

"Contrary to popular belief, I wasn't born into an Armani suit," I replied. "I have been outside of the city, you know."

Conor's face softened into a teasing smile. "Are you sure about that? Because you looked awfully comfortable slipping cash to the maître d' here. That's not something a North Carolina boy learns how to do."

I felt my own cheeks stretching. "I'm a man of many talents. Some of them happen to include retiring several beloved pairs of Vasque Sundowners, believe it or not."

"Ah, the classic boot," he said with a chuckle.

"And which do you wear?"

"Depends on the trail and conditions. Most quick hikes around home, I actually wear a pair of trail running shoes. I don't have ankle problems, and they're lighter and quicker. If I'm doing something extreme, I wear my Scarpas. Do you backpack too?"

I leaned back and took a sip of wine before responding. "Haven't in many years."

"Too busy working?"

The question came from Conor, but James scoffed in response. As if he knew me. I ignored him.

"I've chosen to take my vacations other places," I said, trying not to grit my teeth.

Conor opened his mouth to speak, but James beat him to the punch. "What's been your favorite spot?"

I thought back to something I'd read about Conor's college semester in Peru.

"Machu Picchu."

Conor's entire face lit up, which almost caused me to spill my drink.

"Really? I love Machu Picchu! When were you there? Oh my god,

I spent a—" He seemed to recall who he was talking to and reined in his enthusiasm a little bit. "I mean, I like it too. Saw it in college. Beautiful, isn't it?"

I met his eyes. "Yes. Very beautiful."

"I'd love to go back sometime. I always wanted to take my mom." Conor hesitated, like he'd been about to say more but had reconsidered.

There was a beat of awkward silence before James picked up the conversation in his stead. "Speaking of the Appalachian Trail—that reminds me of the most ridiculous date I ever went on. Conor, did I ever tell you about Anthony's Nose?"

"Who's Anthony? And I don't think you've told me about anyone's nose," he said, crinkling his own.

"No, it's a hike. Part of the AT, actually, nearby in Hudson Valley," James corrected with a warm smile. "I took a date on a hike there one time and it was a disaster."

James glanced at me before he continued. "I mean, don't get me wrong, the guy is a total sweetheart, but he's a bit of a bad-luck charm, really. He has the worst luck in dating of anyone I know."

Conor leaned forward to take an olive from an antipasto tray that had just been delivered. "What happened on the hike?"

"It started off okay. I picked him up from his place in Brooklyn, and we headed out of the city. This was several years ago. It was early fall, and I was looking forward to seeing if any of the trees had changed yet."

He took a sip of the cocktail he'd ordered and continued. "I'd rented a Zipcar, and I want to say it was like a little Ford Focus or something. I wasn't super familiar with it, but I was driving just fine. As we crossed the George Washington Bridge, he decides to change the radio station. No big deal, right? He leans over to fiddle with he knob and somehow loses his balance, falling into my lap and knocking my arm and the steering wheel."

"Shit," Conor chuckled. "Did you wreck?"

James nodded, grinning. "I swerved toward the oncoming traffic, but there was a cement barrier there. My date panicked when he saw the barrier, so he grabbed the wheel and yanked it toward the opposite side instead."

I frowned. This story was beginning to sound familiar somehow.

"But then he realized the opposite side was the damned Hudson River, so he yanked again. At this point, I was screaming at him to let go and fighting to keep his hands off the wheel. Cars were honking and screeching to a stop around us. It all happened so fast. In the end, we'd sideswiped three other vehicles, the center barricade, and clipped off the side mirror on one of the big metal tubes that make up the right-hand side."

"That's terrible. The poor guy. He must have been mortified," Yvonne said with a laugh.

"No, that's just the beginning," James said. At this point he was regaling the entire table with the tale. His cultured voice carried across the rest of us without sounding like he was making an effort. "It seems there were witnesses to the preceding events, and when the police arrived on the scene, two different parties informed them that the cause of the accident had been my 'boyfriend' performing 'sex acts' that led to my loss of control." He'd used finger quotes to imply the date had been neither his boyfriend nor administering oral pleasure at the time.

Shame.

Everyone around the table snickered, including Conor. But I could only stare dumfounded at the storyteller. Because now I knew why the story sounded so familiar. I'd heard it before. But from the other participant's point of view. The other participant being Oscar Overton, my last regular fuck buddy.

What were the fucking chances this guy had dated Oscar as well?

That we'd both dated the same guy?

Now I knew why James seemed to have a problem with me. Things hadn't ended well with Oscar. He'd been the one who'd wanted more—a relationship, commitment, emotions. I'd broken things off with him without discussion.

James caught my eyes and held them.

"Needless to say, it turned into a mess very quickly."

"What did you tell the cops?" Conor asked.

"That's where it went off the rails," James explained, keeping his eyes locked on mine. "You see, Oscar—that was my date—thought it would help if he cut in to take full responsibility for what had happened. He told the police he'd leaned over to give me a—" He glanced around at the table and cleared his throat. "—a 'sex act' without my consent. I guess his assumption was that his confession would prove the accident wasn't my fault."

Conor groaned, his eyes shining with laughter. I found myself staring at him, unable to look away. He was stunningly expressive.

James continued, his own smile betraying his enjoyment of entertaining the group with the outrageous story. "Only, the police mentioned charging him with attempted sexual assault. So of course Oscar panicked. He tried to backpedal, which only made things worse. He wound up accusing *me* of attempted sexual assault, then realized what he was saying. He apologized and must have decided it was the *witness's* fault for even bringing the idea of a 'sex act' into the conversation. So then he accused *her* of flashing her breasts at us, explaining that's what had really caused the accident."

At this point the entire table was laughing. I found myself chuckling as well. I could just picture Oscar on the side of the bridge waving his hands in the air wildly while attempting to concoct the best explanation for the accident. He was a character. For a split second, I realized I missed seeing him around. It was too bad things had ended the way they had. The guy was funny as hell and great in bed.

I glanced at Conor again. A crinkle of confusion marred his smooth forehead. "Wait, is this Oscar who you dated before Richard?" Conor asked.

James nodded. "Yeah. Great guy. Once we finally cleared everything up with the cops, we continued on to Anthony's Nose and had an incredible date. That was the beginning of our dating relationship, short as it was. Now we're just good friends." His eyes turned to me.

"Did he ever tell you that story, Wells? I mean, when you and Oscar were together?"

Everyone else turned to stare at me, but it was Conor who spoke. His eyes held a flash of surprise.

"You... you're gay?"

9

CONOR

I couldn't keep the shock from my voice, although I wasn't sure why I was so surprised or why it even mattered. I quickly moved to apologize for the blurted question.

"Don't answer that. I'm sorry. It's none of my business."

Wells's eyes were like lasers on me, as usual. "It's fine. I'm out. Been out for a very long time."

I looked down at the table where my fingers were stroking the heavy handle of the knife at my place setting. My cheeks felt like they could be used to cook our dinner if the kitchen stoves somehow stopped working. Why was hearing him confirm his sexuality affecting me?

I was gay. So I couldn't help but wonder if that made things weird between us, made a possible attraction even more... possible. Nope. No need to even think about something so ridiculous. I shook my head but kept my attention on my place setting.

"Conor." Wells's voice rumbled over the table to me. "Look at me."

My eyes jumped up to him immediately, which only made my face redder. The man intimidated the hell out of me.

"It's okay," he said in a softer voice. "Really."

I stared at him as if no one else was sitting with us at the long table. Why did he care what I thought?

"Me too. I mean, I'm gay too." I heard James kind of groan and chuckle under his breath. My intention had been to... what? Offer some kind of quid pro quo to the stuffy executive across the table? But my words had come out sounding stupid at the very least and desperate at the most. "I only meant—"

Before I could finish, he cut me off with a grin.

Huh. The man could grin. Who knew?

"It's okay, Conor. Really. But one word of advice? Stay away from men named Oscar unless you're ready to tie the knot."

James's face dropped into a scowl. "God forbid someone wants to be loved instead of fucked," he muttered under his breath so only I could hear it. I flashed a startled glance at him. "Tell you later," he murmured.

I wasn't sure if I wanted to hear it or not.

Dinner continued with one of the Grange BioMed lawyers at the table sharing the story of his own date gone wrong until the awkward moments between me, James, and Wells had faded. I couldn't help glancing back over at Wells every now and then as if seeing him through new eyes. But no matter how hard I tried to see him from a different angle, I couldn't help remembering everything I'd read and everything my mom had ever told me about him: he was ruthless, cold, only ever in these acquisitions for the money.

For some reason, every time I glanced at him, he seemed to be studying me. A memory of watching an old period drama about King Henry VIII with my grandmother flashed through my mind. The actor who'd played the young, virile king had an intense stare that made everyone around him do his bidding like a stage of intricately controlled puppets.

Wells Grange had that same intensity to his gaze. And whenever he turned it on me there was something about it that made me want to do whatever he said.

He excused himself from the table with a polite nod, allowing me to finally let out a breath and relax.

"That guy is scary," I murmured to James.

"Stay away from him, Conor," he whispered back. "He's nothing but trouble."

I turned to look at him. "How so?"

"Broke Oscar's heart. Apparently the man doesn't have an emotional bone in his body."

The familiar vibration in my pocket bumped my heart rate up. I slid the phone out and glanced at it under the table.

Sexy Stranger: *I can't stop thinking about you naked and begging. You have twenty minutes to text me a full nude from your hotel bed.*

My heart launched into the stratosphere.

Conor: *Leaving restaurant now.*

I noted the time on my phone before shoving it back in my pocket. "I have to go," I blurted, trying to mentally calculate how far it was to my hotel and how long it would take to get back. Should I call a cab? Try to walk it?

It wasn't like I needed to wait around for the check or anything, and dinner had long since been cleared from the table. What were we all still doing there?

I stood just as Wells slid back into his seat. My knee hit the edge of the table, causing a clatter of half-empty wineglasses. He lifted a brow at me.

"Sorry," I said. I noticed my hands were shaking slightly as I tried to fold my napkin. "I, ah..."

"Is it your mom?" James asked under his breath, reaching out to squeeze my arm.

"No, no, nothing like that."

He looked at me expectantly, as if waiting for me to explain. He wasn't the only one; the entire table was staring at me.

"I have a... thing. To do. A person." James's eyebrows shot up and I realized what I'd said. "Not like that," I scrambled to correct myself.

"Not a person to do. I mean at least not the way you're thinking." My cheeks were blazing. "It's more of a—"

James squeezed my arm again, laughter twitching the corners of his lips, and I stopped rambling. I cleared my throat. "I just... have to go. I'll see everyone in the morning."

I turned to Wells and tried to act like a calm adult. As if. I couldn't even meet his eyes. "Thank you for dinner," I mumbled in the direction of his tie.

He said nothing immediately, which forced me to look up at him.

The moment my gaze landed on his, he nodded. Was that a smirk at the edges of his mouth? "Enjoy your evening, Conor."

As I bolted away from the table, I couldn't help but shiver at the way he'd said my name. It echoed in my head as I burst out onto the streets of Manhattan and started speed walking to my hotel. For several blocks I replayed that moment: his silence, the way it forced me to look up at him. To meet his eyes. The way it had felt like, for the briefest moment, I was the only other person at that table who mattered to him.

The thought made my lungs squeeze. I was so lost in the moment that I wasn't watching where I was going. My toe caught a crack in the sidewalk and I tripped, stumbling several steps before regaining my balance. It was enough of a jolt to startle me out of the fantasy I'd been conjuring and back into reality.

Of course I mattered to him, I thought with a shake of my head. I was the one who could decide to turn over the rights to my mother's patents. That's what he cared about. Not me.

I needed to forget about Wells Grange.

I glanced at my phone. Twelve minutes to make it back to my hotel. I started jogging.

Eight minutes later, I was on my knees, naked, holding my cell phone in front of my crotch and trying to figure out the best angle to photograph myself when my mom's face suddenly appeared on the screen. I let out a squeal and practically threw my phone across the room in horror.

It took me a second to realize that phone had flashed her picture because she'd been calling. Thank god, I thought, blowing out a breath. I pressed a fist to my racing heart and scrambled from the bed to retrieve my phone.

Great, she wanted to FaceTime. I looked down at my deflating cock and quickly grabbed a shirt from the back of a chair. I tugged it on over my head and swiped to accept the call.

"Hey, Mom, what's up?" I asked, being very, *very* careful to keep the screen pointed up and not letting it dip anywhere near my exposed nethers.

"Hi, honey. Just calling to check in on how the meeting today went." She turned her head, coughing into her elbow. I narrowed my eyes, studying her. It was difficult to tell on the small screen, but she looked paler than usual, the skin around her eyes bruised. And her voice sounded raspier.

"It went fine. How are you feeling?" I asked her.

She waved a hand, brushing me off. "Fine. Tell me more about the meeting. Have y'all come to any terms yet?"

"Wells—" I began. She lifted her eyebrow at my use of his name, and I cleared my throat. "I mean, *That Asshole* wants to go over a few more logistical details before making the official offer. Should come in the morning."

She nodded. "Good. And you're sure everything went well today? That Asshole wasn't too much of a jerk, was he?"

I shrugged. "He's actually not as bad as I expected him to be."

She snorted. "That's because he's a psychopath, and psychopaths are especially skilled at appearing normal when they want something. Don't fall for it." She started coughing again, and this time it went on longer. I noticed she was out of breath afterward, her lips pale.

"Mom, where's your oxygen?"

She waved a hand again. "In the other room. I'm fine, sweetheart. Don't you worry about me."

Except I knew that tone of voice. And I especially knew that phrase. She only told me not to worry about her when there was actually something to worry about. "What happened?"

"We can talk about it when you get home. You have enough on your plate right now."

"You know I still have the log-in information to your patient portal, right?" I told her. "I can go in there and read your medical records myself, or you can tell me what's going on."

She hesitated, then gave a resigned sigh. "I have pneumonia again."

The world around me froze as the bottom dropped out of my stomach. My mother had a rare autoimmune disorder that had significantly weakened her lungs. The concoction of drugs she'd been on for the last several months had been helping to keep her lungs strong, but we'd known that eventually it wouldn't be enough. We'd just been hoping that the treatment would work long enough for some of the newer drugs in early laboratory stages to enter the clinical trial phase.

This was too early. Too fast.

"Mom—" It came out as a croak. I jumped from the bed and rushed to the closet to grab my suitcase. "I'm coming home."

"Conor Matthew Newell, you stay right where you are. And put on some damned pants while you're at it."

My cheeks blazed red. I'd forgotten I was still half-naked. "Sorry," I mumbled, quickly tugging on a pair of shorts. But I didn't stop packing.

"I'm being serious, Conor," she snapped, sounding stronger than she had earlier. "I don't want you coming home right now. I have everything under control. I already have an appointment to get screened for a promising new treatment."

I paused my packing. "When? I want to go with you."

"Friday. I scheduled it for after you flew in because I knew you'd want to."

"But if they can see you earlier—"

"They can't. Not with the pneumonia."

I opened my mouth to argue again, but she cut me off. "Listen to me. I'm going to be okay, Conor. This is just a minor setback."

I slumped on the bed. I hated being so far away. Hated that I wasn't there when she got the news. "I wish I were there."

She smiled and it lit her eyes. "Me too, sweetheart. But I need you up there right now. The doctor's been fighting with the insurance company, and so far it's not looking good. We may have to fund this on our own, in which case we're going to need the money from the printer patents."

My chest tightened at the thought. I'd known how critical this deal was, but having such a visceral reminder of its importance made me anxious. I hated that she'd been put in this position—that rather than donate the patents to a nonprofit that could make the treatment available to anyone who needed it at a reasonable cost, she had to sell it to a corporation that would price the technology out of most people's reach.

I forced a smile, not wanting her to see the strain I felt. "I know, Mom. I'll take care of it."

Her expression softened. "I know you will, sweetheart. You've always been able to excel at anything you've put your mind to."

It was such a mom thing to say. Her faith in me was absolutely unshakeable. I just wished I had the same faith in myself. We talked for a few more minutes about what was going on at home, but I could sense her energy flagging. It was one of the side effects of her current meds: she tired easily. And the pneumonia certainly wasn't helping. But she didn't like to admit weakness.

So I yawned and told her I needed to turn in early. We said our goodbyes and I love you's and ended the call. After hanging up I sat for a while, staring at my phone, trying to collect my emotions.

I glanced at the time. It was late. I'd been supposed to text my sexy stranger half an hour ago. I flipped to my messages, wondering if perhaps he'd reached out when he didn't hear from me. But there was nothing. I tried not to feel disappointed, but it was difficult.

For a moment I considered putting my phone in sleep mode and going to bed. I wasn't sure I'd be good company. But at the same time, I didn't like the idea of being alone.

I quickly typed up a message and hit Send.

Conor: *Hi. You there?*

It felt lame, but I didn't know what else to say.

Sexy Stranger: *That took longer than expected. I was just about to put my phone down for the night. You can make it up to me by sending me a picture of that gorgeous cock of yours.*

I wanted to. More than anything. I would have loved to have lost myself in his words and what they did to my body. It would be so much easier than thinking about what my mother just told me. But I couldn't. I looked down at my poor flaccid penis and circled my fingers around the base of it, giving it a half-hearted tug.

Nope. Wasn't gonna happen.

Conor: *I'm sorry, something came up.*

Sexy Stranger: *Hopefully you, though not the coming part. Just the up part. You know the rule.*

Conor: *Actually that's the problem. I'm... uh... not going to be able to perform tonight.*

I cringed, despising the idea of disappointing him. I quickly added:

Conor: *I'm sorry.*

Sexy Stranger: *What happened? Between the restaurant and hotel. Something happened, that's why you were late texting. What was it? Are you okay?*

The intensity of his concern overwhelmed me. Suddenly, I felt my throat tighten as his words struck something deep inside me. By default, I wanted to answer yes, that I was fine, but I hesitated. I was a people pleaser; I tended to be agreeable. I didn't like to burden others with my problems. Which meant I rarely shared just how deeply my mother's illness affected me.

But was I really going to share all of that with this stranger? He was supposed to be an anonymous hookup, nothing more.

Sexy Stranger: *NotSam, answer me. Are you okay?*

Except he seemed to genuinely care how I was doing. I thought about this afternoon, the banter as I was walking back to the hotel after the presentation. That had been more than sex. That had been... friendly. He'd actually asked me about myself, like he cared about more than pictures of my cock and getting me off.

Maybe he was exactly who I needed to talk to about all of this. It would be such a relief to no longer be carrying around the burden on my own. I was about to type out my response when his next text came through.

Sexy Stranger: *Answer me or I'm FaceTiming you.*

Panic threaded through me. I wasn't ready for that. Once I saw his face, this whole thing would be real and that would break the magic of it.

The only reason I was able to be so bold, so open, was because this was anonymous. That made it feel somehow safe. I didn't want to lose that.

Conor: *Wait! No! I mean, I'm okay. Don't call.*

I held my breath, waiting for my phone to light up with his call. Knowing that if it did I wouldn't be able to resist answering. Fearing that would be the end of things. There was a very, very long pause. The three dots appeared on the screen, then disappeared, then reappeared again. I felt myself growing more anxious each time.

Sexy Stranger: *Ok. Then tell me what's going on. Please, NotSam. You have me worried. I don't like being worried.*

Conor: *I was getting ready to text you to start our... uh... whatever you call it... when my mother called.*

Sexy Stranger: *Oof. Awkward timing. But I understand—family is important. You made the right decision to take the call.*

I smiled. Another kernel of information about my sexy stranger: family mattered to him. It made me like him even more. I couldn't imagine being in a relationship with anyone who wasn't close to their family.

Not that I was imagining being in a relationship with my sexy stranger. That would be ridiculous.

Conor: *Thanks for understanding.*

I hesitated, still not sure how much to share.

Sexy Stranger: *Somehow I think you're not telling me everything, NotSam.*

I took a deep breath and typed up a response. If my talking about this was too much for him, he could say so. But he'd asked, and I was going to take him at his word that he was genuinely interested in hearing what I had to say.

Conor: *My mother's sick. Really sick. She found out today that the drugs she's on aren't working anymore.*

There was another long pause. I spent every millisecond second-guessing my decision to share the information with him. Wondering if I'd sent him screaming for the hills.

Sexy Stranger: *Oh, baby. I'm so sorry.*

Those words. That text. It almost broke me. I felt my eyes welling with tears. *I'm so sorry.* It was such a simple statement, and one I'd heard a million times in the course of my mother's treatment. But never had I *felt* the force of it. Never had the meaning penetrated my heart.

Conor: *Thank you.*

My response seemed so inadequate when compared to the impact his words had had on me. But what else could I say?

Sexy Stranger: *Is there more you can do? Are there other options?*

Conor: *Yes, but they're experimental and expensive. Insurance won't cover them. That's actually why I'm in the city. I'm hoping to close a business deal that will give me enough money to pay for it. That's what my presentation today was about.*

I figured there was no reason not to tell him the truth so long as I kept any identifying details vague.

Sexy Stranger: *Oh, fuck. No wonder you were so nervous. I didn't know. I'm sorry.*

Conor: *Anyway, that's why I'm not able to... er... perform tonight. I'm sorry to disappoint. Rain check?*

Sexy Stranger: *You've never once let me down, NotSam.*

Sucker punch right to the gut. How did this man seem to know exactly what I needed to hear? For the first time I wished I hadn't lied about my name. Just so I could have seen it written out in that text.

I didn't know how to respond. My instinct was to deflect. To tell him to give me time and I was sure I could come up with something.

Conor: *Speaking of disappointment, you'd said earlier today that I might be able to do something to earn your name tonight (and I definitely spent half the day wondering what that might be). I'm sad I won't have that opportunity. Unless you're willing to reconsider?*

Sexy Stranger: *I'll consider it. In the meantime, tell me about your mother. What's your favorite thing about her?*

The question surprised me, and it took me a while to figure out how to respond.

Conor: *Why? I mean, don't you have work in the morning?*

Sexy Stranger: *Yes. So?*

Conor: *I just assumed that since I can't... I mean since we won't be... you know. Doing the thing. That you'd want to go to bed.*

Sexy Stranger: *Doing the thing? What thing would that be?*

Conor: *You know. Between us. Using... parts. Our parts. Down there parts.*

Sexy Stranger: *Yes, but I'd like to hear you say it.*

I blushed. Forced myself to type out the words.

Conor: *Sex. ting. Sexting. With our penises. I mean, not actually sexting with them, that would be difficult. Unless you had a pencil dick. Which you certainly do not. No way you could text with that thing.*

I forced myself to stop rambling.

Sexy Stranger: *Are you blushing right now, NotSam?*

I growled under my breath. How in the world could this anonymous man know me so well?

Conor: *How did you know?*

Sexy Stranger: *I take that as a yes. Good. I like making you blush. I look forward to doing it more often.*

My cheeks blazed even hotter, and my heart pounded a little faster. *More often* meant he wanted more. It meant that he liked me. Perhaps as much as I was growing to like him.

Sexy Stranger: *Now tell me a story, NotSam. I cleared my schedule to spend tonight with you and I still intend to do so. Even if we're not doing *the thing*.*

I stared at the words, my heart swelling. If he kept talking like this, I might grow to do more than just like him. I glanced at the clock. I had more meetings at Grange BioMed starting early in the morning, but now that James had taken over negotiations, I didn't have to do much other than sit there as a visual representation of the Newell family.

I could easily afford to lose a few hours to my sexy stranger. I flipped through my mental Rolodex of embarrassing stories and landed on one guaranteed to make him howl with laughter. Then I started typing.

10

WELLS

My finger hovered over the Send button. It was almost sunrise, and I'd been texting with Conor all night. My eyes burned, and my thumbs ached from pecking on the screen hour after hour. I didn't want to stop, but I knew I had to. Both of us needed some sleep before starting the day.

I read through our last several texts.

Wells: *Sweet dreams.*

NotSam: *They'll be of you.*

Wells: *Except I'm not sweet.*

NotSam: *Except you are. You just don't like to admit it.*

I'd snorted at that. I'd been called many things in my life. Sweet wasn't one of them.

Wells: *We'll see how you feel after tonight.*

NotSam: *Tonight?*

Wells: *9pm. Be on your knees by the bed. Hard. Send me a picture holding yourself so I know you're ready for me.*

NotSam: *Yes Sir.*

Even rereading his response my eyes fluttered shut, and I almost groaned. If he knew what those two simple words did to me. How much it made my insides roar with satisfaction.

He'd then sent the sleep emoji—the little head with z's drifting up from it. I'd typed up my own response but was hesitating. I hit the Send button before I could overthink it.

Wells: *You can call me Trace.*

It may not have been my real name, but it was what my mother had called me when I was little. I hadn't realized until years later she'd actually been saying "tres," the Spanish word for three since I was Wellington Grange the Third. Conor had more than earned the nickname tonight with his earnest honesty and willingness to share himself.

When he didn't respond immediately, I felt a vague sense of disappointment, but it was only fleeting. That meant he was asleep, and he needed it. I took satisfaction in imagining him tucked in his hotel room, curled under the comforter, dreaming of me.

The only thing that would have made the fantasy better was if I was there with him, curled around him, pulling him against me.

And now I was fantasizing about cuddling. This was getting out of control. But I didn't seem to be able to help myself.

I didn't know how I was supposed to sit with this man in a conference room all day and not think of him naked. Not think of him squirming underneath me, begging for release. Or hell, think of the funny stories he'd told me about himself. We'd talked about everything tonight, though always careful to keep any identifying details vague. He'd asked a few probing questions about my family, but I'd skirted around the edges of them.

He'd made it clear in his refusal to FaceTime that he wanted our texting relationship to remain anonymous. Which was a good thing. I'd been consumed with worry when he hadn't responded to tell me he was okay, and had been seconds away from initiating the call.

It would have been disastrous if he'd learned the truth. Especially like that. Even more so now that he'd confessed how ill his mother was. Never mind that he'd been the one to initiate the dynamic between us, he'd accuse me of using our sexual encounter as a means of getting information from him. He'd think I was manipulating him for the purposes of a business deal.

It didn't matter that I hadn't been. The deal had been the furthest thing from my mind when I'd asked Conor about his mother. I'd only been thinking about him and how upset he'd seemed. I'd only wanted to know more about him.

Which was a problem. Because this deal was too important to fuck up. And I was coming perilously close to doing so.

There was just one problem: I wasn't sure I wanted the deal anymore. Not in the same way. And certainly not at the risk of his mother's health. I stretched out on my bed, staying on top of the covers. I wasn't planning on sleeping more than an hour. I had a lot to think about and even more to plan for.

But for now, I closed my eyes and imagined Conor asleep beside me, one leg thrown over mine and his hand on my chest.

WHEN MORNING CAME I woke up feeling strange. Something had changed. Normally, I sprang out of bed ready to take on the day like a fucking tiger—maul anyone who wanted to get between me and success. But this morning suddenly everything seemed too much. The sheets were too soft, the granite tile in the shower too hard. My coffee was too strong, and my favorite suit felt like a costume.

All the while I prepared for the day, I couldn't shake the sense of something itching just under the surface of my skin.

Maybe I just needed to get laid. Thoughts of Conor had kept me on the edge of arousal for so long, I probably just needed the release of sex. Real sex. Not texts and the familiar feel of my own palm.

I thought about any friends with benefits in my contacts list, but none of the names excited me. If anything, the thought of them left me feeling even more unsatisfied.

My mood soured as I made my way to the office. The day was overcast, threatening snow, the clouds pulled tight around the city, making the streets feel claustrophobic. When I reached the building, I stalked through the skyscraper lobby, unable to stop my eyes from sliding in the direction of the bathrooms.

The image of Conor's cock covered in cum, his shirt shoved aside, his Dalek tie barely visible, flashed in my mind. I wondered if he'd be nervous again today. If he'd take another detour in that direction to relieve his anxiety before our meeting.

A part of me wanted to linger. Wanted to sneak into one of the stalls and pull out my phone to direct him toward the empty stall next to me, just so I could hear the sound of him as he stroked himself off. So I could hear his muffled groans and gasps as he came.

I shook my head and reached for my phone to check the time. I had at least an hour before our meeting. I wasn't going to waste it in a fucking bathroom like a lust-struck teen. As I boarded the elevator, I let my thumb slide to the messages app. There was no alert, no reason to expect any new messages.

But just in case.

Our conversation from this morning filled the screen, the last text I'd sent about my name sitting lonely at the bottom. No response yet from Conor. Even though he had to be awake. Even though he had to have read it.

I ground my teeth. The itch under my skin intensified, making me feel raw around the edges. Sending him my name had been an impulse. It wasn't my legal name; it was something more personal. A name only those closest to me had ever used.

I'd wanted to give him something. Something that mattered to me. Something real.

At the time I'd enjoyed imagining his surprise at the unexpected gift. His delight. I'd pictured gushing texts from him, effusive thanks.

His silence was torture.

And it reminded me why I kept such strict rules. Sex. Nothing more.

Certainly no emotional involvement or attachment.

When I reached my office, Deb noticed my foul mood. But instead of steering clear the way every other employee was, she merely greeted me with a raised eyebrow. "Rough night?"

She nodded at my face, and I lifted a hand to my cheeks. Dammit. I'd forgotten to shave. Again. This was the second day in a row. I grunted my response as I paced to my desk.

She didn't back down. Instead, she followed after me. "How was dinner?"

"Fine."

She eyed me for a moment, clearly something more on the tip of her tongue. Whatever it was, she thought better of it and instead pulled out her tablet to start going through the day's agenda. When she was finished, she slid two folders toward me. "The information you requested yesterday."

I glanced at them. The tab on one said Dr. Elizabeth Newell. The other read Conor Newell. I hesitated, my thumb tracing across the name before I realized Deb was still there and had likely seen the gesture. I cleared my throat, setting Conor's folder aside. "Fine. Thanks. Let me know when the others arrive for the meeting. Close the door on your way out."

When she was gone, I opened the file on Dr. Newell. The front page was a summary. I cringed reading it. She was sick. A chronic autoimmune disorder that was weakening her lungs. There was a list of treatments she'd tried that had worked for a time but had ultimately ended up failing. Conor had mentioned there were still possibilities out there, but they would be expensive. And money was apparently already an issue. A financial report on Dr. Newell showed several credit cards already maxed out, a second mortgage on the house, and a few overdue accounts with a nearby hospital.

I turned, glancing out the window. The businessman in me should have been doing backflips. This was information gold—the kind of leverage that would make acquiring Dr. Newell's patents even easier. By buying the rights to her partner's biomedical ink material, I'd managed to make her patents worthless... unless she sold to me.

She didn't want to do so. She'd made that clear on multiple occasions. According to her, companies like Grange BioMed were a scourge, feeding off the most vulnerable, profiting off other people's illness and misfortune. Her intended recipient of the patents was some kind of foundation that would distribute the lifesaving technique at cost, or close to it. And maybe a couple of years ago she would have stood on her principles and refused to sell. But now—now she had no choice. Her research partner had put her between a rock and a hard place.

All I had to do was name my price. She would be forced to accept it.

My eyes fell on the folder with Conor's name on it. I tapped my fingers on it lightly but didn't flip it open. I didn't understand my hesitation. This was business, I reminded myself. Nothing personal. And yet...

A vibration in my pocket startled me. My hand jerked, sending the file skidding to the floor. I ignored it, reaching for my phone instead.

NotSam: *Thank you, Trace. Truly.*

I blew out a breath. The itchiness under my skin receded. Not all the way, but enough to be tolerable. Enough that I felt a smile creeping across my lips. I liked seeing him use my name.

Wells: *I'll see you tonight.*

My text didn't feel like enough though. I wanted to say more—so much more. But I didn't know what or how. I wasn't used to this... this communicating thoughts and feelings business. So I settled on adding:

Wells: *Good luck with your meetings today.*

He sent back the eyeroll emoji followed by:

NotSam: *Thanks, I'll need it with That Asshole.*

I frowned.

Wells: *That Asshole?*

NotSam: *Yeah, it's the nickname my mom and I use for the guy I've been meeting with. She hates everything he stands for and despises the idea of working with him in any way.*

I hesitated, but I couldn't resist.

Wells: *Is he really that bad?*

NotSam: *If you're a fan of soulless, heartless corporate greed types who prey and profit off the weaknesses of others, then no, not at all.*

Something clenched in my chest. So that's how he saw me?

Wells: *He sounds like a real winner.*

NotSam: *At least he's hot. Makes the meetings go by faster. Speaking of, gotta run if I'm going to make it there on time. See you tonight!*

I sat, staring at the words on the screen.

Soulless.

Heartless.

Preying on the weak.

It wasn't like I didn't know my own reputation. It was useful to be seen as cold and unemotional. It gave me an advantage in negotiations.

But for Conor to think about me that way.

It gutted me.

Because that wasn't who I really was. I'd always considered my reputation something I wore like a suit, something I would change out of at the end of the day. Maybe it had started out that way, but suddenly I wondered if I'd been wearing it long enough that it had become part of me. Like a second skin.

Deb knocked on the door and opened it a crack, poking her head in. "The lobby called. Conor Newell and James Allen are on their way up."

I nodded.

She frowned. "You want me to get them settled and come get you in ten?"

I shook my head. "No. I'll be over in a minute."

She looked at me a moment longer, her concern over my demeanor obvious. Then she ducked back out of my office, closing the door behind her.

I stood, reaching for my suit coat on the back of my chair. Something crunched under my foot. It was the file on Conor Newell. Several pages had escaped from the folder when I'd knocked it to the floor earlier. I crouched, gathering them together while my eyes skimmed the top page automatically. I realized I was looking at an application for a line of credit on a building in downtown Asheville.

Conor's game store. He was probably planning to use it as collateral on a loan to get money for his mother's treatment. Of course he was. Because he was generous and loving and caring.

Whereas I was heartless and soulless and greedy.

The emptiness in my chest turned physical, an ache that actually hurt. I suddenly *wanted*. It wasn't desire—it wasn't sexual. It was larger than that. Deeper. I wanted Conor Newell to see me differently. I wanted him to respect me. To like me. I wanted to prove to him that I could be more.

I wanted to prove that I could be enough for him.

11

CONOR

Wells was late to the meeting. Really late. And it was pissing James off. He looked at his watch for the millionth time. "What an *asshole*," he muttered. It was loud enough for the others at the conference room table to hear, and they squirmed, visibly uncomfortable. But none of them protested or corrected him.

I stifled a yawn. I'd been up so late that I'd slept through my first two alarms. I'd barely had time to shower and race out the door, and I certainly hadn't had time to stop and grab a cup of coffee. Wells's secretary, Deb, had offered me a cup when she'd escorted us into the conference room, but I'd declined because my stomach was still too unsteady with nerves.

I was desperately regretting the decision to skip it.

"Do you and Richard want to have dinner tonight?" I asked, trying to distract both of us from the delay. "I'd love to finally meet him if he can spare the time."

It was a lie. From everything I'd ever heard about the guy, he was a spoiled douche. But James seemed to love the man, so asking them to dinner was the right thing to do.

"He has fencing club tonight."

I blinked at him. "He... what?"

"Don't ask. It's some group from college that bonded enough to make it a monthly thing for life."

"Just you and me, then?" I asked. It had occurred to me earlier that I was going to do something stupid and beg my sexy stranger to meet me in the city for hot sex if I didn't stay busy with other things.

James frowned at me apologetically. "Can't. Sorry. I have dinner with my banker to go over some things. Richard wants me to invest in Olielle, and I need to figure out how to make it happen."

"What's Olielle?"

James flapped his hand. "Pfft. No idea. Real estate, maybe? But it's important to Richard, so..." He craned his neck to try peering out the windows to the hallway. "Where the hell is that jackass?" he muttered. "We need to get this deal moving so you can get home to your mom."

James was about to declare mutiny and revolt when the door swung open and Wells strode in. He gave no apology or acknowledgment of his tardiness. Instead, he moved directly to where I sat and deposited a Starbucks cup in front of me before moving to the head of the table. But instead of sitting, he stood behind the chair, hands resting on the back of it.

What the hell?

I glanced at the cup and saw the Sharpie marks on the side noting it was a mocha latte. How the hell had he known I drank a mocha latte?

I snorted to myself. *Don't be ridiculous, everyone likes coffee and chocolate.*

After taking a tentative sip, I let a sigh of pleasure escape. Wells's eyes shot to mine. I couldn't resist the twist in my stomach at the sight of him. I thought about what I'd texted Trace earlier—that Wells might have been an asshole, but he was still hot. It was true. Even more so today. He still hadn't shaved, and two days' worth of stubble turned his jaw to a rugged shadow. It was entirely incongruous with his perfectly crisp suit and piercing blue eyes.

I dropped my gaze to my coffee cup. I didn't need him to notice me gawping.

"Plans have changed," he said without preamble or introduction.

That got me looking right back up again. I found Wells staring at me. My heart began to pound fast and loud enough I could hear the swoosh of it in my ears.

Beside me, James stiffened and leaned forward. "Changed how?"

Wells continued looking at me, even as he answered James. "My offer is off the table."

Panic clawed hot and fierce inside my chest. I was having a hard time breathing. I'd been trying to line up other funding for my mother's treatment just in case, but this deal was still critical. It still needed to go through.

James placed a hand on my arm, trying to reassure me. "Explain," he said to Wells with narrowed eyes.

"I'm done negotiating." He nodded toward Deb, who maneuvered a cart piled high with documents into the room. She began distributing packets to everyone at the table. "I've decided to accept Dr. Newell's original terms. I've had legal alter our draft offer to reflect that, though of course there are still details to be worked out."

When he finished, there was silence in the room. After a moment, one of his VPs cleared her throat. "Mr. Grange, I'm not sure—"

"I am."

"But—"

He ignored her and turned to me. "Do you accept?"

I glanced toward James, feeling entirely helpless. "I don't understand. Accept what?"

James continued glaring at Wells. "What's the trick here?"

Wells held his hands out to the side. "There isn't one."

"I'll want to be involved in drafting the final agreement to ensure there are no surprises in the fine print," James said.

"Of course," Wells told him. "My attorneys will be happy to work with you on that. Any questions should be resolved in favor of Dr. Newell."

Several members of the Grange team sucked in a breath at that. Two began murmuring to one another, casting furtive glances at Wells.

Something had seriously changed here and I still didn't understand what it was. "Can someone please explain what's going on?"

"He's accepting your mother's terms," James told me.

I met Wells's eyes. There was something there. That hunger again. The one I'd seen the previous morning. It made something inside me burn, my skin flushing. "Why?" I asked him.

It took him a moment to answer. "Because this deal is critical to Grange BioMed's future, and I don't want to risk losing this technology."

For some reason, the answer disappointed me.

"There is a condition, however," Wells added.

"Of course there is," James sighed, rolling his eyes.

Wells ignored him, keeping his focus on me. "We'll go over the new arrangements through lunch today, and then this afternoon, while the attorneys hash out the rest of the fine print, I would like to spend some time getting to know you, Conor. If this deal goes through, our company will be working closely with your family to get this tech to market in a reasonable time frame, and it's important we start that relationship off on the best foot possible."

It was the last thing I expected to hear him say. He wanted to spend the afternoon with me? Like, just the two of us? My pulse kicked up a notch even while my stomach twisted with nerves.

I glanced at James. He'd already started flipping through the stack of documents Deb had placed in front of him. He had a look of incredulity on his face.

"What do I do?" I asked him in a low voice.

His answer was simple. "You say yes."

MY BRAIN WAS STILL REELING after lunch when I found myself in the dim hush of a town car sitting next to Wells Grange as the city crowds moved around us. The back seat was spacious, but still it felt too small, as though I could shift ever so slightly and accidentally brush against him. His smell dominated the space between us, that mix of masculine cologne and his own warm body. It made it difficult to concentrate.

Wells cleared his throat. "What would you like to do?" he asked. "Anything in particular you'd care to see while you're in New York?"

I stared at him. "What, like a tourist thing? The Statue of Liberty or something like that?"

He shrugged, shifting the soft-looking wool of his formal coat across his shoulders. The black coat made his eyes look even bluer, if that was possible. "Or museum or art gallery, perhaps. Whatever strikes your fancy."

I was inclined to be annoyed with him. Had it not been for his abrupt change of plan, my brain wouldn't be wildly scrambling to make sense of the man beside me. I'd gone into the meeting this morning with a game plan, a strategy to win the best terms for my mother possible. And now it was irrelevant. Because I'd won. Somehow, inexplicably, he'd agreed to my mother's price. But why? What had caused the sudden shift?

And why ask to spend the afternoon with me? A part of me wondered if this might be some sort of trap, a way to maneuver me into position where he could ultimately take advantage of me and my mother. If it was, I didn't plan to make it easy for him. He'd succeeded in throwing me off whatever game I may have had going into this. I intended to return the favor.

I struggled to come up with the very last thing I could imagine Wells Grange wanting to do. My eyes drifted over him, from the polished shoes to the perfectly pressed pants to the cufflinks glittering at his wrists. He looked every bit the quintessential New Yorker, born to money and prestige and power.

"Carriage ride in Central Park," I blurted.

It wasn't really true, but his reaction to the cheesy suggestion was worth the lie. He stared at me like I'd just requested a private showing of the pope performing popular hip-hop moves. Naked.

"A what? A carriage ride through..." He couldn't even bring himself to finish.

I opened my eyes wider, trying to appear innocent and earnest.

When in reality I had to bite the inside of my cheek to keep from smiling. "I've always wanted to take one."

He tightened his jaw. "Of course. Hank, Columbus Circle please."

The car turned slowly through the next intersection, driving past the throngs of people making their way toward Times Square. I couldn't even picture Wells Grange among the hoi polloi. God forbid someone accidentally step on his two-thousand-dollar Berluti shoes. Not that I knew what those were, but James had mentioned his boyfriend wanting a similar pair despite having a closet full of them at home.

"Will you be warm enough?" Wells asked, raising a brow at my own coat.

"Just because it's from JC Penny doesn't mean it won't keep me plenty warm," I said defensively, wrapping my own black dress coat around me and trying not to look like a moron.

Wells's face softened. "I was more worried about you not having a scarf or gloves."

I refused to acknowledge the thoughtfulness of that statement. "The carriages have blankets, right? I'll be fine."

His nose wrinkled. "Those blankets have been used by god knows how many strangers since being washed dozens of years ago."

I laughed. "I'm made of stern stuff, city boy."

Wells turned to look out the window. "There's a market in Columbus Circle. We'll pick up a scarf and gloves for you there before getting the carriage."

The warm feelings in my chest needed to get the hell out. I had no space inside for positive thoughts toward Wells Grange. I tried reminding myself of what an asshole he'd been keeping us all waiting that morning, but then the traitorous side of my brain reminded me that he'd only done that because he'd been working out a better offer for my mom.

And he'd brought me a mocha latte.

Dammit.

I closed my eyes, letting out a breath. The man appeared to be making a legitimate effort here; the least I could do was give him a chance.

"Are you from here?" I asked.

He continued looking out the window as he spoke. "Greenwich."

I stared at the back of his head waiting for him to say more. When it appeared no other information was forthcoming, I rolled my eyes. "Sorry," I finally snapped. "Didn't mean to pry."

His head whipped around in surprise, but before he could say anything, the driver announced we'd arrived. I bolted out of the car onto the sidewalk and made my way to the market stalls set up by the entrance to the park. Vendors were selling baby items with funny sayings on them in one stall, apple donuts and cider in another, and various artistic items in many of the rest. Wells moved past me to a stall displaying a colorful collection of hand-knit goods.

"These will do," he muttered.

The woman behind the table looked up at him from her knitting with a relaxed smile. "Good afternoon. Are you looking for something in particular?"

Before Wells could say something offensive, I reached for a soft-looking scarf made of fat stripes in rainbow colors. As soon as she saw me choose it, the woman's face lit up. "That's my favorite yarn. It's a blend of merino, cashmere, and silk. Feel it."

I ran the back of my fingers across the scarf. She was right. It felt like a dream. "My friend Bill would go nuts for this yarn. Does it come in a sock weight? He likes the fiddly stuff with tiny needles."

She hopped up from her stool and reached up to a display shelf behind her before pulling down a matching pair of socks to the scarf I held. "I even have a beanie and gloves to match. If you buy the whole set, I'll write down where he can get the yarn," she said with a wink. "My name's Kathy, by the way."

"Conor, nice to meet you."

Out of the corner of my eye, I could see Wells watching me patiently as I chatted with the woman and picked out a separate scarf and gloves for myself. I let her wrap up the rainbow set for my friend while I wound my new scarf around my neck. Wells had been right. It made a big difference and warmed me up immediately.

"Is Bill someone special?" Kathy asked with a grin. Wells stiffened beside me. Knowing him, he wouldn't appreciate some random stranger asking him such a personal question.

"Oh, no. He's my mom's neighbor who's been helping us with..." I remembered Wells was there and didn't know about my mom being sick and needing help with meals and doctors appointments. "Shoveling snow... um, when I'm not around and it... snows. And stuff."

"Well, give him my card and tell him I'd love to hook up with him on Ravelry."

When it came time to pay for everything, Wells shoved his credit card at the woman before I even had a chance to grab my wallet. "I got this," he said.

"Absolutely not," I replied. "Are you crazy?"

He glanced at me. I was expecting his face to carry an expression of annoyance or pity, but instead there was something else in his gaze. Something that made my chest tighten.

Possessiveness, I finally realized.

Like I was somehow his to take care of.

I found myself drawn to his eyes, unable to look away. He smiled, the movement slow and languid, the corners of his lips tilting up, one side higher than the other. As though he'd won some game I hadn't even realized we'd been playing.

Fuck that.

"Wells, you may be richer than god, but I can afford my own damned gifts, thank you very much. Especially after this morning."

I turned back to Kathy, with the sugariest smile I could manage. "Don't mind him," I said, reaching into my pocket for my wallet. "Here." I thrust several bills toward her. "Keep the change."

She looked from me to Wells and back again before shrugging and plucking the money from my hand. "I appreciate it," she said, returning Wells's card to him unused and handing me the package. "Enjoy the rest of your afternoon."

We said little to each other as we left the market and strolled along Central Park South. Wells kept his hands in his pockets, a frown pinching the skin between his eyebrows and his attention lost to the sidewalk as if trying to puzzle through a complicated problem. I didn't interrupt. I didn't particularly have much to say to him anyway.

If anything, I was considering suggesting we forget the whole "bonding" thing and go our separate ways when Wells steered us toward an empty carriage. An attractive young man stood next to the horse while the animal drank from a bucket of water. "Carriage ride?" he asked with a big smile.

I began to nod when Wells asked, "How much time will it take?"

The man's smile didn't drop but his eyes moved to me before returning to answer Wells. "It's a forty-minute loop through the park."

The corners of Wells's lip turned down briefly before he let out an impatient sigh. "Fine," he said, stepping forward to hand me up into the carriage.

I hesitated. "Do you have somewhere else to be?"

He seemed surprised by the question. "No. Why?"

"Then why does it matter how long the ride will be?" I asked.

He opened his mouth to answer and then closed it. Then he frowned. "I'm just... not used to spending time idle I guess."

I lifted an eyebrow. "This whole afternoon was your idea," I reminded him. "Carriage rides are supposed to be fun."

He gave me a long look, his expression unchanging. "Yay," he finally said in the most deadpan voice I'd ever heard.

I blinked at him. "Did you just make a joke?"

He quirked an eyebrow. "If you tell anyone, I'll deny it."

Before I could respond, he waved his hand, still outstretched and ready to help me up into the carriage. I took it, wishing for the briefest moment we both weren't wearing gloves.

Once we were both settled, the driver turned and smiled. "My name is Scotty, and I'll be your tour guide this afternoon. There's a blanket there if you'd like it. Let me know if you have any questions as we make our way around. I'll point out some places of interest, but feel free to ask me anything in the meantime."

He faced forward and began directing the horse to do a U-turn right there in the middle of the Manhattan city traffic.

I turned to Wells and saw him clutching the side of the carriage as it lurched around. He was so clearly out of his comfort zone I couldn't help but grin. This was going to be fun.

"Blanket?" I asked, reaching for the faux-fur monstrosity on the seat in front of us.

12

WELLS

There was nothing more humiliating to a New Yorker than looking like a damned tourist. I avoided nonsense like this because it was bullshit meant to separate people from their money.

Conor, however, was in full tourist mode. "Oh look! A real-life dog walker," he said, pointing to a young woman struggling to manage six different dogs on various leashes.

"Do you have a dog?" he asked, turning toward me. I leaned over to tuck the ends of his new scarf into the front of his coat and caught a whiff of the patchouli scent coming off it from the market stand where he'd bought it. It was normally a smell that completely turned me off, but of course on him it was intoxicating. I needed to get control of my attraction to him before I did or said something inappropriate.

I finished tucking the scarf before clearing my throat and glancing away. "No."

He continued to look at me as if expecting more. I clenched my hand into a fist and cleared my throat. "No, I don't have a dog."

Conor laughed again. "Do we need to score you some weed? Or a few shots of tequila? Or would this be a good time to remind you that this whole 'getting to know each other' bullshit was your idea."

I blew out a breath. He was right. "I'm sorry. I'm just... this isn't what I'm used to." I met his eyes. "But I do want to get to know you."

He studied me for a minute. "Why?"

I was saved from answering by our driver pointing out the building where Lady Gaga apparently owned a penthouse.

Conor leaned forward. "Ooh, where?" he asked. The driver pointed, launching into a story about the time he'd actually seen her. Or someone who looked a lot like her at least. Conor listened with interest, and it took me a moment to realize it wasn't feigned interest either.

"You a Lady Gaga fan?" I asked when the driver finished his story and Conor settled back in his seat.

He shrugged. "Isn't everyone when you're drunk on the dance floor?"

I didn't have an answer to that. I couldn't remember the last time I'd been somewhere with a dance floor.

My expression must have been enough for him to read my mind because he chuckled. "Yeah, I don't picture you as the clubgoing type. You seem more like a..." His eyes roved over me, taking me in from head to toe. I resisted the urge to shift and pull my shoulders straighter. "Private-club kind of guy. Expensive cigars, ridiculously expensive wine. Ungodly expensive scotch."

He wasn't entirely wrong. "The Brandy Library is my preferred haunt."

Conor leaned closer to the carriage driver. "Have you heard of that one, Scotty?"

The man nodded. "It's over in Tribeca."

"Let me guess, pretentious as hell?"

"Let's just say if James Spader is ever cast in a remake of *Pretty in Pink*, you'll find him there with an elbow on the bar. Oh, and he'll be hanging out with the bro dudes from his old fraternity who are all iBankers now. And they'll be trading war stories about where they were when they heard the inheritance tax went up."

Conor laughed, full-throated with his head thrown back. It was a beautiful sight. My eyes dropped to the patch of skin under his jaw, just visible above his new scarf. I wanted to lick it, I realized abruptly. To press my lips against it and feel the sound of his laughter infuse me.

He caught me looking at him, and I did nothing to hide my interest. His laughter quieted, ending with a sharp intake of breath. Tension suddenly crackled between us. He licked his lips, pressing them together for a moment before clearing his throat. "Why me?" he asked, repeating his earlier question.

Because of moments like this, I wanted to tell him. When he laughed with abandon. Or when he noticed the parts of the city others overlooked. Or the fact that he already knew our driver's name, and when he expressed interest in his stories, it wasn't out of a sense of obligation or feigned politeness, but genuine curiosity. Or the fierceness with which he cared for his mother, willing to sacrifice everything for her.

Conor Newell was a man who lived his life. Followed his passions. Experienced things. Felt things.

Being around him made me want the same.

But I couldn't say any of this. Because as far as he was concerned, we were practically strangers. He didn't realize just how much I knew about him from our many hours of texting. He didn't know just how difficult it was for me to sit here and pretend that I didn't know about the time he'd gone skinny-dipping in the French Broad River when a raccoon had made off with half his clothes. Or about the time he'd tried to cook Mother's Day breakfast for his mom as a kid but confused the measurements, resulting in fried balls of flour paste his mother had to choke down with a smile.

Holding all of this back was making me act like an ass, but I couldn't seem to stop.

I gave him the only answer I could think of. "You're the one holding the patents to the printer." I didn't realize how harsh the explanation sounded until his eyes clouded.

He lifted a shoulder, glancing off to the side. "The printer is my mom's baby. To be honest, I just sell board games."

I shifted closer, leaning toward him. I started to reach a hand for his arm but at the last minute dropped it onto the seat between us. "I thought I heard a rumor that the 3-D printing was actually your idea."

He paused, either the cold air or being put on the spot making his cheeks bloom pink. "Well, yeah. I guess, technically it was. I was super into the technology at my gaming store. I..." Conor peered over at me through his thick lashes, seemingly hesitant to say the next part. "I use it to print custom game pieces."

I'd never heard of anything like that before. "Like the little dog in Monopoly?"

He smiled. "Kind of. But more like the Assassin from Citadels or Tordek from D&D." When he saw my face, he laughed. "Or... like if you wanted to play chess where the game pieces were Muppets instead of the usual king, queen, rooks, etc. I could print those pieces for you. Well, not the actual Muppets since they are protected by copyright and trademarks, but you get the idea."

"Ah, I see. You can design new pieces and actually create them using the 3-D printer."

His eyes brightened. "Exactly. It started as a hobby, but then people in the gaming community found out about it and began commissioning pieces from me. The business is doing well. Eventually, I'll need to hire some help. I run it from the space above the game shop which helps a little. Asheville is a small town, but I've done well there."

His enthusiasm for the subject was infectious, and I was about to ask him to tell me more when something occurred to me. "How are you managing two businesses while you're up here negotiating this deal for your mother? It can't be easy."

His expression faltered a bit. "It's... fine." His voice cracked and he cleared his throat, repeating, "I'm fine."

Well, that was an obvious lie. I wondered if he needed help, if he had much support back home.

"Conor..."

He cut me off, pointing past me. "Oh look, it's the fountain from *Friends*."

"Actually," the driver cut in, "it's not the one from the television show."

"Really?" Conor asked. "That's insane. It looks like the same one."

As he spoke back and forth with the driver about the other parts of the show that hadn't been real New York locations, he leaned across me to get a better view of the fountain.

"It sure is pretty though," he murmured. "This whole park is. So much quieter than the hustle and bustle. Having such a wide expanse of natural beauty in the middle of the crazy city... it's unexpected. Don't you think?"

He turned as he asked the question, but because of our proximity, the white puffs of our exhales mixed together between our faces.

His front teeth quickly came out to bite at his bottom lip, which sent a hot spike of need through my gut.

"Sorry," he breathed, sitting back into his spot beside me. "Guess I'm acting like the stupid tourist after all."

"I like it," I admitted. "Seeing you get excited about the park makes me realize how much I've come to take it for granted."

"Really?"

I nodded. "I jog here most days and don't even notice it. But you're right. It's a peaceful break from the noise on the city streets." I looked around, trying to see it through Conor's eyes. The cyclists whizzing past, the young mothers walking together with their fancy strollers, and the city residents jogging for exercise. The large expanses of dormant grass and rocky boulders peeking out from beneath children's scrabbling hands and feet. Tiny dogs in sweaters led a pair of older women down a path toward several benches where the matching set of older men waited.

It occurred to me that I hadn't enjoyed much of anything New York had to offer lately. It made me want to see more. Experience more.

With Conor.

"Have you seen any shows here?" I asked. "I could get us tickets."

Conor snorted, which caused the driver to chuckle.

I frowned. "What?"

"I can't picture you at a show, no offense."

"What? I do take offense. I like shows," I insisted.

Conor raised a challenging eyebrow. "Okay, then, what was the last one you saw?"

I thought back. "I saw *Fiddler on the Roof* at the Broadway Theater recently," I said defiantly.

The driver hooted with laughter before speaking directly to Conor. "Cutie, tell your boyfriend he needs to see something written this century. That show closed two years ago. "

"Not possible," I argued, ignoring the assumption we were together—like that. "I went with my sister, Win, and she..." I realized I was getting ready to say she'd been pregnant, but then I realized my niece was almost three years old. How had time passed so quickly without me realizing? I made a mental note to reach out to my sister and ask her to another show. She loved them and knew the words to all the songs.

"Hmm," I conceded. "I guess it's been a while."

Conor leaned into my shoulder, still sporting a grin. "It's okay. You're a workaholic. Everyone knows that about you."

I frowned. "Pick a show. We'll go while you're here."

Conor studied me, his eyes flicking between mine. "Why are you doing this?"

"I assume you don't have access to Broadway shows in Asheville," I said, deliberately misunderstanding him.

"No. Why are you suddenly trying to be my tour guide?"

Because I want to spend time with you. Because I think about you all the time. Because it's easier when you're around.

But I said none of those things. "You... seemed stressed yesterday during the negotiations," I said instead. "I wanted to give you a chance to get out of the office and relax while the attorneys hashed out the details."

Conor's expression shifted, the openness suddenly shuttering. "You act like I can't hold my own during a damned business meeting. I'm not a kid. And I do actually have a business degree. Moreover, I own two—"

I reached for his arm without thinking. "Stop. That's not what I meant."

Time seemed to stop as we both looked at my hand on the sleeve of his winter coat.

"Sorry," I muttered, releasing it quickly and folding my hands together in my lap. I clenched my jaw. I was fucking this up. "I just thought you could use a break. And I damned sure thought I could use one. It has nothing to do with how capable you are or aren't."

Conor looked away, off toward Central Park West. "What happened between you and Oscar?"

I was taken aback by his question. What did the guy I used to have sex with have to do with anything? "Why?"

He shrugged. "I'm curious."

"He wanted a relationship. I didn't. End of story."

Conor frowned. "But if you were dating, weren't you already in a relationship?"

"Oscar and I weren't dating," I clarified. "He's just a guy I used to—"

He held up a hand. "Don't say it. That's rude as hell. Not everyone is like you, Wells. Some of us do actually prefer a relationship over a convenient fuck."

I opened my mouth to argue, but what could I say? The only inaccuracy in his statement was the implication that I'd been indiscriminate in my choice of sexual partners, that I was someone who just slept around, jumping from bed to bed. Nothing could have been further from the truth. I'd chosen each sexual partner carefully, making it clear up front what I expected out of the arrangement. I'd never lied to any of them. I'd never promised them anything more. And if I felt like they might have started expecting more I ended it because I didn't want to lead them on.

I'd broken things off with Oscar because it wasn't fair to let him want something he would never have from me.

Ultimately, however, Conor was right. I didn't do relationships. I never had.

I never would.

I pressed my lips together, saying nothing.

Something like disappointment flashed in Conor's eyes, and he quickly looked away as we approached the completion of our tour.

Great. Somehow in forty minutes I'd managed to make him think even less of me than he had before.

No wonder I wasn't cut out for this shit.

When Conor hopped down from the carriage, he gushed his thanks to the driver before giving me a perfunctory nod of thanks and walking into the park. I paid the driver and followed Conor, ignoring the driver's teasing comment about getting Oscar's number.

"Conor, wait," I called to his back. "I'm sorry."

He whipped around. "For what?"

I opened my mouth and closed it before settling on what to say. "I don't like to talk about my private life."

His burst of laughter startled me. "You are the master of fucking control. What are you so goddamned afraid of? That someone might realize you're an actual person behind that Armani suit and take advantage of you? That you might lose out on several million dollars in a multibillion-dollar deal? Lighten up already. Jesus. The deal is already done. We're not negotiating anymore."

I stared at him. "Brioni."

"Huh?"

"It's not Armani. It's Brioni Bespoke."

Conor's face morphed from confusion to amusement. He was so expressive, so engaging. I wanted to touch him. I wanted to sink my nose into the crook of his neck and inhale him.

"You're a piece of work," he said through his laughter. "What the hell is Brioni?"

I shrugged, allowing myself to laugh too. "Italian suit maker. It's only a couple of blocks from here on Madison Avenue. Want one?"

Conor's eyes sparkled in the cold air. "That depends. Do you have a coupon?"

I was reminded of his money situation, the fact he'd attempted to mortgage his own businesses to cover his mother's medical expenses.

I couldn't begin to imagine the stress he was under, yet here he was smiling in Central Park. With me.

I wanted to reassure him about his mother, make promises that she'd be okay, that I would *make sure* she was okay. But of course I couldn't. First of all, he didn't know that I knew about her illness. And secondly, I could no more stop the effects of her autoimmune disorder than stop the tides from turning.

But there was something I could do. I could distract him for a bit, and since he was clearly drawn to the expanse of nature in the park, I could escape into it with him for a while longer.

I pointed off to our left. "Have you ever seen the movie *Elf*? The snowball fight happened over there by that footbridge."

Conor began walking in that direction, turning around to face me while stepping backward down the path. "Now you sound like Scotty. And no offense, but I can't picture you sitting still for the movie *Elf*."

"It came out while I was in college. Those were the days I was still trying my hardest to be straight, and my girlfriend wanted me to take her to see it."

Conor stopped walking, and I nearly ran into him. I reached out to steady myself using his shoulder and he brought his hand up to clasp my forearm. Our eyes met and my chest tightened.

"I thought you said you didn't like to talk about your private life," he said softly.

Only with you.

I released my hold on his shoulder and stepped back. He reluctantly let go of my arm. "Well, I'm not revealing state secrets exactly. Don't most gay men go through a denial phase like that?"

"I didn't," he admitted. "But I know plenty of people who have. I guess I never would have figured you for someone who gave a shit what other people thought about you."

The subject was getting a little too close for comfort, so I changed it quickly.

"Tell me how you got into gaming."

13

CONOR

I told Wells about how I'd started the game store, which led into a conversation about what I did for fun, which had us trading stories of hikes, rafting trips, and other outdoor adventures we'd been on. We had more in common than I ever would have guessed, and I'd begun to feel like the man by my side in the park wasn't at all the man my mother had been griping about for years.

He spoke of his own family, his European mother and his American father who'd met in college in Massachusetts before starting their family in Greenwich, Connecticut.

"Your dad's an investment banker, right?" I asked.

Wells nodded. "He's worked on Wall Street since before I was born. Not sure he'll ever retire. The man's a workaholic."

I stared at him. "Pot, meet kettle..."

Wells snorted softly and looked away.

I was about to ask him more about his father when he abruptly changed the subject, asking, "Do you like Indian food?"

I blinked at him. Hadn't we just eaten lunch at the office? I looked around us and only then realized the sun had set. How long had we been wandering around the park? I took stock of my body and realized the front of my thighs were frozen and I couldn't feel my toes in my dress shoes.

"Yeah. I like Indian, especially if it'll warm me up quickly. You know a place?"

He pulled out his phone to send a text, and within moments his town car coasted to a stop a few paces ahead of us. Wells opened the door for me before speaking to the driver.

"Bengal Tiger, Hank."

Hank snorted quietly but didn't say a word. It sounded like the noise one made in place of saying "duh."

Wells turned to me, and suddenly I was overwhelmed with guilt at second-guessing his motivations earlier in the day. "Thank you for this. I think... I think I built you up in my head to be all about business success at whatever the cost, and I didn't allow you to actually be... normal."

He tilted his head in question. "I'm not sure what to say to that."

I cursed under my breath before looking back up at him. He really was a beautiful man, but this was not the time to take notice of it. "I didn't mean it as an insult. At least, it was meant to insult myself, not you. What I'm trying to say is... I prejudged you. I assumed you were the corporate asshole the media and my mother have always made you out to be. That's on me. I should have given you a chance without coming to the table thinking I already knew who you were. That was my mistake."

Wells's face softened. "I'm sorry too. I actually *am* the corporate asshole everyone has made me out to be. But... that's not necessarily who I want to be."

As the car made its way through the crowded city streets, I thought about his words.

"Why do you do it, then?" I asked in a low voice, as if by speaking softly I wouldn't anger the scary beast.

Wells looked out the window on his side of the car. His hands lay clasped calmly in his lap over the rich folds of his coat. Something about his hands looked familiar, and I found myself staring at them.

"It's a long story," he said after a moment.

I rolled my eyes. "Right. I forgot you didn't like to talk about your personal life." Despite the fact he'd been doing so most of the afternoon.

Wells turned to me, creases of concern marring the otherwise smooth skin of his forehead. "No, Conor. I'd like to tell you, but I'd rather wait until we sit down to eat if you don't mind."

His words were stilted and overly polite, another unexpected tone from him. I was beginning to feel like I'd stepped out of the Grange BioMed building and into an alternate universe.

"Here we are, sir," Hank said from the front seat as he slid to a stop next to a narrow brown awning. "Text me when you're finished and I'll be by to collect you."

We made our way upstairs into a narrow, crowded restaurant. I could tell right away from the smells inside that I would love it.

"God, it smells amazing in here. It reminds me of Chai Pani back home," I mumbled as I unpeeled the warm layers of coat and scarf.

Wells spoke to one of the men behind the counter, who showed us to a small table in the corner immediately. From the nasty glares pointed our way, I gathered we had some kind of reservation or were receiving preferential treatment.

"Come here often?" I asked with a grin when I settled into the seat.

Was that a blush on Wells Grange's handsome face? Now I knew I was in an alternate reality.

"Hank swings me by for takeout at least once a week."

I looked up from the menu to gawp at him. "Why not send just him or get it delivered?"

He shrugged and looked at the menu. As if he needed to see it. Coming here so often, surely the man had the damned thing memorized. "He'd have to park the car, which is impossible. It's a long walk from the office, but it's right on my way home. It's no problem for me to run up here and grab it."

I peered out at the street, orienting myself from what I knew of the city and where the office was. "You live on the Upper East Side?"

He shrugged. "Not even that far. More like Lenox Hill. Near Bloomingdale's if you know where that is."

I shook my head. "I only know where some of the subway stations are. Oh, and this one game store near the Empire State Building."

"Lexington Ave subway station. That's my stop," Wells said with a wink, looking back down at the menu. "Not that you'd ever catch me riding the trains."

Was he flirting with me?

"Of course not," I teased. "How plebeian."

When a young woman came to take our order, I let Wells make the decisions. I was overwhelmed enough from the crowds, the city, and the nearness of such an imposing personality. The last thing I needed to add was stress over which dishes to get.

After Wells finished ordering for us, he added something unexpected. "And the usual for Hank, please. To go. Thanks, Angel."

I stared at him in disbelief. This man who didn't seem to notice or care about many of the people around him had just gone out of his way to get food for his driver. And apparently did so often enough that there was a usual dish he ordered.

He must have misunderstood the look on my face.

"What? Her actual name is Angel. Don't look at me like that. I'm not a creep."

After I finished laughing, I clasped the metal cup of cold water in front of me before biting the bullet and asking what I really wanted to know. "Do we have time for your long story?"

Wells smiled and sat back in his chair. When that man broke out a real smile, it was enough to start excited bees buzzing in my stomach.

"The short version is I trusted the wrong person."

I thought back to what I'd asked him. "Wait... that's the story behind why you're a corporate asshole?"

Wells's long fingers forked through his hair as he coughed out a laugh. "Pretty much. I mean, I was always competitive, don't get me wrong. I worked my ass off in school and graduated with high marks. Earned my way into the Ivy League for both undergraduate and my master's. But while I was in business school, I met a guy in my apartment complex named Mark. We quickly became best friends and were interested in the same type of business challenges, took several of the same classes. We graduated and started a company together based on a business plan we'd created for one of our entrepreneurship courses."

Hearing about Wells as a student was strange. It was hard to picture him without the mantle of corporate success around him.

A server delivered us bowls of soup and refilled our water cups before hustling away again. Wells took a taste of soup before speaking. I ignored the way his throat moved as he swallowed. Or at least tried to. But the man had a beautiful neck. In fact, he had a beautiful everything. If I allowed myself to follow that train of thought, it might lead me somewhere I didn't want to go, so I forced it from my head and focused on Wells's story instead.

"The company specialized in express pharmaceutical supply transportation and logistics," he explained. "Mark and I worked very well together, and the company grew like magic in that first year. I remember spending Christmas at my parents' house a year and a half in. My father had invited Mark's entire family to celebrate with us, and everything seemed perfect."

He hesitated a moment before clearing his throat and adding, "He, ah... he met and fell in love with my sister during that visit."

He glanced away, looking so vulnerable, it made me feel unsettled. I didn't like seeing him that way. It made me want to reach across the table and place my hand on his—anything to give him a modicum of comfort. But I wasn't sure how he would take the gesture, so instead I kept my fingers clamped around my spoon.

"Wow. That sounds perfect," I said, wondering why he looked so unsure. "Everything falling into place."

His lips twisted slightly. "Yes, well. My parents raved about Mark's and my success that Christmas, and I remember feeling like it was the first time they were actually proud of me. I imagined a long life of kicking ass with Mark by my side, and when Mark and Win got together... he even became family. Everything we touched was gold."

His voice sounded ragged as he told the story, and I wondered at the emotions behind it.

I remembered reading about Wells's early success with a business called PharmDash that eventually became Grange BioMed.

"Then what happened?" I asked.

"I caught him cheating."

He said it so matter-of-factly that it took a moment for it to sink in. "On your sister?"

He hesitated. "That too. But first I discovered he was siphoning some of the pharmaceuticals in our custody chain for personal use. One day I saw him accept a package from one of our drivers. I gave him the benefit of the doubt, of course. I assumed it was a package that needed special handling or had been loaded into the wrong vehicle. Something like that. But then it happened two more times. Same type package, same driver."

"Shit," I said, putting down my soup spoon and pushing the bowl away. The food was delicious, but the story dampened my appetite. I was beginning to see how deeply affected Wells had been by the events.

"Yes. So I interviewed the driver, discovered he'd been told to deliver a 'sample' each week from a certain shipment to Mark for quality control reasons, and determined the 'sample' was a specially packaged delivery of six bottles of a narcotic pain medicine from the manufacturer. When I finally got to the bottom of it, I learned the manufacturer's rep had agreed to the side deal in exchange for better transportation rates from our company."

I sat back in my chair, oblivious now of the hustle and bustle going on around us in the cramped space. "Jesus, Wells. What did you do? Did you call the authorities?"

He nodded. "I had to. When I confronted Mark, he lied to my face about it. Blamed it on my sister. Said she'd manipulated him into it because she'd become addicted to the pain meds after gallbladder surgery or something like that. And the worst part?"

He paused, glancing down at his hands. The muscle along his jaw ticked as he clenched his teeth, as though the anger from long ago still sifted under his skin.

Then he blew out a long breath, and I realized it might not be anger that was causing his hesitation, but the fact that he was about to share something personal. He seemed almost skittish, as if this was a story he wasn't used to telling. I said nothing, letting the silence stretch, afraid that even moving might scare him away from telling me.

"I believed him," he finally said softly. His lips twisted. "Why wouldn't I? We'd been best friends for years. And he always knew exactly what to say to get me on his side. Mark was good at many things; instilling loyalty was one of them. So I went to Win and told her I knew her secret—told her she needed to get help for her addiction. She denied it, of course, but I didn't believe her. It wasn't until she had her doctor call me to tell me she'd never had gallbladder surgery that I realized the truth—that Mark was the one with the problem."

He shook his head. "I can't believe I trusted Mark over my own sister." It was obvious how upset the admission made him.

I couldn't help it—I reached across the table and placed a hand on his arm. He immediately tensed and I almost jerked away, but then his hand landed on top of mine. He looked up, his eyes meeting mine. And the intensity of his gaze was like a physical force. I couldn't have looked away if I'd wanted to.

"You can't blame yourself," I told him. My voice was barely more than a whisper, but still he heard.

The corner of his lips ticked in a rueful smile. "Yes, I can."

"You can't control the world, Wells."

The smile grew larger. His hand covering mine felt somehow heavier. As though he could hold me in place. "Yes, I can."

It felt as though suddenly the conversation had shifted in a new direction. Clearly we weren't talking about his sister or his former business partner anymore. My mouth dried, something inside of me flaring at the possessiveness of his touch. There was something so familiar to it, as if my body were responding to a question I hadn't realized he'd been asking. It left me feeling off balance, my skin too tight.

I needed the comfort of familiar ground, and so I slid my hand out from under his and reached for my spoon, hoping he didn't notice it trembling slightly as I raised it to my lips. "Mark sounds like a grade A asshole," I said, trying to steer the conversation back on track.

When he said nothing, I found myself babbling. "I despise liars," I continued. "There's nothing worse—especially in a situation like that. To throw your own sister under the bus like that? Just to cover up his own personal failings? I mean, how low can you get? He was basically fucking you coming and going. Lying not only about your business but also your personal life? What a motherfucker!" I shook my head. "I can't imagine anything worse."

A frown pinched the skin between Wells's eyebrows. "Yes, well." He glanced away for a long moment and then back again. "I realized I was in way over my head. That's when I called the police. It was only because of my father's suggestion of a crisis management firm that we were able to keep the bulk of the story out of the media. Which was a damned good thing once all the details came to light. Mark was a piece of work. Was sleeping around with... all kinds of people."

I noticed his nostrils flare in disgust. Apparently Wells could negotiate a brutal business deal that left people in tatters, but the idea of marital infidelity was abhorrent.

"Your poor sister," I said. "Is she okay now?"

Wells's face cracked into a sweet smile. "She's happily married to a good man, and they have a wonderful daughter. Her husband is a schoolteacher in Danbury, Connecticut. Win is a stay-at-home mom."

"How the hell can they afford that on a teacher's salary?" I blurted without thinking.

And Wells fucking Grange blushed to the tips of his ears.

Was it possible this selfish corporate asshole supported his sister's family? I wasn't sure I could wrap my head around the idea.

"Sorry," I said before he felt even more put on the spot. "None of my business."

"No, it's fine. I made sure that Mark's half of the business went to my sister. And then I worked my ass off to grow the business so she'd never have to rely on someone else ever again."

There was something in his voice that startled me. I felt like for one split second there in the bustling restaurant I could see right into Wells's deepest need. His eyes flicked down to the table where he drew designs into what was left of his soup with the spoon. Once again, my gaze was drawn to his large, capable hands.

The silence that descended wasn't uncomfortable or strange, at least for me. I enjoyed the opportunity to take in his close presence as my perception of him continued to twist and click like a giant tumbler lock seeking its opening.

As soon as the entrees were delivered, things went back to normal. Only this time, being with Wells Grange was easier. I wasn't as intimidated by him. In fact, I was intrigued. I wanted to learn more, hear more. As he spoke about living in New York, I found myself leaning in and responding with tiny jokes and teasing remarks just to see if I could get him to smile again.

It was almost, but not quite, a date.

And it wasn't until my phone buzzed much later that I realized I hadn't thought about my sexy stranger all day.

14

WELLS

The day was passing at mach speed. It was the first time in years I felt so compelled to stay in one person's company as long as I could, regardless of the ramifications.

And there *were* ramifications.

Because I found myself starting to want more. So much more. More time with him, more stories from him, more smiles and laughs. I wanted to take him home to my apartment and slowly peel the clothes from his body, so that I could see more of him.

Taste more of him.

I already knew what he looked like naked. I'd practically memorized the photos he'd sent me when he thought he'd been sexting his anonymous wrong number. As we left the restaurant, stepping out onto the cold streets of the city, I couldn't get the image of his hand wrapped around his cock, the tip glistening with precum, from my mind.

I wanted to turn, press him up against the wall of the restaurant, and close my mouth over his.

But I couldn't.

Because I was a fucking liar, and as I'd learned at dinner, he found liars abhorrent.

He'd made it very, very clear that for him there was little worse than someone who lied and manipulated to further advance their own agenda, be it personal or business or, god forbid, both.

And that's exactly the position I found myself in.

I was going to have to figure out a way to fix it. And I would, I felt confident of that. It's what I did for a living: I fixed problems.

But that would come later. After we finalized the deal and there wasn't as much on the line for us both. For now, I wanted to enjoy this moment alone with Conor on the streets of New York City.

I dropped Hank's food off at the car and turned us toward the Four Seasons only a few blocks away, giving Hank a chance to eat while we walked. The night was brisk, the straggling commuters walked hurriedly with their collars turned up and their hats pulled low. But I didn't feel the cold. Not while Conor strolled by my side.

"So, tell me more about your family," I ventured.

There was a long pause, and then he lifted a shoulder. "You already know about my mom; she invented the medical printer."

I waited for him to say more, and when he didn't I asked, "Are you two close?"

Another pause, as though he were choosing his words carefully. "Relatively."

Again his answer was succinct. Which confused me. I knew from our text conversations that they were more than close—Conor adored his mother.

"Do you see her often?" I already knew the answer. He'd told me —or rather Trace—that when his mother had gotten sick, he'd moved into the apartment above her garage to be nearby and therefore saw her almost every day. If not for a doctor's appointment, then to drop off groceries or run errands or just check in and spend time with her.

He shrugged, his eyes glued to the sidewalk ahead. "More or less, I guess. As often as you might expect living in the same smallish town."

I had to force myself to keep walking when what I wanted to do was clamp my hand around his arm and pull him around to face me, force him to meet my eyes, and tell me what was going on. I didn't understand why he was being reticent. He'd been so open with Trace about his relationship with his mother, the struggles he faced in dealing with her illness.

But when it came to sharing those same feelings with me—with Wells—he clammed up.

As though he didn't trust me.

I clenched my jaw, thinking of everything I'd shared with him. About my sister and Mark. Sure, I'd held a few details back from the story, but still—I'd told him more than I'd ever told anyone else.

It looked like Conor wasn't willing to do the same with me.

I didn't like that.

I was about to press for more when my phone buzzed in my pocket. With a frustrated huff I yanked it free, intending to send it to voicemail until I realized it was Deb. She knew better than to call when I was out of the office. Normally she would text unless it was important.

"The office," I told Conor as I stepped away and swiped the screen to answer the call. "Should be quick." I held the phone to my ear and growled, "What?"

She didn't bother apologizing. She rarely did. "Legal is done with the paperwork. They've left several stacks of documents in the conference room for you and Conor to review before the deal can be finalized."

"Why can't they take care of it all?"

"I asked. Something to do with liability and due diligence and other things that you don't pay me enough to pay attention to."

"I pay you fine," I told her.

"I'll always take more." I could hear the smile in her voice.

"When do they need it done?"

"According to them? Yesterday. But they said by tomorrow morning should work as well."

I cursed under my breath, my eyes sliding toward Conor. Normally I wouldn't think twice about returning to the office this late at night. Actually, normally I wouldn't have even left the office at this point. But I didn't like the idea of cutting my time with Conor short.

"Is everyone already there?" I asked Deb. "I don't want to get back to the office only to have to wait."

There was a brief pause. "Legal's left for the night. So have I for that matter. Everyone assumed that... ah... you wouldn't be back in until tomorrow."

So the office was empty. "What about Conor's lawyer, James? Did he stick around?"

"Apparently something came up. He said to tell you that if you and/or Conor touched any of those documents without him being present, he would sue you ten ways to Sunday."

I let out a laugh. "He's welcome to try."

"That's what I told him. More or less." She cleared her throat. "So should I let everyone know we'll be digging into the documents first thing in the morning?" There was a hopeful note to her voice.

I turned and eyed Conor. He stood by the curb, head thrown back as he stared up toward the sky. I followed the path of his gaze, but all I could see was an expanse of blackness past the glare of the street-lights. He looked so striking and lonely that something in my chest squeezed.

"No. We'll take care of it tonight."

Deb cursed under her breath. "Of course. Because I was just pulling up to the McKittrick Hotel. You do realize I plan to submit my bill for the Sleep No More tickets and the rest of the evening's activities for reimbursement."

"Don't bother," I told her.

"Oh, I plan on bothering. If you think I waited four months for these tickets only to leave before we even get to the bit with the naked bull flailing around covered in chocolate—"

"No," I cut her off. "I mean, you don't have to bother coming in. I'll take care of things."

There was a long pause. "Do you... even know how to turn on the lights in the office?"

"I'll figure it out."

She let out a chuckle. "If you say so."

"Give my love to the naked bull."

"Oh, I plan on it. Trust me."

I hung up the phone and turned to Conor. He stood in profile, puffs of his breath framing his face in a soft halo of clouds. His cheeks were pink from the cold, his bottom lip plump from worrying it with his teeth. I could see hints of exhaustion around his eyes, a slight bruising of the delicate skin underneath. I remembered, then, that it had been a long day for him. For us both. After an even longer night.

Briefly, I thought about sending him back to his hotel and tackling the paperwork on my own. But selfishly I didn't want him to go. I wasn't ready for tonight to end. I'd started the day with the goal of proving to Conor that he could trust me, and given his reticence to tell me about his mother, I'd failed.

But the day wasn't over yet.

He glanced toward me, and I wondered if he realized I'd been staring. He lifted an eyebrow. "Everything okay at work?"

"We're needed back at the office."

His eyes widened. "*We?*"

"Paperwork to go over. Apparently it involves both of us."

"Just the two of us?" The pitch of his voice was a little higher than usual. It was adorable.

I smothered a smile. "Unfortunately your friend James had other plans. He said to continue without him." It wasn't exactly what he'd said, but close enough as far as I was concerned.

Conor worried his bottom lip again, and I had to look away or else I wouldn't be able to stop myself from staring at the way his teeth worked the sensitive flesh. "Okay. I guess... I guess we might as well get it done."

What I wanted to say: *hopefully that's not all we get done.*

What I did say: "Good. I'll text Hank."

～

I'D SPENT the last forty minutes hard as a rock, not even the rote mundanity of the paperwork able to put a dent in my lust for Conor. It was torture to sit across the conference room table from him and not be able to touch him. I wanted to sweep the stacks of documents to the floor and bend him over the gleaming expanse of wood. I wanted to rip the shirt from his shoulders and drag my fingers down the column of his spine as I pressed my cock against his ass.

I shifted, my pants growing even more painfully tight. I wanted him. Badly. But I couldn't have him. Not yet. It would complicate the negotiations and potentially bork the deal. Once the contracts were signed, he would be mine. But until then…

I sighed, shifting in my seat. If only my brain could get the message to my cock. I wasn't sure how much longer I could stand to be in the room alone with Conor, the sound of him… the sight of him… even the smell of him invading my senses. Like the outdoors on a crisp winter afternoon.

I forced myself to focus on my computer, struggling to make sense of a column of numbers on some spreadsheet summarizing laboratory test results. But I didn't care. That was the problem. It was boring. While Conor… Conor was everything but.

My eyes flicked across the table. He'd been methodically making his way through a thick stack of documents, not once breaking his focus to glance my way. Clearly my presence wasn't nearly as distracting for him as his was for me.

I decided to change that. I was afraid it would be too obvious if I used my phone to text him, so I muted notifications and slipped it into my pocket. Then I clicked open the text program on my computer, pulled up my recent conversation with him, and started typing.

Wells: *How has your day been?*

His phone vibrated against the table, the sound loud in the silent conference room. He jumped, letting out a squeak of alarm. "Sorry," he mumbled, snatching it and thumbing it open.

I watched as he read my message. A smile tugged at the corner of his lips. Something swelled in my chest at the sight of it. Something possessive. That smile was mine. I'd been the cause of it, and I wanted more.

NotSam: *Good. Busy, though. Sorry I haven't been able to text more.*

Wells: *I understand—work comes first. Have you at least been thinking about me?*

His smile grew, accompanied by a soft flush to his cheeks. It made him look fucking adorable.

NotSam: *Yes.*

Now it was time to make him squirm.

Wells: *Have you been thinking about me fucking you?*

His eyes went wide, and I watched him bite his lip as he struggled to school his features. He cleared his throat before typing.

NotSam: *Yes.*

I decided I liked watching him get my texts. I liked seeing him struggle to contain himself, knowing I was the one causing those reactions. It made me want to push harder, further. I focused again on the screen and typed another message.

Wells: *What would you want me to do to you, if I were there in front of you?*

Conor let out a kind of strangled whimper, the tips of his ears flaring a bright red. I glanced up at him again. "Everything okay?"

"Yes. Yes, yes. I mean, yeah. Yes. Fine. Things are fine. It was just

a... text. That... you know. I got and... anyway, yes. Everything's okay."
Now his cheeks had begun to glow as well. Excellent.

I returned my focus to my computer, pretending to concentrate
on the minutia of the spreadsheet, but instead every sense was tuned
on Conor. I watched out of the corner of my eye as he typed up a
response, and then I clicked over to the text screen.

NotSam: *Now's not really the best time. I'm still in that meeting.*

Wells: *With your hot boss?*

NotSam: *He's not my boss.*

I faked a cough to hide my smirk before responding.

Wells: *But he is hot, yes? Describe him to me.*

Conor's eyes flicked up. I kept my attention on my computer,
pulling up an empty Word document and typing gibberish to make it
look like I was actually working. I could feel him studying me, his
gaze tracing over my features in an almost physical caress.

NotSam: *He's tall.*

I waited for more.

Wells: *That's it?*

He let out a frustrated breath. Then he hunched over his phone
and started typing. And typing. To the point that I began getting
nervous.

NotSam: *Fine. His eyes are that crystalline blue that seems impossible
and wildly unfair they're so beautiful. I used to think they were cold but
then the sun hits them and... I don't know. It's like standing on the edge of*

a boat in the middle of the ocean and staring down into the water and realizing that below you is a depth greater than you could ever comprehend and it's full of so much beauty and life that no one's ever seen before and if you just dove in... maybe... maybe you could catch a glimpse of it and you think maybe you should just jump but then you remember that the ocean is a dangerous place and more than likely it will kill you instead.

I stared at the words. Somehow, it had become difficult to breathe. It took everything I had not to look up, not to want to stare at him until his eyes met mine. And then what?

I didn't know the answer to that question.

NotSam: *Also I'm fairly certain he has a rockin' bod if the way his suits fit is any indication.*

And just like that, the tension of his previous text dissipated. I had to bite the inside of my cheek to keep from laughing.

Wells: *Would you fuck him if he asked?*

Out of the corner of my eye, I saw Conor's hands freeze. He glanced toward me and then away, his top teeth worrying his bottom lip. He typed out an answer and then stared at his phone for a long moment before deleting it. My heart pounded. Suddenly that answer meant everything to me.

15

CONOR

I stared at my phone, the last text reverberating through my head. Would I fuck Wells Grange if he asked? My feelings about that were different after having spent the day with him. I snuck a glance at the man, the tips of my ears searing with embarrassment from even considering such a question. He sat on the other side of the table, his coat off and tie loose, shirt cuffs rolled up to reveal strong wrists and tanned forearms dusted with hair. He worked on a laptop, fingers flying across the keyboard, his focus on the task at hand absolute, completely unaware that only a few feet away I was imagining what he would look like naked. What it would feel like to have his hands caress down the front of my shirt. Then lower. Sliding my belt free, flicking open the button, reaching inside...

I cleared my throat and shifted in my chair. His eyes flicked toward me, and I had a moment's disorientation. I'd been telling the truth when I'd described his eyes like the ocean. They promised depth but also danger, and both were equally titillating and terrifying. And they were so, so easy to get lost in.

"Is something up?" he asked. I hadn't noticed his hands pausing on his keyboard.

The same hands I'd been picturing around my cock seconds

earlier. My cheeks flamed and I glanced away. Of course something was up, I wanted to shout at him. My fucking dick!

Instead I said, "Up? Me? No." I forced a laugh that came out as a squeak. "I'm down, totally down. But in a good way, like the slang way. Not the sad or depressed way. Like, I'm cool. Normal. Totally fine."

A small smile curled his lips and he dipped his head, returning to work.

Trace: *You're taking a long time to answer the question. It should be a yes or no—does the idea of his cock in your mouth appeal to you?*

Conor: *He's a potential business partner. I shouldn't be thinking about him in that way at all.*

Trace: *But you have, haven't you?*

I ground my teeth together. Yes, of course I'd thought of him that way. It was impossible not to, especially after this afternoon.

Conor: *Why does it matter?*

Trace: *Because I want you to imagine he's me.*

No way I read that correctly.

Conor: *What?*

Trace: *Imagine the man sitting across from you is me. And tell me, in detail, what you would do to me. What you would want me to do to you.*

I swallowed a helpless squeak. I couldn't help it—I glanced toward Wells. He was frowning at the computer screen, so rigidly focused I doubt he even realized I was still in the room. My heart began pounding harder as I thought about what it would be like if Wells Grange were my sexy stranger.

If all those sessions of him telling me what to do, all those photos of that gorgeous cock, belonged to him.

Of course it was a preposterous idea. My sexy stranger may be controlling when it came to sex, but he was also caring and interesting. It wasn't always just about him the way it was with Wells.

But that didn't mean I couldn't imagine Wells's body—use him for my fantasy. Indulge in what it would be like to fuck him. It wouldn't be the first time I'd had such thoughts.

I let out a trembling breath and tried to keep my fingers from shaking as I struggled with what to write. Where to begin.

Conor: *You would lean back in your chair, your hands clasped behind your head casually. And you would tell me to stand up. You would order me around the table until I was standing in front of you. You'd make me stand there a minute while your eyes traced over me. Then you'd tell me to drop to my knees.*

Trace: *And would you do it?*

Conor: *Without question.*

Trace: *Then what?*

Conor: *You'd tell me to unbuckle your pants. To pull out your cock. You'd already be hard. Straining against your pants and I would let the knuckles of my hand brush against you as I took my time with the zipper. And you'd curse under your breath for me taking so long because you'd want to feel my fingers wrapped around you, my palm cupping your balls.*

Across from me Wells cleared his throat and shifted in his seat. He'd been so still, the only movement his fingers on the keyboard, that the sudden sound startled me. His eyes met mine, and I quickly glanced away, afraid that somehow he would know if he studied me too long.

I started to push from the table. "Sorry," I said, holding up my phone. "It's my uh... work... and there's a thing I have to—thing. It might take a while, so I'll just go to the lobby so I'm not distracting you—"

"No." The sharpness of his response seemed to startle us both. He let out a tense breath. "Stay. You're not bothering me. Please." He gestured for me to sit.

I hesitated before sinking back into my seat. Standing would have exposed my raging erection, and I was glad to keep it hidden under the table. "Okay. Thanks."

He nodded, focus back on his computer. Leaving me forgotten once again.

Trace: *You mean the way I'm currently cursing at you taking so long to tell me what's next?*

I bit my lip in an attempt to keep my smile in check.

Conor: *I haven't... been... with many men. I'd want to take my time with you. With your cock. I'd want to explore it. With my eyes. My lips. My tongue. I'd start soft and slow. Maybe the first thing I'd want to do is taste. Just with the tip of my tongue sweeping across your slit. Just to see if there was anything to taste yet.*

Trace: *There would be.*

I couldn't stop my eyes from flicking toward Wells. He sat, staring at his screen, a frown pinching the space between his eyes. His fingers hovered above the keyboard, whatever he was reading having captured his attention completely.

I wondered what he would think if he knew that I was currently sitting here imagining what he tasted like. My mouth watered at the thought, and I clenched my phone tighter, wishing it was Wells's cock I was gripping.

Conor: *You'd want to put your hands on my head and push me down, push yourself into my mouth. But you wouldn't.*

Trace: *I wouldn't?*

Conor: *Not yet. Because I like the idea of your nails biting into the armrests of your chair. And I like the idea of your frustration. I like knowing that it's me causing that.*

Across from me Wells shifted, a hand moving to the armrest of his chair, knuckles burning white from clenching it. I smirked. If he only knew how perfectly he was playing into my fantasy of him.

Conor: *I like to tease so I'd run my lips down the side of you. So lightly you'd probably feel it more as breath than anything else. And when I got to your base I'd have a decision to make. Do you like having your balls cupped? Sucked? Licked? Ignored?*

Trace: *Sucked and licked.*

Conor: *Then I would take one of your balls into my mouth, feel it heavy on my tongue as I sucked, my fingers dancing back up your cock. I'd keep going until I could hear you groan, until you thrust against me, desperate for more. But I wouldn't be done teasing.*

Trace: *If I had my way you would be.*

Conor: *But this is my fantasy, remember? I'd run my tongue back up your cock, circle it under the lip of your head to see if you're sensitive there.*

Trace: *I am.*

Conor: *Good. Then I'd wrap my lips around you, teasing your tip, letting you get a hint of the wet warmth of my mouth. Make you crave it.*

Trace: *I would be. I am. Why are you not here doing this to me?*

I smiled, liking that he wanted me there. Enjoying the fact that I was turning him on. It was taking everything I had not to slide a hand under the table and press it against the bulge straining my pants. I was so fucking hard, almost painfully so. I wasn't sure how long I would be able to last before excusing myself.

I glanced again toward Wells. He was flipping through a thick stack of documents, searching for something with focused determination. He'd loosened his tie even more and unbuttoned the top of his shirt. His cheeks were flushed, a light sheen of sweat visible at his temples.

I watched him a moment out of the corner of my eye. Wondering what it would be like if I ever acted on this fantasy. What Wells would do if I stood up and came around the table toward him and dropped to my knees. Placed my hands on his thighs and pressed them apart.

I let out a soft sigh at the thought and realized only belatedly that Wells had gone still. He stared at me, his eyes a storm-tossed sea. That hunger was back with an intensity that caused a shiver to race down my spine, that made my balls contract with desire.

I couldn't stop myself; I glanced down at his lips. They were full, fuller than they should be for such an angular face. As if he could read my mind, he traced his tongue around them. I swallowed a groan, my cock straining even more. Imagining those lips taking my crown, sliding down the length of me.

I typed without thinking.

Conor: *I would take you all at once. Without warning. Without hesitation. I would take as much of you into my mouth as I could and then more.*

Trace: *All of me.*

Conor: *Yes.*

Trace: *And I would hold you there like that, with me filling you.*

I let out a groan, not even trying to hide it. There was no way Wells wouldn't have heard it. But when I looked up at him, he had his elbows on the table, his head cupped in his hands, his fingers thrust into his hair as he hunched over his laptop. The muscle along his jaw twitched.

He didn't look my way, and I hastily returned to my phone.

Conor: *Yes. And when you let me go you'd be wet from my mouth, slick, and you'd spin me around and swipe the documents from the table, letting them shower down in a rain of paperwork. You'd put the palm of your hand between my shoulder blades, pushing me over, your other hand reaching around me, tearing open my pants and freeing my cock and I would be so fucking hard for you.*

Wells sat up abruptly, slamming his computer shut with a sharp click. "I think that about does it for the night. Don't you? We can finish up the rest of these documents tomorrow." He started to stand but then changed his mind and pulled his chair closer to the table before reaching for the various stacks of documents.

I blinked, glancing at the work we hadn't gotten to yet and then back at him. "Are... you sure?"

"Yes."

I didn't move, confused by this sudden change of plans. Finally, he looked up at me. "You should go back to the hotel. Good night."

I thought about my sexy stranger. Back at the hotel I would be free to indulge in my fantasy of him. But I also felt a pang of something like disappointment at leaving Wells. I'd been enjoying sitting across the table from him, imagining him naked.

Except he'd just made it clear he wasn't interested. Wells was the one telling me to leave. And I'd told himself a long time ago that when someone tells you they're not interested, you should listen to them. I swallowed, my throat feeling oddly tight. "Okay, then. I guess... I guess I'll see you in the morning."

Wells barely glanced up long enough to grunt.

Feeling dismissed in such an abrupt and uncaring way seemed to negate all the warmer feelings I'd begun having toward Wells that day. Earlier, in the city together, we'd finally seemed to find common ground. There had been brief moments of connection, and at one point I'd even caught him looking at me in a way that made me wonder if he found me attractive.

But now? Now he was acting like I was an annoyance again. Which only served to put me right back where I was when I'd arrived in the city two days before. I felt unsteady and unsure of myself. Out of place.

And that pissed me the hell off. Without another word, I turned and left.

I pulled out my phone as I stormed out of the lobby and into the frigid night. There was one person in this city who made me feel good. If there was anyone I could count on to get Wells Grange out of my fucking head, it was Trace.

Conor: *My meeting ended earlier than I expected. I'm free for the rest of the night.*

I took a deep breath. Held it. Then typed some more.

Conor: *I could... come meet you. Continue our previous session in person.*

There was a long pause. Long enough that I started to regret having asked. My steps slowed until I was standing in the middle of the sidewalk, phone clutched in my hands, waiting. Crowds of late-night revelers surged around me, but I ignored them.

Why wasn't he answering? This shouldn't have been a difficult question.

Three dots appeared on the screen and I held my breath.

Trace: *I don't think that's a good idea.*

I sucked in a breath, my stomach dropping in disappointment. It wasn't the answer I'd been expecting. I blinked several times rapidly, trying to clear my head. I had to respect his desire to keep this anonymous, right? At least that's what I told myself. Especially since I'd originally felt the same way.

My fingers felt numb, but I forced them to move, to respond to his text. To pretend that what he'd just said hadn't gutted me.

Conor: *Oh. Okay. I'll text you when I'm back in my hotel room then.*

Another long pause.

Trace: *I don't think that's a good idea either. I think maybe we should take a break from this.*

Everything around me froze; even the sounds from the street traffic vanished. I read the message again in case I'd misread it the first time.

Stupidly, I felt my chin begin to wobble. I looked up at the crowds on the sidewalk. There were couples and families, groups of friends and people chatting animatedly on their phones. It was one of those moments where it seemed that everyone had someone in their lives but me.

But what had I really expected would happen? Where could things with Trace have ever gone? Trying to have any of my relationship needs met by some random stranger in a city hundreds of miles away from where I lived was ridiculous. He could be married for all I knew. Or a criminal. Or prefer DC over Marvel. I felt a gurgle of disgust escape my throat. I was pathetic.

By putting expectations on my sexy stranger after a couple of texts, I was grasping at straws.

Screw him. Screw all of this, even Wells with whatever the fuck kind of games he'd been playing with me today. I was done. With all of it. Done waiting for other people to solve my problems. To come to my rescue.

Despite my fears about my mother's health, I powered down my phone completely as I made my way to the hotel. I'd checked in with her before arriving back at the office after dinner, and she'd been tired but stable. She and her caretakers knew what hotel I was staying in, so they'd be able to reach me there if they needed to. Meanwhile, I needed to keep the temptation of Trace's texts far away from me for the night.

I needed to remember he wasn't mine.

16

WELLS

I sat there staring at my phone—at the last text I'd sent. I couldn't bear to have Conor out there thinking Trace didn't care about him. I quickly typed out another message.

Wells: *Wait, hold on. Let me explain.*

I waited for him to respond. Obviously we couldn't meet, that much was clear. But I could have found a better way of telling him. This was all going wrong. This wasn't my plan—not that I'd had a plan... yet.

I'd been stupid. I'd pushed things too far, sitting across the conference room table from him while playing at being both Wells and Trace simultaneously. Essentially, I'd been lying to his face, and if there was one thing my day in the city with Conor had made crystal clear, it was that he would never forgive me for not confessing to being his anonymous sext partner. He'd been very forthcoming with his feelings about dishonesty and had admitted to initially having concerns about my own integrity.

Not only would admitting to him I was Trace make him feel betrayed personally, it would also support his assumption that Wells

Grange was a liar, an unethical user. Based on how he felt about me coming into this whole negotiation situation, there was no way he'd give me the benefit of the doubt.

And it wasn't like I deserved it anyway. Because I *had* lied to him. I *had* led him on.

I'd even let the personal information I'd learned as Trace affect the negotiations. Albeit in Conor's favor, but still. I'd blurred the lines between the two. Used what I'd learned in one relationship to impact the other.

Because of that, Trace and Conor could never meet. He could never learn the truth. Which is why I'd had to break off the "anonymous" text conversation. It was the only way to protect him from inadvertently revealing anything else personal to me when I knew that had to be the last thing he wanted.

After his reluctance to tell me in person about his mother, I realized I could no longer play both roles with him. I couldn't continue to hear his innermost confessions about his fears for his mother as Trace and be denied the same intimacy as Wells. It was like only getting half of him, when I wanted so much more.

There was no easy solution. I could possibly continue working on getting to know him better in person, but even that felt like a lie now. The texts we'd shared sat heavily between us like a fat, cumbersome elephant that was impossible to deal with but too sweet to ignore.

I left the office with a lead weight in my gut and a hole in my chest the size of the Holland Tunnel.

I kept my phone gripped in my hand, waiting for it to buzz that he'd responded, but it stayed silent. When I got into the car, I flicked open the messages app. Still nothing. I bounced my knee up and down, nervous energy curling inside me. It wasn't like him to ignore my—Trace's—texts. It had me worried.

I couldn't help but text him again.

Wells: *You okay?*

As soon as I hit Send, I regretted it. Was it arrogant of me to assume that the reason he wasn't responding was because of me? What if he was just busy? Out somewhere, maybe.

The thought had me clenching my jaw. Out where? With whom? Familiar possessiveness churned in my chest. What if something happened to him? What if someone took advantage of him? He was in unfamiliar territory in this city, and he was too trusting by far.

I leaned forward in the car. "Hank, do you mind swinging by the Four Seasons on the way home?"

He nodded with a murmured, "Yes, sir." He was kind enough not to point out that we'd already passed the hotel, which meant he'd have to do a U-turn to get there. Not at all on the way home.

I sat back. Absently, I ran my hand across the supple leather of the seat, my eyes drifting to where Conor had sat earlier today. There'd been a moment when his hand had pressed against the expanse of leather separating us. I'd let my own hand fall next to his until there was little more than a breath of air between our fingers. I'd wanted to reach out with my pinky and run it down the side of his palm, across the delicate bones of his wrist.

I groaned, squeezing my eyes closed against the memory. What the fuck was wrong with me?

I was saved from answering the question by Hank. "Here we are, sir," he said, pulling the car to the curb near the entrance to the hotel. He started to get out so he could come around and open my door, but I waved him off.

"I'll only be a moment," I told him as I stepped out onto the sidewalk. The night had deepened, turned colder. I hunched my shoulders, pulling my coat tighter around me as I strode toward the revolving door. Just before I reached it, I hesitated.

What was I doing here? What was I hoping to accomplish? It wasn't like I could demand to know why he wasn't responding to my text messages. As far as he was concerned, I was Wells. I had nothing to do with Trace.

I just want to make sure he's okay, I told myself. There was nothing wrong with that. It's what any friend would do.

Except I knew I wasn't just a friend.

Maybe I wasn't even a friend.

I didn't know what I was to him. Or what he was to me.

I just knew that I needed to see him.

I pushed my way inside and up a short flight of steps to a marble foyer with soaring ceilings. Ahead of me another set of steps led up toward a seating area and a half-empty bar. Tourists and businessmen mingled, murmuring in low voices while soft music played from hidden speakers.

I hesitated again, second-guessing myself. It was an unfamiliar feeling. One I despised.

A large family of tourists surged past me, clad in garishly colored overstuffed coats and talking loudly and laughing. One of them bumped my shoulder, and I started to glower when she turned and pressed a hand to her chest and gushing, "Oh my goodness, sweetie, I am sooooo, so sorry." Her thick Southern accent washed over me, and the genuine look of apology in her eyes made me think of Conor. Instantly my aggravation at her eased.

"It's no problem, ma'am," I found myself automatically replying.

She smiled, but the expression caught and she tilted her head to the side. "You okay, sugar? You look like a tick that can't find a bum to bite."

I lifted an eyebrow.

She laughed, loud. "Lost, love. You look lost."

"I'm fine." My response was clipped.

She winked. "Everyone but you knows that's a lie, hon."

I ground my teeth, about to protest when I looked up and saw him. Conor. He was walking past the bar, toward the bank of elevators tucked around the corner. Without thinking, I started after him.

Behind me I heard the woman laugh. "Looks like that tick found a nice bum. You take care with it, you hear?"

I ignored her, my focus only on Conor. I pushed my way through the rest of the tourists and took the short flight of stairs in two steps. I reached the top just as Conor arrived at the elevators. He stopped. So did I.

He stood still a moment. So did I.

This was as far as my plan had taken me. I'd told myself I just wanted to make sure he was okay, and now I had my proof. I could turn around and leave without him seeing me. It wasn't like I could call out to him. How in the world would I explain what I was doing there?

Instead, I reached for my phone. I typed the first thing I could think of.

Wells: *I'm sorry for earlier.*

I held my breath, waiting for his phone to buzz. Wanting to see his reaction to what I'd written.

But there was nothing. He merely shifted from one foot to the other. Then the elevator doors slid open. He stepped inside. And was gone.

I stared after him. An unfamiliar feeling in my chest. Something hot and tight and unpleasant.

I glanced back at my text and that's when I noticed that instead of the usual blue of an iMessage, I saw the unusual green bubble of a text. It was the same thing that happened when I sent Deb a text while she was on a plane or had her phone turned off for some other reason.

So maybe Conor wasn't ignoring me. Maybe his phone had run out of juice. Or maybe he'd turned it off. Except he'd never let that happen, not with his mother being ill and possibly needing to reach him.

That's when I remembered the one time Win had blocked me—when I'd accused her of being an addict. The same thing had happened to the texts I'd sent her then: they'd turned green.

Which meant it was also possible that Conor had blocked me. That he didn't want to hear from me. Not now and maybe not ever again.

I reread my text, suddenly second-guessing myself. Again.

Since when did Wells Grange ever apologize to anyone?

My father's words echoed in my head. Rather, they were John

Wayne's words in *She Wore a Yellow Ribbon*, and they were etched into my father's very soul. *Never apologize and never explain—it's a sign of weakness.*

And here I was showing my belly to someone who, by all accounts, should be my business rival.

But Conor Newell was the furthest thing from a rival. Hell, I wasn't even sure he'd be considered a rival to a competing game shop owner in his small town. He'd probably invite the person over to co-market and collaborate. Conor was a nice guy.

Which was another reason I had no business thinking of myself with him. He wasn't the kind of man who wanted the same thing I did.

I fucked. Conor loved.

He'd make a better match with that damned horse carriage driver, someone chatty and fun. Not Glacial Grange.

I needed to stop this stupid obsession. To get this deal finished and Conor Newell out of my head.

I turned and strode from the hotel, back out into the cold night and into the waiting car. "Home," I told Hank.

When he didn't immediately shift the car into gear, I looked up, meeting his eyes in the rearview mirror. "Are you sure?"

No.

"Yes."

He hesitated again, but I pointedly stared out the window, avoiding eye contact. Silently, he maneuvered the car into traffic and drove me home.

When I got up to my apartment, I poured myself a Macallan and stood at the windows looking out into the night. It was a sight that had always symbolized my success. To be able to have this kind of view in Manhattan meant I was somebody important, successful. I was living the life my father always imagined for me. Money, prestige, and power.

I snorted at the thought. There'd been a time my father had been deeply, irrevocably disappointed in me and my accomplishments. I felt a slow burn make its way up my neck and flush across my cheeks at the memory. It had been the day I'd realized the extent of Mark's treachery, the extent of his lies and subterfuge. I'd been forced to do the one thing I'd always sworn I would never do: go to my father for help.

Throw myself at his mercy.

It wasn't that my father was a bad person, he was just cold. Exacting. He could be generous as well, but it always came with strings. It was why I'd tried so hard to build a life without relying on him.

Yet there I'd been. Standing in front of his desk in his heavily wood paneled office, the smell of expensive cigar smoke soaked into every surface. He'd known why I was there, but he'd made me say it nonetheless. He'd made me confess the mistake I'd made in trusting Mark, made me lay bare just how deeply the man had violated not just my trust, but the entire family's.

"You do understand that your sister is devastated by this," he said. "Already the gossip mills are talking. She's likely to lose her seat on the board of the foundation, and she certainly can't continue her volunteer work with the League. She'll be lucky to salvage any shreds of her reputation after this scandal."

"Yes, sir." I dropped my eyes to the plush antique rug under my feet. "I should have believed her when she told me she wasn't the one the drugs were intended for."

In the periphery of my vision, I saw him steeple his fingers, pressing the tips against his lips as he considered me. "And why did you believe Mark over your own flesh and blood?"

I winced at the question. "He was my business partner. We worked together for years. It never occurred to me that he could—" I swallowed. "He could betray me like that."

My father barked a laugh. It was so sudden and out of place that I almost jerked back. When I looked up, my father's eyes held a mixture of impatience and annoyance. "You should have realized that the moment he turned his attention to your sister."

My heart ticked up, my breathing becoming shallower. "Sir?" I asked. It came out weaker than I wanted, more squeak than sound.

"You think I didn't know about you two?" He rolled his eyes. "You

weren't exactly subtle the way you looked at him when you brought him home for Christmas. The way you'd come to dinner with stars in your eyes and swollen lips from doing god knows what together."

It felt like the air had been sucked from my lungs. "You knew?"

His expression indicated just how ridiculous he found my question.

"Did Mom?" My chest squeezed tight and I took a step forward, panic churning in my gut. "Did Win?"

"Of course not," he scoffed. "But the moment I saw him toss you over for your sister, I hired a private investigator to dig into his life and follow him." He reached into a drawer and pulled out a thick file. It landed on the smooth expanse of his wooden desk with a thump. "It's all there going back years. The cheating. The drugs. I'm sure the police will find it quite useful in building their case against him."

My knees felt weak. I reached out to grab the back of the stiff wooden chair perched in front of his desk. "But you didn't say anything."

He waved a hand. "You wouldn't have listened. You never did. You've always had to learn the hard way. Decisions have consequences, son. Maybe now you'll remember that."

"What about Win? You let her marry him."

He quirked an eyebrow. "So did you."

"But I—" I swallowed what I'd about to say next. That I'd trusted Mark. Believed in him. Loved him.

Even after he left me for my sister.

I'd made up excuse after excuse for him. Convinced myself I was happy he and Win had found each other, grateful that he was at least still in my life even if he was no longer in my bed. Mark had known me well—better than anyone else. Anytime I'd found myself second-guessing him or pulling away, he'd always known exactly what to say or do to keep me loyal.

I squeezed my eyes shut, the burn of tears threatening. And there was no way I could let them fall. I could imagine nothing worse than crying in front of my father.

"I trust you have learned your lesson?"

"Yes, sir." It came out in a wheeze.

"And what is it?"

My lips were numb. My response automatic. "There is no room for emotion when it comes to business."

My father nodded, a gleam of pride in his eyes. "Exactly. And don't you forget it."

He studied me a moment longer. "I'll pull some strings, call in a crisis management team, make sure the worst of this scandal is buried. Not just for you but for Winifred as well."

My jaw ached from clenching it so tightly. But I knew the words my father expected to hear. "Thank you."

My father stood and came around the desk to face me. Little separated us except for a few feet of stale air and a lifetime of missed birthdays and late nights at the office. He reached out a hand. It landed heavily on my shoulder. "You're the one who brought that man into our lives, Wells. Never forget that the fallout of this belongs to you."

I hung my head. "Yes, sir."

I pulled myself from the memory, a sour taste in my mouth that I tried to wash away with a swallow of scotch. I'd sworn that day to never let emotion impact a business decision. I'd committed myself to building back the business, making enough that Win would never have to think twice about money, that my father would never have to question my commitment or professionalism.

I'd become the person my father wanted me to be in every way.

And I fucking hated it. Because my life was cold and empty and exhausting. Just like his had been.

I once swore to myself that I'd never become my father. But look where I was now: ensconced in a glass tower, looking down on the rest of world, money insulating me from ever having to interact with it. From ever making connections.

Sure I was powerful, but I was also lonely. I reached for my phone, knowing what I'd find but checking anyway. I flicked open the messages app. Nothing from Conor.

Decisions have consequences, son.

Indeed.

17

CONOR

For some reason, I spent more time being angry at Wells than Trace. After an entire afternoon spent getting to know him—the *real* him— he'd ignored me and then dismissed me back to my hotel like I was nothing.

Selfish prick.

Yes, I was annoyed at Trace for not wanting to meet up. But that was physical disappointment. So I wouldn't get laid tonight by a sexy man who wanted to hold me down and fuck my brains out. That didn't hurt nearly as much as the rejection by a man who'd been so approachable and easy just a few hours before. When Wells had turned into the dismissive asshole again in the conference room, it had occurred to me maybe I'd been keeping him from someone important.

Maybe he had someone waiting for him at home.

And that thought burned with the angry heat of a thousand suns. It made me want to beat the shit out of some faceless asshole. Or pick a bar fight. Or... or *something.*

I didn't even get a chance to shove the hotel door open. The doorman opened it gracefully with a polite "Welcome back, sir."

Without thinking, I made my way to the bar for something strong and was startled out of my funk by the familiar bartender.

"You," I squawked, staring at the man whose phone number had started it all.

"Hey, cutie. What can I get you?"

"Did you give me a fake phone number the other night?"

The man's smile lit up the room around him as he leaned across the bar to speak quietly to me. "Dude, why the hell would I have done that? I was desperate for you to call me."

My face heated. "I texted... but it went to someone else."

The bartender grabbed another scrap of paper off an order pad like he had the other night and jotted his number down on it. "Here, call it right now."

"Can't. My phone's battery died," I lied.

"Use the house phone," he said with a wink.

While I dialed the handset he gave me, he reached under the bar for his cell. Sure enough, it started ringing, but my eyes stayed glued to the paper. The green lined paper was distinctive, and I realized the number I'd used the other night to text him had been on a scrap of plain *white* paper.

Where the hell had that number come from? I wondered if someone else had left their number on the bar and I'd picked it up by accident. That would mean Trace had been in this very bar. Could I ask the bartender to... what? Tell me if a guy with a hot dick and a controlling attitude had been in for a quick drink?

I was crazy.

"Sorry," I said, smiling up at him in apology. "My mistake."

"Tonight, then? I get off at—"

"Sorry, no. I'm off to bed now for a very early meeting. But thank you." I gave him my best "it's not you, it's me" face before turning and leaving to make my way up to my room alone.

I did an amazing job of ignoring my phone while I showered and changed into clean pajama pants and T-shirt. And I did an even better job of ignoring it while I wandered over to the window to stare out at the city lights surrounding the relative darkness of Central Park.

But I did a piss-poor job of ignoring my hurt feelings. Without realizing it, I'd spent hours in that park getting to know an interesting and complicated man. I'd hung on his words as he'd described places he'd been and things he'd studied in school. I'd ached to know more about why he seemed to hold himself to such a high standard. Why he didn't seem to let other people in.

And then in the conference room, he'd met my eyes and I'd thought... I'd *thought* there was something there. I'd thought for one brief moment he was going to let me, of all people, in.

I was an idiot.

And then there was Trace. The man who got my blood rushing in every direction and who made me insane with lust. But who was a complete stranger, an internet phantom.

I glanced over at my phone, a dead brick on the stark white bedding. If I turned it on, whose name would I want to see appear? Whose message would I want to read most?

And what the hell would I do if there was no message at all?

I groaned and faced back out the window into the night beyond. The park called to me, reminding me my place wasn't there in the big city with either of those men. It was back home in the North Carolina mountains where the Blue Ridge Parkway crossed the French Broad River and where dense rhododendron always made me feel at home on the hiking trails. I closed my eyes and tried to put myself back there in Pisgah Forest, stepping over knobby roots and rain-worn rocks. One of the only reasons I could spend so much time in my game shop was knowing those familiar paths and vistas were right at the edge of town waiting for me.

In real life, I wasn't the kind of guy who could jet up to New York and coordinate a multimillion-dollar business deal without losing my shit.

In real life, I was scared, confused, and alone. So fucking alone. And I hated it.

I blew out a breath and turned away from the city. After shoving my phone into my suitcase to get it out of sight, I took its place in the middle of the bed.

If there was one thing I was sure of tonight, it was my exhaustion. I could only hope sleep claimed me quickly.

IT DID NOT.

And my attempts at using memories of home to soothe me didn't help at all. I finally gave up and got dressed for my final day in the office at Grange. Putting on a suit yet again chafed in ways I was beginning to resent. I'd done what I came here to do. Even though Wells had, for whatever reason, given my mother everything she was asking for, I'd still worked to represent my mother's interests to the best of my abilities. Now all that was left was signing the papers and getting home to her side.

And if that failed—if Wells Grange pulled the rug out from under us—I'd finally gotten bank approval to put my shop up as collateral on a loan that would at least cover some of the costs needed for her experimental treatment. Not that I'd ever be able to pay it back in my lifetime on what the shop made. But maybe I'd be able to grow my business in other ways. I'd have to ask James to help me brainstorm if the worst-case scenario came to pass.

My gut was in knots and there was no way I could stomach breakfast. With my phone still powered down in my coat pocket, I settled for just a coffee on my way out of the hotel, which meant I had an extra half hour before needing to be at the meeting. Instead of arranging for a ride, I took off on foot toward the office. But only three blocks later, I found myself off the city streets and surrounded by the steady *thumpthump* of joggers' footfalls on the path beside me.

I was in the park again. And I finally felt like I could breathe.

"Back for another ride?"

I glanced up to see Scotty peering down from atop his carriage with his trademark flirty grin.

"It's awfully early for you to be giving rides, isn't it?" I asked with a smile. "I figured you guys wouldn't start until later in the morning."

His cheeky grin was a welcome sight. "Nah. Tourists wake with the sun. Want to make the most of their days. We make a killing year-round if we're willing to hustle."

"I think I'm just walking today, but thanks." I didn't want to keep him from any potential customers.

Scotty hopped down. "Hey. You okay? No offense, but you kinda look like shit."

I shrugged. "Feel like shit. I'm not sleeping well, and honestly, I'd rather be back home. My mom is ill."

He reached into his secret stash of carrots and handed me one to feed to the horse. While he was showing me how to hand it to her, he spoke gently, leaning his shoulder into mine the way a good friend would. "I'm sorry about your mom. Do you want to talk about it?"

His sweet concern unleashed unexpected waterworks. I blinked back tears. "She'll be okay. I'm working on something that will help take care of her. It's just... a lot, you know?"

Suddenly I was engulfed in a hug, my face mashed against the rough texture of his cold-weather coveralls. Even though he was noticeably shorter than I was, his hand had cupped the back of my head and drawn it down to his shoulder.

The funny guy was stronger than he looked, and it wasn't lost on me that I was more willing to open up to this stranger about my mom than to Wells. Why was that? Did I still not trust him?

"Where's your jackass boyfriend?" he teased as he let me go. "He should be the one copping a feel instead of me, not that I mind."

I wiped at my eyes and chuckled. "He's not my boyfriend."

Scotty blinked at me. "Liar."

"Not lying. He's a business colleague."

He grabbed me by the upper arms and met my eyes. "Conor, that man wanted to eat you like a churro, crunch you down in three big bites, and lick the leftover sugar off his fingers afterward."

The image had me laughing again, if only because the alternative was springing inappropriate wood in the middle of Central Park. "He's cute, yeah?"

Scotty met my eyes. "Uh, yeah. Like Chris Hemsworth is cute. Like Adam Levine is cute. Like motherfucking Idris Elba is cute."

I held out my hand. "Stop, I get it. It's just too bad the guy's a corporate drone. He'd probably sell his own mother for a quick..."

The rest of the sentence died in my throat.

Wasn't that basically what I was doing? Selling my mother's life's work for as much money as I could to the last person on earth she wanted to have it?

I stared at the carriage driver without seeing him. I pictured my mother all alone in her bed at home feeling like she was completely out of choices. Forced to sell the patents to her invention rather than donate it to a nonprofit as she'd always intended.

Instead of pursuing some lofty or lucrative career, I'd followed a stupid kid's dream and opened a game shop. Because of me, she didn't have someone like Wells Grange providing for her the way Wells provided for his sister, Win. As much as I'd judged him for being a corporate sellout, he'd done what I hadn't even thought to do: taken care of business. Taken care of his *family*.

"I have to go," I breathed.

Scotty reached into his pocket for a business card. "Here's my number. Let me know how it goes?"

I slid it into my wallet before giving him another big hug. "Thank you. You have no idea how much I needed a friend today."

As I made my way out of the park, back toward my hotel, I thought through what I needed to do. I already knew that refinancing my building wouldn't bring in enough money for my mom's treatment.

But *selling* it and both of my businesses would. And it would give her back the opportunity to say no to Wells Grange. She could keep her patents and donate them to a nonprofit the way she'd always wanted to. So the people who needed the technology the most wouldn't have to go to the poorhouse to get it.

I sent James a text asking for more time, ignoring the texts from

Trace that pinged through one after the other when I turned my phone on. I didn't have the emotional energy for that right now.

James: *What do you mean, more time?*

Conor: *I need to talk to my mom about this again before signing anything. It's a big deal.*

James: *You're right. It is. Take all the time you need. I'll enjoy telling Wells to wait.*

The mention of Wells made my chest tighten.

When I got back to my hotel room, I pulled out my laptop and got to work. The game shop's brick building alone was worth almost two million dollars. I'd bought it for a steal with an inheritance from my grandmother and fixed it up myself while I was in school. Since then, Asheville's downtown scene had only grown more popular, and now I was regularly receiving offers from entrepreneurs and investors interested in buying my building and converting it into something more hip and trendy.

The thought of selling made me feel hollow inside. I loved being part of the scene in Asheville, seeing tourists and locals wander by and decide to stop in just to browse. That was part of what made my day enjoyable. I couldn't imagine a different life than the one I'd built around my shop.

But this wasn't about me, I reminded myself. It was about my mom. And if I sold my building and the business, I could figure out another business to start, or hell... get a job like a real person. Stop trying to have a fun job and go for something more responsible and stable.

I called my mom to explain my plan to her. As soon as I got the basic details out, she cut me off. "Pardon my French, dear, but are you fucking crazy?"

I looked at my phone. Elizabeth Newell didn't use the f-word. "Mom?"

"No. Stop right now. You suggesting selling your companies and that gorgeous building that you put your blood, sweat, and tears into is insane."

Even at her weakest, the woman was feisty as hell.

"But, Mom, hear me out."

"I will not. Go to the Grange office and sign those papers. Now."

"Wait, let me—"

"No. You wait. And you listen to me. I did not spend decades working to improve medical techniques just to let the fruits of my labor sit in a dusty storage room. That printer can save lives, Conor. And selling it to Grange is the only way to get it out there in the world where it can do some good."

"What about your idea for the nonprofit foundation? That man will turn around and charge unreachable prices for it," I argued. "He'll make it impossible for real people to afford. He'll—"

"Then how do I get the biological materials, Conor? Hm? Because the way I see it—" She stopped and began coughing. I held my breath while she tried to catch hers. "The way I see it," she said more slowly, "is that Grange is the one who holds Claude's patents to the printing material. So Grange is the only one who can bring a complete solution to market. It's up to the insurance companies to push back on the pricing. And, Conor, that would be out of my hands no matter who I sold to."

"I thought you hated Wells Grange," I said, ignoring how petulant I sounded.

"I do."

"Why?"

"Because when he negotiated the deal with Desona for their dynamic glucose monitoring technology, he refused to agree to the extra funding needed to adapt the technology for children."

I couldn't square the man my mom described with the guy who'd told me about his three-year-old niece's penchant for wearing a pirate's eye patch every time he saw her.

"I know, but maybe there was a reason we don't know about..."

"Honey, the man only cares about money. About profitability. To him, it's not about saving lives or doing good. Believe me, many business folk are ruthless like that, and you can hardly blame him. He grew up in the culture of money at whatever the cost. His own father is a Wall Street investment banker. That's probably all That Asshole knows."

My brain spun while my mother continued.

"Besides," she continued, "I didn't work my tail off all these years just for you to give up your dreams. You're being ridiculous. Just go sign the papers and come home."

"But Mom—"

"No buts. This is my technology and I get the final say. Got that?"

I let out a long sigh. "Fine," I said, sounding like a moody teen.

We talked a little bit longer about how she was doing before I ended the call and texted James.

Conor: *The deal's back on. Mom wants it to go through. But I need a favor.*

James: *Name it.*

Conor: *Can you finalize the deal without me? I don't want to come in if I don't have to.*

James: *Of course. I can use the Power of Attorney your mom signed. Though of course I plan to make Wells squirm a little longer before I let him know. What should I tell him if he asks about you?*

Conor: *He won't.*

James: *Humor me.*

Conor: *Tell him I'm on my way home.*

There was a pause before James responded.

James: *Everything OK?*

Conor: *Yeah. I'm just tired of being cooped up in that conference room and figure I might as well enjoy my last day in the city.*

We'd been friends long enough that James would know there was more to it than that, but he didn't press the issue. Instead he wrote:

James: *Remember I'm here if you need me.*

I texted him back a grinning emoji and slipped my phone into my pocket.

I may have been brave enough to approve of the deal on behalf of my mother, but I sure as hell wasn't brave enough to face Wells when it happened. I didn't like the way being around him made me want things—made me want *him*. When he'd made it perfectly clear he didn't want me. And even if he did it would just be for a night. According to him, he didn't do relationships.

I wasn't looking for a one-night stand. As it turned out, I was bad at flings. I'd learned that lesson from Trace. I just wasn't cut out to hold back my emotions. It could never just be about the physical for me.

Even as it was, I was teetering on the edge with Wells. I already found myself craving to be around him, wanting to know more about him, wanting to understand him. It would be too easy for me to fall for him. And that was a one-way ticket to heartache.

18

WELLS

I'd arrived obscenely early for the meeting in my best suit. Of course, I knew it was a bit like armor, but I pretended the purpose of donning it was to bolster my confidence in an important business transaction.

Complete bullshit.

I wanted Conor to want me. It was that simple. And that immature.

After everything that had happened between us, both as Wells and Trace, I knew we could never actually be together, but the shallow part of me wanted it to be on my terms.

Which was also bullshit since I knew this was the first time in a very, very long time that I'd felt so out of control.

And I hated every minute of it.

Every single ball was in Conor's court. Which was a position I rarely, if ever, found myself in with my business or personal life. I wasn't handling it well.

The door to my office opened, and I looked up, eagerly hoping for Conor's familiar face but finding Deb's instead.

"Sorry to disappoint you," she said. "James just arrived."

I opened my mouth to ask, but she beat me to it. "Alone."

My teeth clenched. "Thanks."

I went back to the work I wasn't doing on my laptop. "Let me know when everyone is here," I clipped.

She paused for a beat before sighing. "Of course."

When the door closed, I squeezed my eyes together and tried calming my breathing. He was late. He hadn't been late all week. My stomach twisted with worry, and I returned to the litany of concerns my brain had scrolled through all night long.

Was he safe? Was he upset? Was he alone?

I already knew his mother was okay, because I'd had Deb call her house to ask if we could send some gourmet meals over from a local delivery service. The nurse had chatted excitedly with Deb about what Dr. Newell could and couldn't eat.

Another twenty minutes passed and it took all of my self-control not to buzz Deb to ask if she was sure he wasn't here yet.

Finally, just before the thirty-minute mark, Deb popped in to warn me that James's head was on the verge of exploding.

"I'm afraid if you don't go in there, there's going to be a situation," she said. "And I just got my nails done. I'm in no position to fight him."

I stood up and straightened my coat before buttoning it. "Fine. Let's go see what's holding things up."

When I entered the conference room, James immediately laid into me. "Dammit, Grange. What the hell are you playing at? It's hard enough trying to convince Conor to show up, and I can't even get you in the damned room?"

I frowned. "What do you mean about getting Conor to show up? Where is he?"

"He's changed his mind. Says he doesn't want to sell after all."

My stomach dropped. "What happened, is he okay?"

"He was when he texted this morning." James stood, shuffling a blank notepad and pen into his briefcase.

I wanted to leap across the table and strangle him and demand he tell me what was going on. "I don't understand. The terms were finalized. I conceded to everything they asked for. Why is he changing his mind?"

James shrugged. "Maybe he doesn't want to see his mother's life's work used to extort money from desperate patients on their death beds."

I rolled my eyes. "You're exaggerating just to prove a point."

"That doesn't make my point invalid," James countered. "People who need this technology to save their lives won't get it because they can't afford it and they will die." He gave me a sour smile. "But at least you'll get rich in the process."

I felt the blood rise in my cheeks as my anger escalated. "That's not fair. It's because of Grange BioMed that this tech will even make it to market. Without our investment, no one will have access to it."

He gave me an exaggerated shrug. "Well, I guess you'll have to find some other inventor to fleece. The good news for you is that losing this deal will barely be a blip on Grange BioMed's bottom line."

I was about to tell him that I didn't give a shit about the deal, that I was worried about Conor, when James's phone dinged. He held up a finger for me to wait. I rolled my eyes and turned back toward my office.

"It's Conor," he called after me.

I froze before I'd even made it out of the conference room. "Is he okay?"

He didn't respond, his attention on his phone. I wanted to stalk across the room and rip it from his hands, but I held myself still, my body vibrating with tension. The two texted back and forth several times, and I was about to lose my mind and scream for him to tell me what was going on when he looked up at me and slipped his phone back into his pocket.

"Deal is back on," he said. I waited for him to say more, but he just resumed his seat at the table instead.

"Is he okay?"

"Seems to be."

I wanted to throttle that fucking lawyer. "So he's on his way in to sign the paperwork?"

"Nope. I have a power of attorney, so I'll be signing on Dr. Newell's behalf."

"Dammit," I growled. I pulled my phone out and pulled up Conor's number. I was just about to hit the Call button when I realized that I couldn't. Because my number was in his phone as Trace. I couldn't call him as Wells.

I clenched my hands into fists, wanting to punch something. Preferably James if it would make him answer my fucking questions. "Where is he?"

"On his way back to Asheville, I think. He was in an Uber headed to LaGuardia when I finally got in touch with him."

My eyes darted to the door. Everything inside of me wanted to race after him. Instead I ground my teeth together, willing myself to appear calm and collected on the outside when everything inside was raging with alarm. "Why?"

James shrugged. "The deal is done. No reason for him to stick around. Right?" He gave me a look that seemed to imply there was a deeper meaning to his words, and I wondered for the briefest moment if Conor had said something to him about me.

I braced my hands against the edge of the conference room table, steadying myself. I'd expected Conor to be upset with Trace, but I didn't understand what I had done as Wells to send him running. There'd been so much sexual tension between us last night that I'd thought it had been obvious where things were leading. We'd sign the papers, finalize the deal, and then I would take him home and fuck him until neither of us could stand.

But instead he'd left.

He'd left.

Conor was gone. On his way home.

I'd tried to show him that I could be a good person. That I could be worthy of him. That I wasn't Glacial Grange—there was more to me than work and the bottom line. But it hadn't been enough.

He still didn't trust me. In real life I was a corporate raider. He knew from my history that I'd do anything to get the best deal. It turned out that he'd gotten to know me better yesterday and *still* thought the worst of me.

In real life I wasn't to be trusted.

And why did him thinking so little of me bother me so fucking much?

James leaned back in his chair, crossing his arms and appraising me. "Is there something I should know?"

I shook my head, trying to force myself to focus. I'd let myself get distracted. Let my emotions affect my business decisions. I knew better than that—I'd already been burned doing that once before. I needed to remember: this was about the deal. Not Conor.

"No. Nothing," I said brusquely. "He's right. The deal is done. Let's get it formalized and over with so we can move on."

IT WAS DONE. The papers were signed despite Conor's insistence on being a no-show. To say I was disgruntled would be a massive understatement. I was both furious and devastated, so much that I decided to take a visit down to my favorite brandy bar in Tribeca to drown my sorrows in some thirty-year-old Balvenie until I couldn't taste the difference between it and Johnny Walker Black.

Normally I'd soak it up with their rack of lamb or filet, but I couldn't even pretend to have an appetite. So I drank my dinner and then drank my dessert too. I hunched down on the leather chair in my dark little corner and felt sorry for myself, unsure of what I really wanted from all of this. From Conor.

Nothing. That should have been my automatic answer to that question. I shouldn't want anything from Conor at all. I had the patents; the deal was done. That should have been the end of it.

Except that it wasn't because there was still this damn ache in my chest. Like something was missing. It was the same feeling I got when I left the house without my wallet or keys—that sense of something being amiss but not knowing exactly what.

But I did know what was missing. Conor.

I cursed under my breath and searched the room for my waitress. She stood near the end of the bar, piling drinks onto her tray. She glanced my way, and I lifted my empty glass to signal I was ready for another. And froze. Because there was a familiar form hovering behind her, searching for a spot among the crowd to slip through to the bar.

Conor. His cheeks were bright pink from the cold night air, his hair slightly disheveled.

I blinked, sure I must be imagining things. That somehow I'd been craving him with enough ferocity that I'd conjured him out of thin air. But then my waitress turned, and I saw him mumble an apology to her, sidestepping out of her way as she smiled at him in thanks. That's how I knew he was real rather than a figment of my imagination.

His eyes roamed the bar, as though he were slightly unsure of himself and his place among the hipsters and bankers. Something inside of me roared to the surface, the need to soothe the crease furrowing the spot between his eyebrows and protect him over-whelmed my better judgment. Overwhelmed any judgment at all.

I surged to my feet, my knee hitting the narrow table and rattling the crystal lamp on top. It was loud enough to cause several patrons to glance my way. Including Conor. His eyes widened when he saw me. He stood at the other end of the narrow room, close to the door, and I watched as his eyes darted toward it as though considering escape.

Hell no.

I strode toward him, my determination obvious enough for anyone standing between the two of us to hop quickly out of my way.

With every step my mind churned with what I wanted to say to him. I wanted to ask him what the fuck he'd been thinking by blowing off today's meetings. Why the fuck he hadn't responded to any of Trace's texts. And why the hell he'd shown up here, of all places, while I was still feeling raw and exposed.

He must have seen the determination in my eyes because as I approached he steeled himself, his back straightening and his chin lifting. *Good boy*, I thought to myself. I liked that he refused to be intimidated by me, that he seemed willing to stand up to me despite his aversion to confrontation.

But just before I opened my mouth to berate him, he nervously bit at his bottom lip. Every thought in my head vanished, replaced with a desire to reach my hand around the back of his neck and pull him toward me so I could swipe my tongue over the soft flesh his teeth were currently worrying.

Fuck.

He waited for me to say something. But I was too dumbstruck with desire to muster a single word.

"Wells? You okay?" His voice was smoother than the aged scotch and ten times more delicious.

"Fuck, hi. Oh sorry. Conor. Hi. What are you...?" I clenched my mouth shut to stem the tide of verbal nonsense spilling out of me. "What are you doing here?"

His winter-chilled cheeks turned from pink to red. I wanted to cup my palm around the alluring blush but kept my hands fisted by my side instead.

"You'd suggested this place, so I thought I'd check it out." His eyes swung around the room. "Crowded. Must mean it's pretty good." He pushed up onto his toes, craning his neck. "Doesn't look like there are any empty seats."

"Join me," I blurted.

His eyes widened in surprise.

I felt the urge to reach for him, to wrap my hand around his so he couldn't escape. But instead I turned and made my way back to my dark corner, hoping he followed. Wanting to give him the opportunity to choose whether to sit with me or not.

As before, the crowd parted for me automatically, and I felt Conor tuck in behind me, letting me be the one to cut a path. He even reached out a tentative hand, pressing it lightly against my lower back to let me know he was there. And to keep hold of me so he couldn't be separated and swallowed by the throng of people.

When I reached the grouping of leather seats in the far back corner, he hesitated only a minute before sitting. I took the chair across from him. Close enough that I caught a whiff of his unique blend of the hotel Bulgari soaps and whatever supermarket products of his own he'd brought with him. It was a scent I knew I'd never be able to replicate for the rest of my life. It was unique to him and this crazy week.

"Are you okay?" I asked. "Are you well?"

He glanced at me from under his lashes before fiddling with the leather-bound menu book. "I'm okay. Thank you. Just... well. It was a hard day. I'm sorry I didn't come back to the office to sign the papers myself."

I cleared my throat. "I understand. It's a big decision. It couldn't have been an easy one for your family."

Conor's eyes widened in surprise. "Yes. Exactly. Thank you for understanding. But you must..." He glanced at me briefly before dropping his eyes and flipping a page in the book. "You must be excited to be able to move forward with your plans now."

"We have a team already working toward bringing it to market. It will be a while, of course. Hoops to jump through, tests to conduct, regulations to contend with. But it could be a game changer for the industry."

He mumbled something under his breath I couldn't hear. I leaned closer. "What was that?"

Conor met my eyes, and I saw something sharp-edged in his expression. "I said it could be a game changer for people's lives too."

"Well of course," I agreed. "That's a given."

"Is it? In all of your talk about acquiring the patents, it's always been about the industry and the market and potential profits and never about the patients." I started to respond, but he wasn't done. He leaned forward, pressing his point. "Have you ever had someone close to you become sick, Wells? Like, really sick?"

"I... no... I guess I've been lucky," I stuttered, taken aback by the ferocity of his tone.

"Yes, you have been," he said. "It sucks." He pressed his lips together for a moment, then blew out a breath, his shoulders dropping. "My mom's sick. Really sick. I didn't want to tell you before because I didn't want it to impact the deal."

I swallowed, the rawness in his voice causing my throat to tighten. "I'm so sorry, Conor."

He nodded. "When she and Claude developed the printer, their plan was to donate it to a nonprofit so the technology would be available to anyone who needed it. And then Claude sold to you, and my mom's illness grew worse, and the treatments started failing."

It felt like a lie to pretend as though I didn't already know this, and I hated it. But now wasn't the time to tell him the truth. Now was the time for me to sit here and listen.

Even though I already knew the answer, I asked, "Are there more treatment options for her?"

"That's the point. There are. But they're expensive. That's why my mother sold her patents to you. To afford the chance to keep living. Even though she knows that doing so is going to put that tech out of reach for people in a similar situation.

"Don't you get it, Wells? There are people out there like me, people whose mothers are sick, and this printing technology could help them and now they may not be able to afford it."

"That's not going to happen," I told him.

The corner of his lip tipped in a rueful smile. "Isn't it?"

I dropped my eyes to my lap. I didn't know what to say. How to respond.

Conor took a sharp breath and shook his head. "You know what? The deal is done. I'm sorry, I didn't mean to do this. Do you think... maybe it would be okay if we didn't talk business tonight?"

I reached over and took his hand, clasping it between both of mine. I gently squeezed until he met my eyes. "That sounds like a great idea."

His eyes searched mine, and then he let out a breath, his shoulders instantly relaxing. "Thank you."

"Besides, I've already had a couple of glasses and fear discussing business might reverse all the good work this Balvenie has already done for me." I winked at him and squeezed his hand again before releasing it. "What would you like to drink? They do a rare scotch flight if you're into that or a rare bourbons that's great also."

He tilted his head to the side, tapping a finger against his chin. "Do you think they do a good piña colada?"

I blinked at him before looking around to see if anyone had overheard him. "A... what?"

"Oooh! Wait," Conor said, flipping through the book in search of something. "You know what I'm in the mood for? A white wine spritzer."

I glanced at my glass, unsure of whether or not I'd lost count of how many I'd had and was drunker than I'd thought.

The server arrived and welcomed Conor with a flirty smile. "Have any questions for me?"

He shot her large grin. "Yeah, am I in the mood for a sidecar or a glass of that bourbon with the little horsie on top?"

Had I been savoring a sip of the Balvenie, I would have done a classic spit take. As it was, I gawped at Conor as he smirked at me.

That sly motherfucker had been messing with me.

The server laughed her ass off. "Definitely the Blanton's, but if this guy's buying," she said, thumbing over her shoulder at me, "then you need to up your game. Might I recommend the Boss Hog Whistle Pig?"

Conor gave me a look that gave new and filthy meaning to the terms Boss, Hog, Whistle, and Pig. I squirmed in my seat while he decided.

"Screw it. Just bring me whatever he's having," he said. "And bring us an order of those little fancy burgers I walked past please. Thank you."

After she moved away, Conor trained his sparkling eyes on me. "I wish I'd thought to pull out my phone and snap a picture of your face when I asked about those other drinks. You'd have thought I was ordering a whore in a convent."

"Don't you mean a monk in an abbey?"

He nodded, the corner of his lip curving ever so slightly. "I do prefer monks to nuns; it's true."

I took another sip of my drink as the server returned with Conor's glass. "Are you okay though, really?" I couldn't help but ask.

Conor leaned across the small table and rubbed the pad of his thumb across my forehead. "Why are you worrying so much about me?" he murmured. "You had a big day too. Said goodbye to many of your precious millions, didn't you?"

I leaned into his touch, silently thanking the scotch for an excuse to indulge in it.

"That's one thing I have plenty of to spare," I responded, forcing a smile. I waited a moment, feeling the weight of my own words sink in and find purchase before adding, "But we weren't going to talk about that. Sorry."

Conor sat back and took a sip of the Balvenie, meeting my eyes over the rim of his glass. "Mm. Nutty."

His rich voice went straight to my balls as I suspected had been his intent. His eyes bore into mine, making promises I wasn't sure his body was ready to keep.

"You like that?" I asked. "Drink much scotch at home?"

He lifted a shoulder. "Not really. I'm not that manly. I wasn't joking about the piña colada and sidecar. Make it fruity and I'm yours for life."

I laughed and made a mental note. "There's a bar near your hotel that does a killer tequila sunrise."

He grinned. "Now you're talking."

"Or the cosmo. You know it was invented here. I could take you to Long Island Bar."

"Now you're exhausting me. I think I'd rather stay here and drink two-hundred-dollar glasses of scotch with you. It's less effort. Especially if you pay."

We continued bantering back and forth in an easy manner. When he finished his drink, I quickly waved for another.

"Trying to get me drunk?" he asked with a raised brow.

I shrugged. "I'm not comfortable being the only one at the table with a buzz on."

"Afraid I'm going to take advantage of you while you're inca-pacitated?"

I barked out a laugh. "I'm not sure I've ever been incapacitated. Or taken advantage of."

"There's always a first for everything," he teased.

I lifted an eyebrow. "Is there?"

Conor narrowed his eyes, considering me a moment. "Hm. I guess not. Mr. Always In Control is always in control. Why is that? Are you like that in your personal relationships too?"

His question put me on the spot. I stared down at my glass, twisting it between my fingers. I wanted to be honest with him, but I knew he wouldn't like the truth. It would only serve to confirm what he thought he already knew about me.

The urge to not hold back with him surged forward, and I took a swallow of scotch before answering him the best I could.

"I wouldn't say I have to be in control so much as I'm very... selec-tive with the people I choose to trust," I told him.

"Why?"

I shrugged, still studying my glass. "Typical reasons, I guess. I've been burned before."

I waited for him to press for more details, but instead he studied me. I tried not to shift under his gaze, uncomfortable with the thought of what kind of conclusions he might be drawing about me.

He took another sip before asking, "What does someone have to do to gain entry into your trust tree?"

I felt my jaw tighten as unbidden memories flashed. "Don't fuck me over. Don't use me. Don't lie to me or mess with my family."

He let out a soft whistle. "There's a story there. Do you want to talk about it?" His face held empathy, and I already knew him to be a good listener from our day in the city together.

"No."

He threw back his head to laugh, exposing his creamy neck where he'd obviously missed another spot shaving that morning. I wanted to lick it.

"You're a man of few words, Glacial Grange. What does it take to melt you, huh?"

I loved this teasing side of Conor. If two drinks made him flirty, how many would it take before he'd relax enough to let me touch him? I stretched out my leg until my shoe ran alongside his. He didn't move his foot away, so I left mine there.

Our eyes met and stayed together, which made my heart begin to thunder wildly in my chest. I wasn't used to feeling off-kilter with a man, but every minute I spent with Conor Newell left me breathless and unsure. It was time to regain some control over the situation. I wanted him to be the one on edge, not me.

I let the amber liquid swirl around my glass as I met his eyes. "A hot man in bed is good for melting things," I said, causing him to bark out another laugh.

"Touché."

Before I followed this path too far, however, there was something I needed to ask. "Yesterday you said that some people prefer a relationship over a convenient lay," I said carefully. "Does that mean you have a special someone back home?"

Nothing in my research on him had turned up anything about a partner, and I hadn't gotten the impression from NotSam's texts that there was someone in North Carolina warming his bed. But I wanted to know for sure.

His cheeks flushed. "No."

"But you'd like there to be," I pushed.

He blinked and looked away, his fingers idly tracing the rim of his glass. "Sometimes. It would be nice not to have to..." Conor stopped talking and looked down at his drink and shook his head.

I leaned forward. Close enough that he couldn't avoid me. "Nice to what, Conor?" I asked softly. I liked the feel of his name in my mouth and vowed to use it more often.

He met my eyes again and swallowed. "Not to have to always carry life's shit on my own."

The need to protect and comfort roared just under the surface of my skin. Everything inside of me ached to carry his burdens for him.

To use my immense power and wealth to shelter him from the burdens of the world.

But I couldn't. I wasn't the one for him. I knew this truth as well as I knew the mechanics of structuring a lucrative business deal. He deserved a sweetheart. Someone strong but tender who would treat him like a king and take charge when Conor needed to give over control. That would never be me. I was neither sweet nor tender, and he'd already made it clear he thought I was a selfish asshole in real life.

I'd never felt so powerless to help someone in my life.

I took a large swallow of scotch, welcoming the burn of it down my throat.

He snorted softly. His eyes turned molten. "But then again, sometimes I just want to find someone to pin me down face-first onto the nearest solid surface and fuck me like their life depended on it. Go figure."

I choked on the scotch, letting out a wheeze as I struggled to catch my breath.

His intention had been to dispel the tension, but his hot words had only served to ratchet it up a thousand notches. My thundering heart turned its power south until my head swam and my pants tightened.

"Jesus fuck," I rasped, shifting my hips in my chair.

Knowing heat flared in Conor's eyes. "Yeah? That do something for you?" he teased.

"Mpfh." I grunted, eyeballing the back of the leather chair next to him, the one at the perfect height to catch at his hips. The perfect height for bending someone over. Conor caught me assessing the chair and let out a strangled noise from his throat.

"Here you are, gentlemen," the server chirped, setting down a plate with two small burgers on it. "Hope you're hungry. Enjoy."

Without taking my eyes off Conor, I spoke in a roughened voice to the woman. "Definitely hungry. We're also ready for our check."

19

CONOR

I thought maybe I was going to pass out from the anticipation and lust. The heady combination of high-end scotch and Wells's flirting made me feel warm and fuzzy around the edges.

I wanted him so fucking badly. Which was ridiculous since he was an asshole.

But he was such a hot fucking asshole who seemed to reveal shards of non-assholery behind the uptight mask he wore.

Also, I wanted to see him naked.

Like, really really *really* wanted to see him naked.

I briefly thought about Trace, whose texts I still hadn't gotten the nerve to read. He had made me feel the same kind of horny desperation I was beginning to feel for Wells. What the hell was my problem? Was I just hard up? Had my embarrassing dry spell caused this incessant need? Did it matter?

"Do you think Hank can give me a ride to the hotel?" I asked. I'd meant to ask him to take me someplace dark and private and fuck me into the nearest wall, but my Southern manners beat me to the punch.

"Is that what you want?" Wells's voice was gruff.

His eyes pinned me to my seat until I squirmed. Why did I want to reply *No, sir* to this man?

"What..." I swallowed. "What are my options, exactly?"

The foot he'd rested alongside mine moved closer to me until his calf brushed mine. The warmth of his body through his suit pants caused me to let out a needy sound under my breath. He must have heard it because his eyes narrowed even more until I thought I might combust on the spot.

I knew both of us had consumed enough hard liquor to make this a dangerous game, but I also knew we were buzzed enough not to give a shit.

Wells leaned forward across the small round table between us until only I could hear his low rumble. He drew the edge of a pinky finger lightly along the outside of my knee until goose bumps came up all over my skin. "I want you to come home with me. I want to take off your clothes and press your naked body against the windows overlooking the city. And then I want to fuck you until you beg me to let you come."

I closed my eyes as my entire body shuddered. My cock was stiff, and precum dampened my underwear. Fuck, he was incredible. Was there a gay man alive who could say no to that?

"Ungh," I said in agreement.

His face transformed into a smile, but instead of a smile of victory, it was a tender one. His hand moved to my knee and squeezed gently. "Are you sure, Conor?"

His use of my name sobered me, and I wondered if that had been his intent.

"Just for tonight?" I asked, more for myself than him.

He paused for a moment before nodding. "Just for tonight."

It felt a little bit like making a deal with the devil. I knew I wasn't the kind of person who could have an intense sexual encounter with someone and leave it behind so easily. But I also wasn't the kind of person who could say no to Wells Grange when his hands and eyes were on me like that.

"Okay," I said.

As if the answer was ever going to be anything other than yes.

I WOULD HAVE EXPECTED the ride to his place to be filled with awkward silence and regret.

It was not.

The minute the bill was paid, Wells grabbed my hand and hauled my ass out of the small bar and to the waiting town car. The warmth of his hand made my stomach tumble, and when I felt his thumb caress mine, I almost sucked in a breath.

"My place, Hank."

Other than the briefest flash of a smirk, Hank remained professional. Since there was no divider in the car, I expected Wells to keep to one side of the vehicle while I hugged the other. Instead, the minute Wells slipped in next to me, he reached for my hand again to pull me toward him, tucking me against his side and wrapping an arm around my shoulders.

He turned his head and began to murmur soft, filthy things in my ear too low for Hank to hear from the front seat.

"Are you hard for me?"

"Oh god," I breathed.

"Are you leaking? Do you wish I had my hand on you right now?"

"Wells..."

"I can't wait to peel these fucking clothes off you and make you stand before me naked. I want to see every inch of your body."

I let out a soft whine.

"And then I'll trace a line with my tongue from your lips to the tip of your cock. Would you like that, Conor?"

"Ngh."

The low rumble of his laughter felt like warm brandy in the small confines of the car. My panting sounded obscene by comparison.

"Do you want me to fuck you? Push into that tight ass and—"

I couldn't take it anymore, I turned toward him and buried my face in his neck, whispering frantically for him to stop before I embarrassed myself. He smelled so fucking good, and the rich cashmere of his coat was soft against my cheek. I couldn't let myself think about who this was and how inappropriate the entire situation seemed to be.

He was a business partner.

But the deal had been finalized. The papers signed. Besides, his agreement was with my mother, not me. And couldn't my reward for this shitty week be one night of crazy hot sex with the uptight but extremely alluring man? He was only into casual sex, and that was all I needed.

Clearly, the man wasn't relationship material. And lived in New York and was married to his job. And for so many other reasons, all this needed to be was one night of getting each other off before I flew home the following day. Indulging in this insane physical attraction and then putting this whole experience behind me.

"Will that be all, sir?" Hank asked from the front seat. I realized we'd pulled up to the front door of a high-rise apartment building not far from my hotel.

"Yes. See you in the morning. Thank you," Wells said, resuming his professional tone. His *in charge* tone.

Which only made me harder. Thankfully I had my coat to fold around me as I exited the car and followed Wells into the building. Nerves simmered in my gut, and I wondered if I was making a colossal mistake.

Conor, men hook up with other men all the damned time. Just because this happens to be the man you've always thought you hated...

"You okay? It's not too late to change your mind," Wells said softly as he nodded at the doorman and led me inside with a hand to my lower back. "I can walk you back to your hotel. It's only a couple of blocks from—"

"I'm fine," I interrupted. "I don't want to go back to my hotel. I want to go upstairs with you."

He seemed to relax then, as if I'd said something he really needed to hear. We made our way to the elevator and shot up to the fifty-third floor. I tried my best not to feel out of place, but the sleek, marbled lobby alone had been luxurious enough to remind me Wells played at an entirely different level than I did.

When I stepped foot into Wells's living room, all the air vanished from my lungs. Two of the four walls were floor-to-ceiling windows looking out onto the park and the city below.

"Holy crap," I blurted, going automatically toward the view. "This is amazing."

Wells chuckled as he moved around the room behind me, turning on a lamp. Suddenly, the view was harder to see because of the light reflections on the glass.

"Wait," I said over my shoulder. "Can you turn it back off?"

The light disappeared, and I felt Wells approach from behind. Soft lips brushed the skin of my ear as his hands came around to unbutton my coat.

"I spend quite a bit of time staring out of these windows," he said against my ear. His warm breath smelled like the scotch we'd had, which turned me on even more than I was already. If that was possible.

"I can see why. The views are incredible. This place must be worth millions."

"Mm. Sometimes it seems less like home than my office does." There was a melancholy tone to his words.

I turned around to read his face, but it was his usual unreadable default. "Why do you work so much when you already have every-thing you could ever need?"

His eyes met mine, and in them, I saw flashes of the unexpected. Insecurity, exhaustion, *need*.

I leaned in and pressed my lips to his before he could answer. The feel of my mouth on his for the first time made me drunker than the alcohol had. Everything about him was masculine and strong. The feel of his arms sliding around me, the taste of scotch on his tongue, the scent of whatever the hell kind of expensive cologne he wore mixed with the faint sweaty smell of a man's body after a long day.

God, I was so attracted to him, I was beginning to feel desperate. Even more desperate than I was before.

Wells pulled me tightly to him as he took control of the kiss. I felt myself give over to him and melt against his hard body. His hands seemed to roam all over me—my back, my ass, my hair. Little needy sounds escaped my throat while he devoured my mouth. I wasn't sure I'd ever been so consumed by someone's kiss before. It made me crazy, made me want to crawl inside of him and get as much of him as possible.

"More," I gasped into his mouth. "*Wells.*"

He moved from my mouth to my jaw, trailing kisses to my ear before taking my lobe between his teeth. "What do you need, Conor? What do you like?"

The questions sounded strange and awkward on his tongue. Like he wasn't used to asking but more to *taking.*

"You. In charge. No deciding," I gasped.

His eyes met mine with blown pupils in a fierce stare. "Bedroom. Now."

I glanced at the windows. "But I... I thought you wanted..."

"No one sees you but me. Get in there and take off your clothes."

He nodded his head back toward the front door where I'd remembered seeing a hallway off to the left. I hurried in that direction, tugging at my clothes, but I only got to the dark hallway before Wells caught up with me and pulled me hard back against his body.

"Want you so fucking much," he grumbled in my ear before kissing down into my collar. His hands took over from mine on the buttons of my shirt. I tried walking forward, but every step I took made his hard cock brush against my ass. "So sexy. So sweet. The noises you make... you're going to make me come before we get to the bedroom."

I couldn't wrap my head around Wells Grange, multimillionaire CEO of one of the world's most powerful biomedical companies, wanting me. He could probably have any hot piece of ass in the city tonight. Yet he wanted me. I wondered if it was because I'd been easy, already right there in the bar and putty in his hands.

I froze midstep at the thought and felt Wells bump against my back.

"Conor?"

"Why me?" I asked, turning to face him. "Am I just convenient?"

Shut up, Conor. Does it fucking matter? Let the man give you pleasure. Stop questioning it.

Wells's confusion was clear on his face. "Convenient?"

"Yeah. I was there already, at the bar. You didn't have to call or swipe an app. You could just—*mpfh!*"

He shoved me hard against the wall of the corridor, knocking a painting off-kilter and bunching the rug under his feet. His face dropped to mine and I could make out his usual intensity in the dim light from the front hall. His forearm crossed my chest as he held me against the wall.

"You listen to me, Conor Newell. I've wanted you from the moment you stepped into my conference room with your nervous stomach and your little nerdy Dalek tie. I walked behind you to the elevator that day imagining all the things I could do with that sweet, tight ass and that hot mouth of yours. But I tried my best to ignore those feelings because I didn't want you to think I was using you. Didn't want you to think this had anything to do with the deal on the table. But don't for one second think bringing you to my apartment was convenient. I don't bring people here. No one gets to come into my bedroom. Do you understand? But I can't fucking stop thinking of you, and I can't fucking stop imagining what it will feel like to press you down into my mattress and make you cry out in pleasure. It's taken every ounce of my self-control not to come on to you these past two days, and even now I know this is a tremendous mistake. But I can't stay away from you. I can't stop needing you. Trust me when I say you are the *opposite* of convenient."

I stared dumbfounded at him, all the blood having left my brain for warmer climes.

"Then fuck me already," I choked out. "What the hell are you waiting for?"

My feet didn't touch the ground until my half-naked ass was chucked unceremoniously in the center of his large bed.

"Don't make me tell you again to get your damned clothes off," Wells commanded. "Or your ass will have a nice rosy glow on it when I fuck into it."

20

WELLS

This was so wrong. Warning bells were clanging telling me to stop going down this treacherous path. I'd never felt so out of control as I did with Conor Newell in my home. In my bed.

"I want you on your hands and knees," I growled. "Ass in the air."

As Conor scrambled to finish undressing, I struggled to calm my breathing. If I wasn't careful, I'd make a fool of myself before I even got my pants off.

His button-down shirt was already off, and I noticed the T-shirt he wore underneath had the words "Achievement Unlocked" written across the front. I quirked an eyebrow at it. His cheeks flushed. "Xbox reference," he explained. "It's uh... my lucky shirt."

"And are you feeling lucky tonight?" I asked.

"Oh yes," he breathed.

I grinned as I unbuttoned my own shirt in record time and flung it down before ripping my undershirt off and reaching for the buckle of my belt. When a needy sound came from the direction of the bed, I caught Conor staring at me. He'd done exactly as I'd said and his pale, smooth bottom beckoned me from the center of the bed. *My* bed.

"Good boy," I murmured. "So beautiful like that."

I'd expected him to prickle at the moniker, but he didn't. Instead, he seemed to almost purr in contentment. His face lay sideways on the backs of his hands, and his skin was smooth with relaxation.

As I pulled the belt from my belt loops, his eyes widened and his tongue came out to pass over his lips.

"Do you like to be spanked, Conor?" I asked in a low voice.

His eyes turned from interested to nervous, so I quickly amended my question. "Not now, but maybe in your fantasies?"

"Mmm, maybe" was all he said, licking his lip again. I imagined commanding him to pleasure me with that tongue and those alluring lips, but I wanted inside of him too much for that. And I wanted him too dizzy from need to be able to focus on sucking me off.

I opened my pants and walked closer. His eyes tracked my cock as I moved, and it jerked in response to his attention. After pulling a strip of condoms from the box in my dresser, I reached for the bedside table drawer and pulled out a bottle of lube.

"You weren't kidding when you said you don't bring people here, were you?" he asked.

"What makes you say that?"

His eyes flicked to the bedside table. "Your condoms aren't next to the bed. They're separate."

I nodded. "In my top drawer with my socks and handkerchiefs," I said. I placed the supplies on the bed and pulled my pants off before returning my hands to my waist and fingering the band of my boxer briefs to tease him a little.

If the noise he made was any indication, it worked.

"Please," he whispered again. "Take them the fuck off already. Show me your dick."

Instead of doing what he wanted, I walked around behind him and crawled up onto the bed, reaching out to spread his cheeks before leaning in to lick a stripe down his cleft to his tight hole.

"Holy fuck!" Conor yelped as my tongue pressed around his entrance. I held tight to his cheeks to make sure he couldn't pull away. His yelp turned to a moan. "Ohhhh fuuuuuuuck."

I licked, sucked, and nipped at him until the whimpering began.

When I rolled him onto his back, his face was flushed pink and his eyes were half-lidded. His cock begged for some attention, so I licked and sucked that as well. Conor's fingers shot through my hair until he couldn't take it anymore, and he pulled me up to kiss his mouth. His broken voice whimpered my name over and over, each repetition striking something inside of me like a grappling hook.

I ran a hand through his hair as I kissed him, making sure the entire lengths of our bodies were aligned. His hardness pressed into mine through the cotton barrier of my underwear every time he arched his hips up into me.

We were humping like horny teens, and I felt a kind of desperation to touch every centimeter of him at once.

"Get your fucking clothes off goddammit," he gasped. "Why? Why do you still have underwear on? Why?"

His hands tugged at the waistband, but I grabbed his wrists and held them above his head. His eyes met mine with molten heat.

"Because I'm in charge," I told him.

His eyes flashed with defiance. "Who says?"

"*Me.*" It came out a possessive growl.

Conor held my gaze for a beat before making the conscious decision to let go. His eyes finally drifted closed while his entire body was racked with a shudder.

Bingo.

I leaned down and teased the shell of his ear with the tip of my tongue. "Patience, beautiful boy," I murmured. "I want to take my time with you, make you ache for it... make you beg for me to come inside you."

His chest heaved with sucked-in breaths, interspersed with whispered words like *Wells* and *please.*

I lay small kisses down his neck and across his chest, sucked up marks on his collarbone, and teased his nipples into hard nubs. By the time my mouth was back down near his hard cock, his frantic pleading was no longer in complete words, simply noises of need and begging that made my body ache to take him swiftly and without mercy.

When I was finally finished bathing his entire body in kisses and nibbles, I stood back up and stripped off my boxer briefs before climbing between his thighs again. His legs wrapped around my waist and pulled me closer while his hands reached up to cup my jaw.

There was so much expression in his face, I wanted to freeze time and catalogue it. Want and need, trust and curiosity. Heat and tenderness. He was an open book, there in my bed, and mine for the taking.

I'd never felt so overwhelmed in all my life.

I traced a light finger from his temple to the corner of his mouth. "You are so fucking sexy," I groaned. "So expressive."

"Please kiss me." It was whispered and meek. Clearly he was on board with me being in charge, but he still wanted to make his wishes known.

I leaned down and kissed him softly, taking my time before entering his mouth with my tongue. His hands carded into my hair and held on as if he was afraid to let me go. Feeling him wrapped completely around my body, arms and legs, was the closest I'd ever come to knowing what *home* meant.

And that scared the fuck out of me.

Because this wasn't real life. This was temporary, half-fake even, and if Conor ever found out how I'd hidden the truth about our texts from him, he'd know that I was an even worse person than he'd thought.

I pulled back and grunted, nudging him over again onto his belly. Sex. This was sex only. And sex was my damned wheelhouse.

As I lay my body over the back of his and nudged his crease with my dick, I snuck several more kisses down along his spine.

Even if this was meaningless fucking, I was going to enjoy every single second of it.

21

CONOR

I'd passed dizzy several hickeys ago and was well into brainless and debauched by now. Every touch, every kiss from this man set my skin on fire and my heart hammering in my chest. I couldn't get enough. I was drowning and he was air. The minute he'd taken charge, verbally asserted control over me, I'd stopped second-guessing and let myself go.

I pressed my hips back into his dick, begging for it. His hands were like those of a conductor's, sure and precise, urging the rhythm of our joining to bend to his will.

And I was an eager player, desperate to stay in line and give him my absolute best.

"Open for me," Wells murmured against my back. His slick fingers teased my hole, and I did my best to relax against them. "That's it. Just like that."

I tried pressing back against them, but he barked out a command for me to stay still. The ferocious tone of his voice made my cock pulse with precum. It drooled from my tip down toward the pristine bedding. I moved to stroke myself, but Wells's hand came around to grip my wrist and stretch it back above my head on the bed.

"No touching. That's mine tonight. Understand?" He squeezed it hard to make his point before letting it go and moving his hand back to my ass.

"Yes... sir," I gasped, wishing like hell it wasn't just for tonight. "Yours."

"Mm, good. Now stay still while I stretch this tight hole of yours."

"Nngh."

His fingers worked my channel in and out while his other hand smoothed up and down my back with an almost reverent touch.

I'd never felt such frenzy to get someone inside of me before. It was almost like worrying if I didn't get him inside me now, I'd miss my chance for ever and ever. And I *needed* him. Needed him so much, it scared me. Something about this encounter wasn't simply a hookup. What had started out as a one-night stand felt monumental. And that was nonsensical.

Supposedly Wells Grange was a glacier. Cold and calculated. He had walls in front of his walls. The man was known for being stoic and distant, unfeeling and brutal.

Yet here he was worshipping my body as if it was the most exquisite treasure he'd ever laid eyes on. His voice was firm and demanding, but his lips were passionate, his hands gentle, and his soft breaths against my skin soothing and encouraging.

I tried to stop feeling so desperate and frenzied. Instead, I closed my eyes and focused on every nerve ending he was stimulating. His hands were on my ass, my lower back, my hips. His lips were on my spine, the kisses punctuated by little tastes with his tongue and nibbles with his teeth.

When he slid a second and third finger into me, it made me desperate again. I wanted his cock, not his fingers.

"Wells," I begged. "I can't... I... *please.*"

"So patient. So sweet," he whispered. "You ready for my cock?"

I couldn't think, couldn't respond. I was a writhing mass of *need to come, need to come.* When the blunt tip of his covered cock pressed against me, a guttural groan of relief escaped. My body grabbed for him even though the stretch made me hiss. Wells stopped for a beat to let my body adjust before pressing on. And *oh dear god* it felt amazing. The humid heat of his body against my back. The thick stretch of his cock thrusting into my ass. The smooth, cool whisper of the sheet against my cheek. The sounds of our rapid breathing swirling around the room. The feel of his large hand clamped firmly around both of my wrists high above my head.

"Fuck, Conor. So tight, so hot. Your body's like heaven." The words were almost slurred in pleasure, and hearing him start to lose control was even more of an aphrodisiac than everything else he was doing to me.

It was my deepest fantasies made real. Being held down and fucked hard by a powerful man—by *this* man—while I lay there and took it. It was too much.

"Shit, gonna come," I cried.

"No."

"Huh?" I gasped. "But I—"

"*Do. Not. Come.*"

The commanding tone was almost enough to push me over, but the desire to please him held me back. I squeezed my eyes closed and tried to talk myself off the ledge. I thought of terrible things, disgusting things, but nothing helped. The man inside of me was going to get me off without a single touch to my dick.

"Wells," I chanted. "Wells, I don't think—"

His thrusts sped up until I felt his hand let go of my wrists and move to my throbbing cock. The moment his fingers closed around me, I wanted to cry out with ecstasy. I let out a choked moan, the feel of him so perfect. So absolute.

His, I thought. I was his.

"Come for me, baby," he rumbled behind my ear, stroking me twice before I exploded with a scream. My breath completely left my body as my balls continued to empty all over the bed and his hand.

"That's it. Fuck, that's hot. Give me more." Wells's words were strangled. He continued to stroke the last of my cum out until I felt him tremble and thrust hard one last time, calling out my name and holding me tightly to him with a strong arm across my chest.

I felt the pulse of his release inside me and squeezed in response, eliciting an extra gasp out of him. When we were both done, spent and sweaty on the formerly crisp bedding, Wells snorted softly. "Well, I can't say that was unexpected exactly... but... fuck. That was unexpected."

I couldn't cogitate my brain enough to form a word, so I just grunted in acknowledgment.

"You... god, Conor."

He sounded so pleased, so sated. I reveled in his admiration and tried to hold on to the feeling even when he grasped the condom and pulled out.

"Stay there," he said with the return of his bossy tone. I smiled into the bedding. As if I was going anywhere. He'd be lucky to get me to leave by the weekend.

The real life part of my brain tried to remind me I was flying out the following day, but I pushed it aside. There was no room for real life right now when my body was feeling so divinely shattered.

"C'mere," Wells murmured, pulling me onto my back by the shoulder. He had a thick, warm cloth from the bathroom and began to clean me off with sure but gentle strokes. When he was finished, he met my eyes and reached out to smooth the hair from my forehead. It was so tender, my throat tightened.

"Thank you," he said softly.

His simple words floored me.

"For what?" I asked. "You did all the work," I teased, not knowing how else to respond. *My pleasure* sounded a bit too fast-food drive-thru.

He let his fingers trail down my cheek, his thumb tracing the edge of my jaw. "For letting go. For giving yourself to me so fully. I know it couldn't have been easy for you."

His eyes flicked away, his hands brushing the towel against the mess I'd made of his bedding.

You're wrong. It was the easiest, most natural thing I've ever done.

But I couldn't bring myself to say the words. Instead, I swallowed. "Oh, well... yeah. It was... it was good."

Huh. That sucked.

I sat up and clasped his arm to stop his attempted clean up. "What I meant to say was it was incredible. And I trust you. Yeah, that's unexpected, but I do. At least... in this regard. In... in bed."

I sounded like an idiot. But at least I was an honest idiot. He deserved to know that there was nothing held back between us. I gave him all of me, and assumed he did the same. Because I'd felt it. I'd felt the connection between us when our bodies were joined and his mouth was on my skin.

And it had been unlike anything I'd ever experienced.

It had scared me half to death.

22

WELLS

"You're staying," I said, trying not to spend too much time parsing what he'd said about trusting me *in bed*, the implication being that he didn't trust me outside of bed. The last thing I needed to be reminded of right now was the giant secret between us.

Conor looked up at me, still fucked-out and flushed from his orgasm. "I am?"

I nodded. "Move over so I can replace this cover. Get under the sheets; it'll only take a minute." I needed to keep my hands busy or else I would reach for him and bury my face in the crook of his neck and never let go.

He shifted off the damp bedding and pulled the sheets back, looking around my bedroom. "Should I take a shower first? Everything looks so... clean."

"If you'd like." I gave him a pointed look, one eyebrow crooked. "But I don't mind you a little... dirty."

The man blushed, and my heart did a traitorous skip. Conor slid between the sheets and lay his head on the pillow I normally used. His hair was a riot of swirls and tangles from where I'd raked fingers through it and used it to pull his head back for kisses while I fucked him. Just the sight of him there, like that, in my bed made me feel a strange combination of possessiveness and comfort. He was far from the kind of man I usually had sex with.

I was used to men with slick and polish, who approached sex the same way they approached everything else in life: as a deal to be brokered on mutually beneficial terms. Where sex was about hedonistic pleasure contained within the bounds of a mutual understanding that kisses weren't contracts and emotion wasn't in the offering.

Conor was nothing like that. His body was rugged and hard, his muscles earned from hours spent in the wilderness rather than at the hands of some overpriced trainer at an upscale Manhattan gym. To him sex wasn't a transaction, but an exchange. He gave without demanding in return, he trusted where anyone else would harbor suspicion, and he let himself care even when it was inadvisable to do so.

And he was so brutally honest in his reactions, laying bare his vulnerabilities and his desires and his pleasure. There was no guile or subterfuge, no game playing or manipulation. Conor was himself —unashamed and carefree in a way I wasn't accustomed to.

By the time I switched out the comforter and joined him in bed, he was most of the way asleep.

"Warning," he mumbled. "Cuddle whore here. Tell me now if you need your space."

It was on the tip of my tongue to tell him I didn't cuddle, but before the words came out, I realized having him in my arms was the only way I could imagine spending this night in bed with him.

"Bring it on," I said. "I can take it."

He shifted, turning on his side and burrowing his back into me. Without hesitation he reached for my arm and pulled it across him, threading his fingers through mine and holding our entwined hands against his chest. I could feel the steady thump of his heart beneath my touch, the comforting rhythm that caused my muscles to ease and my body to relax against his.

"Mmmmm," he hummed sleepily. "'Night, Wells."

My name on his lips did strange things to my own heart. *I can take it*, I reminded myself.

I couldn't take it.

Having his naked body pressed against mine, his ass nestled against my crotch, for hours on end kept me hard and ready until I couldn't stand it anymore. While he slept, I toyed with his hair and ran my fingers softly over his warm skin. I thought about how perfectly he fit in my arms, how easy it was to lie here with him tucked against me.

How desperately I didn't want the night to end. Didn't want the moment to come when he'd slip out of my grasp and out of my reach.

I closed my eyes, pressing my forehead against the back of his neck, breathing in deep the scent of him. I should have laughed at myself and all of the shitty promises I'd made about this being only one night and there being no future between us.

That wasn't what I wanted.

I imagined following Conor Newell home to North Carolina and begging at his feet for a chance at more. For once in my fucking life, I even considered walking away from my company if that's what it would take to make him consider a future with me.

But every time I tried to picture what a future with him would look like, I was slammed with the memory of our texts. I imagined confessing to him that I was Trace. That I'd known Conor was NotSam since the morning of our first meeting. The betrayal I'd see in his face was too devastating to contemplate. No relationship could start off with such deception—I knew that. But it was especially disastrous considering I was a terrible relationship bet to begin with, without even adding the subterfuge bit to it.

Still asleep, Conor twisted in my arms to face me, throwing an arm across my ribs and wrapping a leg around one of mine. A soft, muffled sigh escaped him and blew warm breath across my bare chest.

I pulled him closer, pressing a kiss to his head and holding him tight just to enjoy what I had for a little bit longer.

He'd said it was only for tonight.

We'd both said it.

But how could I let him go when he was the only person besides my sister who seemed to see through my bullshit? And he was the first person in a decade who'd stood up to me, challenged me, chastised me, made me laugh. He caused me to reassess how I ran my business and what I wanted in life, and he was the epitome of kind and sweet and genuine.

Conor was an entrepreneur like I was, but he didn't let it rule his life. He still had time for family and friends, hiking and adventure.

I let out a heavy sigh, wishing things were different. Wishing *I* were different.

"S'okay," he murmured. I wasn't sure what he meant, but it felt like he was trying to comfort me. Maybe he subconsciously sensed my inner turmoil and knew I needed reassurance. Or maybe his body felt the hammering of my heart against his and worried I was about to stroke out.

I traced a fingertip under his chin, tilting his face toward mine. "I need to tell you something," I whispered, unable to hold it in any longer. No matter what happened between us, I needed this out in the open. He needed to know I was Trace. He needed to hear it from me.

"S'okay," he repeated in a sleepy voice. "'Morrow."

My throat felt thick with unsaid words. "Conor..."

"Mmm." He stretched and yawned, turning again so his back was to me. I shifted into place behind him.

"Conor—"

He grabbed my arm, like he'd done earlier, pulling me closer so that my front pressed against the length of his back. His ass lined up perfectly with my cock, which was still hard and desperate from being so near him. I instinctively thrust against him and groaned.

"Mm-hmm," he hummed.

I kissed the side of his face, his ear, his neck. The kisses were soft and light, allowing him to still choose sleep if that's what he wanted.

He hummed again and arched back into me. He was so warm and soft, pliant and willing. I couldn't resist him.

"Want you," I breathed into his ear. "Want you so much."

"Yours," he murmured sleepily. "Always."

I froze for a beat, unsure of what he meant. Did he think he was with someone else? Someone he truly cared about?

"Conor?" I whispered.

"Wells," he groaned. "So hard for you. Want to please you."

Oh god.

My cock jumped hard against his naked ass. "You do please me, baby. You please me so much."

"Want you inside. Am ready. Please, Wells."

I brought my hand up to cup his face, turning it toward me to take his lips with mine. The kiss was sloppy but real, and I lingered in it until my cock began dragging a wet trail across Conor's lower back. I reached for the supplies on the bedside table and suited up. When I pressed a lubed finger inside of him, I realized he was still plenty prepped from earlier.

I clasped him behind one knee and bent it up in front of him on the bed, staying pressed along his back. When I slipped inside of him, I wrapped my arms around his waist and chest and tucked my face into his neck.

My thrusts began slowly. I wanted to savor the feeling of dragging my cock in and out of him. The sounds of his whimpers turned to a kind of keening with each pass across his gland. He breathed my name into the pillow over and over again and held my hand against his heart so tightly, I thought the shape of it might imprint onto his very soul.

It was the closest I'd ever been to anyone in my life. I felt him everywhere and wanted him there forever.

"Conor," I rasped. "I... I... *Conor.*"

Suddenly he pulled out of my grasp, away from my body and turned to face me, reaching to pull me on top of him so we were face-to-face.

"Like this," he said softly. "Please."

The dim light from an uncovered window illuminated shiny spots on his cheeks. His eyes were suspiciously damp, and I ached to wipe the tears away. But I couldn't bring myself to acknowledge them.

So instead, I did as he asked. I bent his knees up and entered him again, matching his groan of pleasure with one of my own. It felt like coming home again, and when he wrapped his legs around me, I didn't want him to ever let go.

Our eyes locked together in the light of the city night as I pulsed in and out of him slowly and deliberately. His hands moved across my chest and shoulders, my sides and into my hair, but his eyes stayed on mine, solid and open. Trusting and so very present.

There were reams of words I wanted to say to him, confessions to make but also promises. But none of them came. We stared at one another while our bodies wrecked each other, and when I felt the telltale squeeze of Conor's channel around me, I remembered to give him the order.

"*Come.*"

23

CONOR

The middle of the night lovemaking changed things. Oh, how it fucking changed things.

The man above me wasn't at all That Asshole I'd thought him to be. He was powerful and domineering, but he was also kind and soft. He gave me pleasure as if mine was all that mattered, and his was nothing but a footnote to be seen to after the fact.

After we'd both come and he'd gently cleaned me again, he slipped into bed behind me and pulled me against him. One arm wrapped possessively around me, pinning me to his body, and I could have almost sworn I felt his lips move in a soundless "Mine" against the back of my neck.

"Yours," I breathed. I wasn't sure if he heard me, but his fingers tightened around mine as he pulled me closer.

I felt tears threaten again. I let them come. Because the moment was too perfect, too real, and I wanted it to last forever. It was as if Wells's bed had become a bubble removed from the real world. Here it didn't matter that he lived in New York and I had a business in North Carolina. It didn't matter that he was married to his job and I had a sick mother to care for.

It didn't matter that he was a man who eschewed relationships.

Who refused to trust. Who kept emotions at bay because they were the one part of his life he couldn't control.

Tonight he'd let that control falter. He'd let me slip through the cracks. But that didn't mean when morning came he wouldn't revert to who he was before. Seal the cracks, shore up his defenses, double down on his need for distance.

Except I'd seen him tonight. The real him. As he'd rocked into me, his hands twined with mine, my legs locked around his hips, he'd let his defenses fall away. His eyes had shone with the emotion he normally kept so carefully hidden.

He'd let me see his need, his hunger. His pain. All of it.

I'd seen the truth of Wells Grange tonight, and it had caused my heart to swell. To ache. To need.

And I knew with absolute certainty that what I needed was this man in my bed. In my life. In my heart.

He'd felt that need too. Of that I was certain. It had been clear in the way he looked at me. In the way my name sounded on his lips as he came. The way he clung to me as he emptied himself into me.

The way he held me now, his possessive breath warm against my neck. His lips just a whisper away from my flesh.

This had been no one-night-stand sex.

What that would mean when the sun rose remained to be seen. But for now I snuggled deeper into Wells's arms. We would figure it out, I told myself. There was no other option.

I woke to the feel of Wells's lips trailing a path across my shoulder. His hand rested on my ribs, fingers curled possessively around my side. I hummed my appreciation and arched back into him. He was hard and though I was a little sore from the night before, I was ready for round three.

"Morning, sleepy," he mumbled into my ear before taking my lobe gently between his teeth.

I groaned and ground my ass more insistently against him.

His laughter was deep and still a little raw from sleep as he shifted his hand to my hip, holding me in place. "Easy there." He dropped a kiss to the base of my neck, spending an extra moment nuzzling the sensitive skin and causing my breath to hitch.

Then he was gone, the cold air stark against my back. He leaned over me, tucking the sheet around me. "Let me freshen up first," he said, dropping another kiss to the side of my mouth.

I reached for him. "No need to rush off."

"I'll be right back." He winked, the promise clear in his eyes. "I have plans for you."

I sighed as I watched him shuffle to the bathroom, admiring the way the muscles in his ass bunched and flexed with each step, the unexpected tattoos that had surprised me when he'd stripped his shirt off. It made me wonder if there was more to him that would surprise me, things like the ink that might reveal themselves to me in time.

When he disappeared behind the closed door, I flopped onto my back with my arms thrown wide. I knew I must have had a stupid grin on my face, but I didn't even care. Because the Wells of last night —the one who'd opened up and shown me his true self—was still here this morning. He hadn't retreated. He hadn't woken regretting or second-guessing what we'd done.

Which gave me hope for our future.

My heart was fluttering like a fool's. I was having *feelings* for this man. Serious feelings. And I was giddy with it.

Because I was pretty sure Wells had similar feelings for me.

My grin deepened and I turned my head into the pillow, inhaling deep so that his scent filled me from the inside out. I would live in that smell forever if I could.

A chirp sounded from somewhere nearby and I realized it was my phone. I slipped from the bed and stumbled around the room until I found my pants, pulling my cell free. It had been a text from my mother, checking in.

I thumbed open the messages app, intending to send her a quick note that all was well. But my fingers hesitated when I saw the conversation listed below hers.

Trace.

My stomach dropped.

It was time to stop ignoring him.

I thought for a moment before typing up what I wanted to say.

Conor: *You were right to suggest a break. I was looking for something you couldn't give me. But I think I found what I want and need with someone else.*

I smiled, thinking of Wells. I'd have gotten lost in the thought if it hadn't been for his cell phone vibrating against the bedside table, distracting me. I focused back on my texts to Trace.

Conor: *I want you to know that you were exactly what I needed at the time. I'm glad I accidentally texted you and that you responded. You helped me through a difficult time and I will always be grateful for that. Thank you for everything. But it is time I moved on.*

Wells's phone vibrated again and I glanced toward it, wondering if maybe it was something important. I quickly typed up the last text and hit Send.

Conor: *Good luck and I hope you find what you're looking for in life.*

Almost instantly Wells's phone vibrated. Something hollow began burrowing through my chest. Thoughts began churning at the edge of my mind, whispering suspicions that seemed too absurd to be true.

And yet... I couldn't shake the doubt that suddenly gripped me.

My fingers tightened around my phone. I realized my hand was trembling. Slowly, carefully, I stood and moved around the bed until I could get a clear view of Wells's phone.

There were three alerts. Three texts.

The last one read:

NotSam: *Good luck and I hope you find what you're looking for in life.*

I let out a cry of alarm and stumbled back.

My mind was a shock of white static, my entire body on fire with the feeling of betrayal.

From the bathroom I heard the sink turn on and the unmistakable sound of Wells brushing his teeth.

Soon he'd finish. And he'd walk into the bedroom. And I would have to face him. Knowing the truth.

Panic gripped me. I couldn't. I just couldn't.

I scrambled for my clothes, yanking them on without checking to make sure they were right side out. It didn't matter, I didn't care. All that mattered was getting out of here. Leaving before Wells walked out of that bathroom.

24

WELLS

I stared at myself in the mirror. My hair was disheveled, my lips still swollen from Conor's greedy kisses the night before. The perpetual scowl that normally pinched the skin between my eyebrows was gone, and I sported the most ridiculous grin ever.

Anyone who set eyes on me would immediately know I'd gotten laid last night. But it was more than that. I'd had plenty of sex in my life, and it had never left me looking like this. Feeling like this.

This... contentment, excitement. This sense of a puzzle piece finally settling into place was new.

It was Conor.

I glanced toward the door. Knowing he was just on the other side, still wrapped in my sheets, made me eager to get back to him. I'd call Deb and tell her to push my morning meetings, and I'd spend the time with Conor instead.

We'd start in bed, finishing what I'd initiated when we'd woken up. I'd take my time with him, showing him with my body how I felt about him. How much I wanted to be with him.

How much I needed him.

After that... I didn't know. The last time I'd been in a relationship with a man had been Mark and it had just happened. We'd been friends then housemates and then business partners—it had been easy to add being lovers into the mix.

There hadn't been any obstacles like my job, like Conor's business, and his mom.

Like the secret I was still keeping from him.

I fisted my hands against the bathroom counter. The muscle along my jaw in my reflection ticked, the scowl reappearing between my eyes.

I had to tell him. Before anything else. Before I touched him, before I asked him to cancel his flight and stay longer, before we crossed the bridge of how to navigate a potential relationship.

He had to know the truth. He had to have the option to leave me. Or, hopefully, forgive me.

My fingers trembled as I wet them in the sink and ran them through my hair, trying to bring some order to the wavy mess. I was stalling. I knew it. Another one of my father's favorite John Wayne quotes came to mind. "Courage is being scared to death but saddling up anyway." Taking a deep breath, I straightened. Gave myself a silent nod of encouragement. And stepped into the bedroom.

The bed was empty, the sheets cast aside in a tangled heap. I swiveled around, wondering where he'd gone. "Conor?" There was no response.

I pushed out of the master into the living room, wondering if he'd gone to the kitchen in search of breakfast. But both of those rooms were empty as well. "Conor?" I called, louder. My heart began hammering in my chest and my breathing shallowed.

I jogged toward the guest rooms, thinking that maybe he'd been using one of the extra bathrooms. But they were all empty and silent.

Conor was gone.

After circling the apartment twice, I found myself standing dazed by the bed. I pressed a hand against the sheets where I'd last seen him. There was still a trace of warmth which meant he hadn't been gone long.

I didn't understand. Why had he left? What had changed in the brief time I'd been in the bathroom. I reached for my phone, intending to call him to make sure he was okay. And that's when I saw it. The texts on the screen.

There were three of them, one stacked on top of the other.

NotSam: *You were right to suggest a break. I was looking for something you couldn't give me. But I think I found what I want and need with someone else.*

NotSam: *I want you to know that you were exactly what I needed at the time. I'm glad I accidentally texted you and that you responded. You helped me through a difficult time in my life and I will always be grateful for that. Thank you for everything. But it is time I moved on.*

NotSam: *Good luck and I hope you find what you're looking for in life.*

Oh god. I sucked in a breath, but my lungs seemed incapable of processing oxygen. He'd seen. There was no other explanation. He'd texted Trace and my phone had vibrated and he'd seen his own texts appear on my screen.

I felt light-headed, my knees weak. I sank onto the side of the bed, numbness spreading through me as I read and reread the texts.

I think I've found what I want and need with someone else.

Me. He was talking about me. The words physically hurt, stabbing me in the chest.

He'd texted Trace to call things off.

And instead he'd learned the truth. That I'd lied to him from the very beginning.

Now he was gone, and I didn't know how I was going to get him back. I reached for the pillow he'd slept on and pulled it to my face, burying my nose in it in search of his scent.

For once in my fucking life, I had no idea what to do. Did I go after him? Beg him? Chase him? What could I possibly say that would explain the situation in any terms other than ones that made me look like the bastard I was?

I couldn't feel my fingers, my face. A dull roar thundered in my ears. Why was I surprised this was happening? What the hell had I expected?

I took a deep breath and called him. It went straight to voicemail. The sound of his familiar, relaxed voice cut straight through me.

Hi, you've reached Conor Newell...

I hung up and typed with shaky fingers.

Wells: *Conor, please let me explain.*

I cursed myself for typing practically the same thing I had before, when he still thought I was Trace, someone separate from Wells.

Wells: *I tried to tell you. I tried to tell you so many times. It's why I couldn't sleep last night.*

Wells: *I'm so sorry, Conor. Please understand that I didn't mean for this to happen. I thought... I thought it was some anonymous fun at first until I realized it was you... and even though I knew I should, I couldn't stop. But then I got to know you in real life and...*

I let out a stuttered breath.

Wells: *and I started having feelings. Real feelings, Conor. Please talk to me.*

I hit Send and stared at the small screen, willing it to light up with his response.

When it finally did, my numbness exploded into shards of acute pain.

NotSam: *Don't ever text me again. I'm blocking this number.*

I read his message again and again. Until I couldn't see the words anymore because they'd blurred together from the tears.

It was over.

25

CONOR

Blocking his number may have not been the most mature thing to do, but it was the only way to ensure I wouldn't fall prey to his bullshit words.

God only knew how I found my way to the airport and onto the plane. When the flight attendant asked me what I wanted to drink, I apparently told her my street address. The young woman in the seat next to mine moved away a little bit so our arms no longer touched. Wondering if heartbreak was contagious, I glanced at her before looking back up at the flight attendant and ordering sangria. In the end, she had mercy on me and handed me a bottle of water. Unfortunately, it did not come with a side of sleeping pills.

My head couldn't stop spinning through all the possibilities. How the hell had Wells Grange been the anonymous man I'd texted? It wasn't like I could blame him, of course, since I'd been the one to initiate the texting. But still... had he somehow bribed the bartender to flirt with me and then give me Wells's own number? That seemed awfully convoluted. Had Wells been in the hotel bar that night and slipped me his number without me noticing? That sounded even more ridiculous.

And even if that were the case, what would have Wells hoped to accomplish? Some kind of elaborate scheme to get more power during the negotiations? If so, how? He'd ended up paying full price anyway. What did he get out of sexting with me behind the scenes? Bribery material for the future?

My stomach soured as I thought about the photos I'd sent him. Heat rushed to my cheeks in embarrassed shame. What had I been thinking? Sure my face wasn't in any of them, so there was no way to identify the cock in the picture as mine, but still. If Wells had wanted blackmail material, he certainly had it in spades.

He wouldn't do that to me, I automatically thought.

Except how could I possibly be sure of that? He clearly wasn't the man I thought he was.

Or maybe he was. Maybe he'd always been That Asshole and I'd just fallen prey to his charm offensive. Maybe I wasn't the only one he'd even done this to. The thought of Wells seducing another man made me ill.

I pressed my fingertips against my temples, what-if scenarios spinning through my brain.

I thought back through every interaction we'd had as NotSam and Trace. Remembering Trace's... *Wells's* commanding tone with me that first night we'd texted had me squirming in my too-narrow airplane seat. All the woman next to me needed to really lose her shit was to see me with a sudden erection.

I took a deep breath and closed my eyes. I needed to stop thinking about Wells. To stop torturing myself with what-ifs and recriminations.

Focus on Mom, I told myself. She was the person who should be getting all of this mental energy from me, not him. Never him.

But that was easier said than done. I remembered texting Trace about my mother, about how sick she was, and then...

My eyes shot open as I made the connection. And then the next morning he'd been late. He'd come in announcing an end to the negotiations because he'd agreed to our price.

I'd told him we needed the money from the deal to pay for her treatments, and he'd turned around and made sure we got it. No more haggling. No more delays.

Then he'd asked to spend the day with me. My chest squeezed at the memory. There'd been no reason for him to make such a request. The deal was done, only the technicalities left to be arranged. He could have been done with me as well. But he hadn't been.

I struggled to come up with a business reason for him to have spent the day with me. I couldn't.

Maybe... maybe he'd just wanted to spend time with me.

Dammit, there was something in my eye. And throat. And fucking heart.

I shook my head. No. He was not a good man. He wasn't. He was a user. A cold-hearted bastard. And even if he thought he was having feelings for me, he'd made it very clear he didn't do feelings. Hadn't James even said that was a well-known thing around town?

Wells "Glacial" Grange was a fucker, not a lover. Everyone knew it.

That fucker.

I turned to look out the window. But it was hard to hold on to my self-righteous rage. Because I kept remembering the smaller moments of kindness. The way he'd cleared the conference room during my presentation when I'd accidentally flashed the wrong slide on the screen and almost fainted. The way he'd tucked my scarf into my jacket during the carriage ride. The way he'd listened and asked questions when I'd told him about my game shop. The way he'd always kept a hand on my lower back when the crowds around us threatened to separate us.

The kind of things that people did when they cared for one another.

What if...?

No, I told myself again. Men like Wells didn't change. They didn't. And, hell, even if they did, it wasn't like I had any interest in leaving everything that was important to me and moving to the city. Just the thought of moving far away from my quaint town, the rugged paths of my favorite hiking woods, and my ill mother made me feel nauseous.

No, New York wasn't a place for me. And I couldn't imagine Wells Grange being happy anywhere else.

So, it was a nonstarter regardless of anything that may or may not have passed between us.

In real life, a relationship between the two of us would never work.

"WHERE IS SHE?" I asked Bill the moment I walked through the side door of my mom's house. "By the way, I got you something at this cool market stall in Central Park. Give me a minute to say hi to Mom and I'll—"

I stopped talking when I noticed the look on his face. My stomach dropped, and I began to shake.

"Bill," I croaked. "Where is she?" I took a step deeper into the house, getting ready to call out to her, when he grabbed me by the elbow.

"She's okay. She's at Mission," he said, referring to the local hospital. "I told her I'd take you there as soon as you got back."

"I could have driven straight there from the airport. Why didn't you call me?"

"I didn't want you to freak out and drive like a maniac. And there's no rush. She's okay."

"Obviously she's not okay," I barked, letting some of my emotion from the day escape. "She's in the fucking hospital. What the hell happened?"

I could hear the panic and desperation in my voice and knew if I didn't get myself together soon, I'd be a soppy mess on the floor in a curled-up ball. And that wouldn't help my mother at all. I took a breath, trying to calm myself. Right now I needed to be strong for my mother. Later, when I was on my own again, I could fall apart.

"She was having trouble breathing from the pneumonia. They're giving her some breathing treatments and IV antibiotics. She's doing much better, but they want to keep her a few days. They're being extra cautious because of her compromised lung function."

As he spoke, he led me back out the door and took the keys from my hand, opening the passenger door of my own SUV and urging me in.

When we got to the hospital, he dropped me off out front with instructions on where to go once I got inside.

"I'll meet you in there after I park."

I raced past the welcome desk to the elevators and made my way to the right floor. When I finally got to her room, I could hear soft music playing. Bill must have remembered to bring her Bluetooth speaker. She'd been hooked on a soothing Spotify acoustic channel before I left on my trip, and from the sounds of it, she was still enjoying the same playlist.

"Hey," I whispered, pushing the curtain aside. "You awake?"

Although she looked pale and small, my mom had her usual bright smile for me when she saw who was visiting her.

"Conor, you're back."

The familiar sound of her voice soothed me more than any acoustic music ever could. "I come bearing millions," I teased softly, pulling the visitor chair close to the edge of the bed so I could sit and hold her hand.

She pressed her palm against my cheek. "While I'm not going to turn away the millions, what matters is that you're here now."

I could feel tears threatening and was afraid that once they started, I'd never be able to stop them. The wound from Wells's betrayal was still too fresh. So I swallowed around the burning in my throat and forced a smile. "You had one job while I was gone," I told her, laughing. "Stay out of the damned hospital."

26

WELLS

I had fifteen tabs open on my browser. Two of them were for airlines with flights to Asheville leaving in the morning. Five of them were for flower shops and chocolatiers. And the rest were too stupid to mention. I'd just opened a new tab, intending to find a charter jet company who could fly me down to Asheville tonight when the door to my apartment swung open. I didn't even have to turn from the wraparound kitchen bar to know who it was. Both Deb and my sister had a key to my apartment, but it was only Win who walked with such purposeful strides. Deb was stealthier than that.

"Well, you're alive, then," my sister said as she crossed to where I sat.

I didn't look up from my computer. "Was that in doubt?"

She tossed her purse and coat onto one of the chairs and stood, arms crossed, facing me. "Deb called me. Said you hadn't come in and weren't responding to her texts or calls. She sounded pretty panicked."

I felt a moment's concern for causing Deb to worry. But I didn't let that stop me from reaching for my phone to call the charter plane company.

Before I could dial the number, Win's hand closed over mine, tugging the phone from my grasp.

I stood. "What the fuck, Win?"

Her eyes traced over me, her expression morphing from mild annoyance to concern. "I could say the same to you. You look like shit. What happened?"

I held out a hand for my phone. "Give it back."

"I will in five minutes." She pointed to me. "Now sit. Explain."

"None of your business," I growled.

But it didn't matter because by that point she'd seen the windows open on my laptop, the top one belonging to a women's magazine sporting the title "Lost your man? How to win him back in five easy steps!"

I waited for her to laugh. Instead her forehead creased with sympathy. "Oh honey." She reached for me, squeezing my upper arm. "What happened?"

My throat tightened. For a moment I wanted to let her pull me into a hug and tell me it would be okay like she had when we were kids. But instead I dug my fingers into my hair and stood up to pace. "I think..." My voice cracked and I swallowed. "I think I fucked up."

"Well, that's not surprising," she said with a sardonic laugh.

I shot her a mock glare, and she shrugged. "What? I'm your sister —you want me to lie to you?"

"No I want..." I blew out a breath and let my hands fall to my sides. I felt utterly defeated. "I want you to tell me how to fix it."

She gave me a long look, then nodded. "Have you eaten?"

I rolled my eyes. There wasn't a problem in the world my sister didn't think you could cook your way out of. "I'm not hungry."

She waved a hand and started for the kitchen. "You'll eat anyway. Now," she said, digging into the pathetically bare refrigerator, "tell me what happened."

So I did, while she chopped an anemic-looking bell pepper and a carton of very sad mushrooms and added them to a sauté pan. She was in the middle of beating several eggs together when I got to the part about Conor finding out the truth about Trace's identity, and she paused, sucking in a breath. "Wow, you really did fuck up, didn't you?"

I sunk back down onto one of the barstools ringing the kitchen counter. I felt totally deflated. "I did. But if he would just listen he would understand. Yes, I hid that one little detail from him, but I also provided for him," I argued. "I gave him financial security. That's what should matter."

Win set down the bowl and turned to me, her expression full of pity. She stared at me in silence long enough to make me itch.

"Oh honey, he wants your love, not your money."

I blinked at her, not sure how to respond. She leaned forward and took my hands between hers. It was the same gesture I'd seen her pull with my niece when she wanted her complete focus to explain an important lesson. "Look, Wells, you've been very generous to me and my family, and I can never express my gratitude enough. Because of you, we have complete financial security, which is a real gift. But that's not how I know you love me."

I started to protest, but she cut me off. "Think of it like this: my daughter adores the big Thomas train set you got her for Christmas. But you know what brings the biggest smile to her face? When her Uncle Wells sweeps her up in his arms and spins her around in the air. That's love."

Thinking of my niece's giggles whenever I burbled raspberries to her cheeks brought a smile to my face.

Her eyes brightened. "That smile right there," she said. "That's what life is all about. It's the moments you spend with the people you love. The memories you make with them." She chuckled. "Don't get me wrong, money can certainly make life much easier. But it isn't love. I would give all of my shares of Grange BioMed away if it meant keeping the love of my husband and child. The money means nothing without them. Do you understand?"

The words caused something to squeeze in my chest. "But what if I can't give him love?"

She mock scowled at me. "Wells Grange, I've known you my entire life. You are capable of great love, if you'll just allow yourself to feel it. And Mark doesn't count. Don't give that fucker one single thought when we're on the subject of love."

Her nostrils flared in old anger left over from when I'd finally admitted to her about Mark's and my relationship. She'd been gutted, and it had taken a long time for the two of us to find our way back to each other after so many awful confessions.

I crossed my arms, wanting to believe her but not sure I could. Regardless of whether or not Mark had deserved it, I'd loved once before and it had gone terribly wrong. "What if it's a fool's errand in the end? Conor has his business in Asheville, and he's a country boy at heart. I can't imagine him ever happy living here."

She didn't look up as she slid the finished omelet onto a plate. "Could you be happy living there?"

I started to tell her that it was a ridiculous question. My life was here. My company, my apartment, everything I'd worked so hard to build after Mark had nearly destroyed it—all of that was in the city.

But was that what I wanted my life to be? I'd been so consumed with proving to everyone else that Mark's betrayal hadn't torn me apart or kept me from living out my dream, that I didn't stop and wonder what my dream really was.

Win lifted an eyebrow, waiting for my answer.

I told her the truth. "I don't know."

She placed the omelet in front of me. "Maybe that's something you should figure out. But, here's the thing, Wells. You have to accept that you can't control how Conor feels about you. You can't make him love you back. All you can do is lay your heart at his feet and tell him it's his if he wants it. But you can't force him to take it."

I opened my mouth to argue, but she held up a finger, cutting me off. "You can't control love, Wells." She shoved a fork in my hand. "Now eat. Then we'll figure out how to show Conor how much you love him."

"I never said I loved him," I said around a mouthful of cheesy eggs.

She smiled. "You didn't have to. I knew the moment Deb called that there were only two things that could keep you from the office: death or love."

I SPENT the rest of the afternoon exhausting my sister with various schemes I could attempt to convince Conor I was worth loving.

"What if I bought him a plane?" I asked, getting excited at the thought. "That way we can go back and forth whenever we want. Hank knows a guy who—"

I noticed Win's pinched face.

"What? What's wrong with a private plane? I can afford it. If it would make his life easier, it would be worth it. Plus, we could fly his mom wherever she needed to go for the best treatment." I wondered if I could get Deb on this right away.

"Stop," she said, rolling her eyes. "You're being an idiot."

I blinked, not sure what I'd said that was so wrong. "How?"

She sighed. "You're equating money with love again, Wells. That's never going to work with a guy like Conor. He doesn't want a damned plane."

"Preach," a sarcastic voice said from the entryway. Deb. She came into the living room and kicked off her high heels before giving Win a hug.

"Shouldn't you be at the office?" I asked.

She raised an eyebrow in my direction. "Shouldn't you?" she asked as she headed toward the kitchen where I knew she'd put on a pot of coffee whether she wanted some or not.

"You look like shit, by the way," she called back. "And my Spidey sense told me there were plans afoot. If you're planning something, you need me. I'm the planning queen."

It was true.

"Plus," she said, coming back into the living room and pulling a black sweater on over a pair of trendy blue jeans that had miraculously replaced the suit she'd arrived in. "I gathered some new intel on our target."

She shoved the suit into her big bag and curled her legs under her on the sofa before grabbing the nearby throw and dragging it over her lap.

I frowned. "What target? What are you talking about? The 3-D print deal is over. It's done."

Deb exchanged a look with Win. "Yeah, not that kind of target. I'm talking about Conor."

I didn't understand. "Right. Like I said. I don't need any more intel. The project is... wait. What kind of intel?"

Win sighed. "Men, I swear to god."

Deb held out a hand for a fist bump before turning back to me. "His mom is back in the hospital and—"

I jumped to my feet, cutting her off. "What? Is she okay?" Conor had to be going out of his mind with worry. I hated to think of him sitting all alone in the hospital, trying to handle everything on his own. I began to pace, trying to figure out what I could do to help. Where was my phone?

Deb held up a hand, trying to corral me into place. "She's going to be fine. She has pneumonia, and she needed stronger antibiotics than they could give her at home."

I blew out a relieved breath. "That's good news, then."

Deb bit her lip. "There's more. One of Conor's game shop managers just quit."

My stomach dropped. "Seriously?" I resumed my pacing. I needed to keep moving or the mental and emotional exhaustion would take over. "How is he supposed to hire a replacement while he's helping his mom?"

Deb hesitated before speaking. "I could contact a placement agency..."

"No," I barked. "He'd never accept that." I noted the startled look on her face and tried to soften my tone. "But thanks for offering."

I escaped to the kitchen to pour myself a cup of Deb's coffee, and when I returned, Win and Deb were discussing something about love languages.

"No psychobabble. I beg you," I said, taking a sip of the hot, rich blend. I hoped the caffeine would perk me up and bring me some kind of miracle solution.

"It's not psychobabble," Deb said. "Love language is how you show and perceive love. You know, like whether someone telling you how they feel about you or surprising you with a thoughtful gift makes you feel more loved."

Win turned to me, a calculating look in her eye. "Maybe financial support is your love language, Wells." She tapped a finger against her chin. "But what's Conor's?"

I thought about all the little details I'd learned about him in the short time we'd known each other. Somehow, I didn't think 'being told what to do in bed' was what she was looking for. "How the hell would I know?"

Win rolled her eyes. "And you wonder how you lost him," she grumbled under her breath.

Deb ignored her. "How does he show his mother love?" she asked with exaggerated patience.

"By taking care of her health and taking over her work when she can't do it," I said after thinking a minute. "I think he would have even taken on some of her bloody experiments if it meant easing her burdens. And the poor guy gets queasy when he sees blood."

Win and Deb exchanged a look. "Well, I think you have your answer, then."

I frowned. "I do?"

Deb threw up her hands. "Acts of service." She turned to Win with a sigh. "Men, I swear," she grumbled. "Let's go get greasy appetizers and cocktails," she said to Win. "I have Wells's business Amex —he can treat in absentia."

Win stood and patted me on the shoulder. "Yes, you do. Now go show that man how much you love him." She started toward the front door while Deb slipped her heels back on.

I swallowed, suddenly nervous and unsure of myself. "But what if it's not enough?" I called after her.

She turned and smiled. "Remember, Wells, you can't control love.

All you can do is give it freely and unconditionally." She blew me a kiss. "Let me know how it goes."

I spent a long time after they left sitting in my living room, staring out the windows at snow-shrouded Central Park surrounded by the crush of skyscrapers. It was such a familiar view that I often took it for granted, not really seeing it even when I was looking right at it.

In many ways, that felt like what had become of my life. That I was living it the same way: only making a passing acknowledgment of its existence every now and again. Never stopping to truly take it in and appreciate it. After Mark's betrayal, I'd been so intent on proving to everyone—my father, Win, the world—that I was okay. That I didn't need a partner to succeed.

I'd never taken the chance to wonder what I really envisioned that success looking like. I thought it meant money. A penthouse with the right address and impressive views. The right kind of job with an influential company. Power.

I had all of that now, and somehow it wasn't enough. I'd thought that if I just worked harder, earned more, grew the company faster, it would somehow fill the empty place inside me. I'd been wrong. Because it turned out the only person who could fill that spot was Conor.

And I'd fucked it up.

I had to figure out a way to fix it.

But I had to figure out a way to fix my own life first.

27

CONOR

I'd spent almost every minute of the first several days after I left New York at the hospital with Mom or on the phone with the specialty clinic in Chicago, trying to arrange for her to be admitted to a new experimental treatment program they were starting in a few weeks. It was one of the reasons we'd been in such a rush to close the deal with Grange and get the money in the bank. Technically the admission window for the program had closed, but my mother was a perfect candidate and I was trying to get them to make an exception.

Finally, just this morning they'd agreed to take her. It probably helped that I'd pledged several of the millions she'd made from the Grange BioMed deal to fund future studies. I was ecstatic until I learned the only weekend they could admit her was the same weekend as ICECon in Minneapolis. It was a no-brainer which obligation I would choose, but it had meant scrambling to try and find someone to cover for me at the con as best they could. ICECon was supposed to be the big launch of my game piece printing business in the gaming community. I'd invested thousands of dollars in premium booth placement, advertising, swag, and even a speaking opportunity.

To give that up wasn't easy.

Thank god for James and his love of all things nerd and geek.

When I'd called him in a panic, he'd immediately agreed to stand in for me at the con. That man never could turn down an opportunity to cosplay.

I left the shop that afternoon to swing by the house only long enough to grab some things for my mom before joining her at the hospital for dinner. When I stopped for gas, I considered asking the attendant behind the register what the best energy drink was for someone who'd basically gotten no sleep in days and had no expectation of sleep anytime soon. Every minute I wasn't at the game shop, I was at the hospital. And every moment I was at the shop, I was balancing a tightrope between covering for my shitty-ass manager who'd up and quit while I was in New York, and trying to prepare a huge game piece order that had come in right before my trip.

But instead of asking about the energy drink, I just grabbed my usual bottle of Mountain Dew and a protein bar. Hopefully that would tide me over until I could find something semi-edible at the hospital cafeteria for dinner later.

As I pulled into my mom's driveway, my only thought was of grabbing the fleece pajamas she'd asked for and racing back out the door. Instead, I was greeted by a cherry-red Subaru with a white cross logo and the words LIFE SUPPORT! printed across the side. My heart began pounding, and by the time I parked and stumbled out of the car, I was almost in tears.

"What happened?" I croaked.

A woman with a similarly branded red shirt waited for me on my front porch. She stood and smiled as I approached. "Are you Conor Newell?"

"Yes, just tell me. Did something happen? Is she okay? Did she—" I couldn't even finish the sentence.

Her expression morphed to confusion.

"Aren't you here about my mom?" I waved at the bright red car. "From the hospital?"

She slapped her palm against her forehead. "Oh goodness no. I'm here to fix your problems."

I blinked, completely unable to follow what she was saying. "Huh?"

She resumed her original perky smile. "I'm from Life Support! Our job is to be your number one support system."

She was way too perky to be bearing bad news. My heart rate slowed, but my confusion remained. "I don't understand."

"My job is to help you. I'm Karen, by the way." She held out a hand. "I'm your new life manager."

I stood silent a moment. Clearly my lack of sleep was playing games with my brain. "Life manager?"

"Yep, anything you need, one of my colleagues or I can take care of it. Well, within reason of course. Obviously nothing illegal." She winked. "Think of us like your extra pair of hands. You can have us clean your house, run errands, organize clutter, cook. We also have specialists on staff who can help with bills, finances, taxes, anything accounting related."

I shook my head. "As wonderful as all of that sounds, you must have the wrong person. I'm pretty sure I'd remember if I'd hired you."

She continued her overly friendly smile. "Our services are a gift from a friend. He said you had a lot on your plate and sounded concerned about you."

There was only one person that came to mind. My jaw tightened, but my heart also stutter-stepped. "Was it Wells Grange?" It was just like him to try to use money to buy his way back into my life. I wasn't about to give him that chance. I didn't want anything to do with the man.

"He... ah... preferred to remain anonymous," she said, the perky smile fading.

That surprised me. But it didn't change things. "As wonderful as your service sounds, I'm sorry, I can't accept this."

She hesitated. "Mr. Newell—"

"Conor," I corrected.

"I know it's none of my business, Conor, but sometimes it's the people who don't ask for help who need it the most." She gave my arm a brief squeeze. "If it helps, the man who hired us said you'd probably refuse, and if so he'd pay us to sit in your driveway for eight hours a day, seven days a week for the next two months. Which frankly sounds boring as heck." She grinned. "Since we're going to be here anyway, you might as well use us."

I shook my head. Fucking Wells Grange. I hated to let him win, but Karen was right. It was time I admitted that I needed help. I unlocked the front door and held it open for her as the adrenaline spike left me feeling even more exhausted than I'd been before. "Welcome to Chez Newell. Sorry it's a wreck; I haven't really been here."

Her smile widened. "Then that's what I'll start on first."

"By the way, you should really rethink the name of your company," I muttered, stepping over the threshold. "Or at least carry a set of defibrillator paddles just in case."

∼

THE FIRST LETTER arrived the next day. I found it sitting on the freshly polished front hall table after getting home from visiting Mom at the hospital. The house was spotless, the scent of banana bread drifting in from the kitchen. It was heavenly.

I didn't realize who the letter was from at first, only that it was handwritten which meant it wasn't likely junk mail. I slid it into my back pocket and forgot about it until I got ready for bed that night.

I opened it, expecting maybe a handwritten note from a neighbor offering a casserole or something, and was shocked to see it was signed by Wells.

DEAR CONOR,

I know you said not to text you, so I decided to try contacting you this way in the hope you could simply choose not to open it if you didn't want to hear what I had to say. First of all, the most important thing is an apology. I discovered the first morning of our initial meeting that you wore the same tie as my sexy texter. Once I realized it was you, I was afraid to tell you in fear you'd hold it against me during the negotiations. And... there was some-

thing about NotSam that I couldn't resist. I should have cut the texts off then, but I wasn't strong enough. I wanted what I had with NotSam—the easy conversation, the steamy connection, the late-night confessions. It was the first time in a very long while I didn't feel so alone.

But all of that means I was selfish, pure and simple. I didn't tell you because if I did, I'd lose something precious. Which is ridiculous since I ended up losing it anyway. I'm so very sorry for hurting you, Conor. You deserve better than a man who would keep that from you. You deserve someone who will always put you above all others, including himself.

You asked me in our texts what my name was, and I told you it was Trace. That's the name my mother always called me. There's something about a child's connection to his mother that makes her special name for him more... real somehow. As if she, more than anyone in the world, knows the real person beneath all masks.

But I didn't tell you a funny story about the name. When I was very young, maybe four or five, my mother took me overseas to her hometown of Andorra la Vella between Spain and France. While we were there, every time my mother introduced me to someone new, they commented 'Très adorable.' I didn't speak French, nor did I realize until years later that 'Trace' had come from the Spanish 'tres' since I was the third Wellington Grange. Meanwhile, I came home from that trip thinking my middle name was adorable. Whenever someone called me Wellington Archibald Grange the Third, I'd pout and correct them. "I am très adorable!"

On that note, I'll say au revoir. Je suis très désolé. Tu occupes toutes mes pensées,

Wells/Trace

AFTER LOOKING up the French phrases to discover they meant "I'm very sorry" and "you are in all my thoughts," I almost caved and texted him. But to what end? I really was too tired to even put two thoughts together. And I had approximately six hours before I had to be back at the shop in the morning. A broken heart over someone I'd basically known all of five minutes simply couldn't take priority over my mother and the businesses I was attempting to keep afloat.

I was asleep before I even thought to take the rest of my clothes off.

The following day brought more chaos at work, but that didn't mean I didn't think long and hard about the letter and gesture of help from Wells.

Every time I thought about him—which was at least a billion times a minute—my chest ached with such acute pain that I'd considered asking one of the doctors at the hospital if there was something physically wrong with me. It didn't seem possible that heartache could be so literal. But it was.

"Excuse me, do you work here?"

I looked up from where I'd been paying some bills to see an older gentleman and a boy about nine years old standing at the open door to my tiny office in the back of the shop.

"Sorry, sir. Yes, I work here. Do you need help?"

"I'm looking for a basic chess set for my grandson here, and the lady up front was busy helping all the customers in line. I hate to bother you..."

I smiled at him. "It's no bother, and I have a couple different ones I'd love to show you. My grandfather taught me how to play chess too," I admitted. It brought back some warm memories that helped pass the next couple of busy hours in the shop before I took a long lunch break to visit Mom in the hospital.

When I got to her room later that afternoon, I told her about the pair. "They reminded me of Pop and me," I said, settling in and unwrapping the sandwiches I'd picked up. I told her about my day at the shop while we ate. I was glad to see her appetite had picked up a little and her coloring was better.

"I heard from Deborah Hines earlier this morning," Mom said when I stopped talking long enough for her to get a word in edgewise.

I glanced up at her. "I don't know who that is. Someone at the university?"

She shook her head. "She's Wells Grange's assistant in New York."

The sound of his name churned the food in my stomach. "Oh. Deb. Yeah. Is um... is everything okay with... ah, everything?"

Mom's face turned serious, and she reached out a hand for mine. "She needed to confirm some contact information, which was odd in and of itself. But she also mentioned during the conversation that they were able to structure the deal in a way that allows me to get on Grange's health insurance plan if I needed better health insurance. Theirs is supposedly some top-of-the-line plan heads above what I have through the university. And she also said they could add you to it. Which... doesn't make much sense since you don't really work for me."

I wondered if she could feel my thudding pulse through our joined hands. "Oh, well... that's good, right? You can always use better insurance."

"My health insurance through the university is already good, Conor. What's going on?"

"Well then. That's settled. They were just probably trying to be nice. You know, since you agreed to sell them your patent." I wasn't really a good bullshitter, but I was especially a bad one where my mother was concerned. She had a built-in Conor Bullshit Detector.

"I finally got around to looking a summary of the final contract terms." Her eyes bore into me. "Conor, they paid *full price.*"

"I told you that," I said defiantly. "I told you they paid what you were asking."

"When you said they agreed to our terms, I thought you meant one of our offers during a negotiation process. I never in a million years thought you meant That Asshole had actually agreed to our *original* asking price!"

"Don't call him that," I blurted, realizing my mistake as soon as the words were out of my mouth. Mom's expression turned from confusion to surprise. "I mean... it's not nice," I mumbled. "And... he's a person, you know?"

"Conor Matthew Newell," she said slowly. "What the hell happened in New York?"

I glanced at her before looking away. "I closed the deal like you asked."

She barked out a laugh that started a coughing fit. "You sure did," she sputtered through her cough. When she got it under control, she studied me. "So, am I hiring you out as the world's greatest negotiator, or is there more to this story you're not telling me?"

So much more.

"I... well..." I looked at the ceiling in the hope I'd find answers there. When that didn't work, I glanced out into the corridor hoping to see a nurse who needed to draw Mom's blood so I could go ahead and faint already. No dice. "I may have accidentally kind of dated him."

She frowned in confusion. "Who? James?"

Apparently the idea I might be referring to That Asshole was so absurd, she'd picked a practically married guy to flesh out the idea instead.

"Not James," I said with a sigh. "Wells."

"Wells," she said slowly. "Wells Grange."

As if there was another Wells.

I nodded.

She pushed herself up in bed. "Let me get this straight," she said, gearing up a head of steam. "I sent you to New York to negotiate an important sales deal and you *slept* with the man to get him to give us full price?"

"What? No," I sputtered. "Are you crazy? Who the hell do you think I am?" I couldn't believe she would even think such a thing. It's not like I was known as a *Man About Town*. I'd barely been on two dates in the last year.

She blew out a breath and sunk back into her pillows. "I'm sorry. You're right. I just... the idea of you falling prey to That Asshole makes me nuts. So, yes. I guess I *am* crazy."

I looked down at my hands, my shoulders falling. "It wasn't like that," I said softly. "I would never do that. How could you—"

Her fingers slipped around mine, squeezing. "I'm sorry. I've been stuck in here watching soap operas all week. I guess my brain jumped straight to the dramatic. I know that's not who you are. Hell, even if it was, as long as the sex was good..."

"Mom!" I cried.

She laughed. "All right, all right. Tell me what happened. What do you mean by 'accidentally kind of dated him'?"

I let out a long sigh, the weight of the past several days and the heaviness of my heart making me feel suddenly more exhausted than usual. "It's a long story."

She made an exaggerated visual inspection of the room before looking at me. "I seem to have nothing but time. Spill."

So I told her an abbreviated version that didn't include my texts with Trace. The last thing I wanted her to know was that I'd accidentally sent a dick pic to a stranger and then proceeded to have mind-blowing sext with him. Instead I basically described Wells's and my getting to know each other on the carriage ride and at dinner together, and I explained that there were reasons he was the way he was. That in reality, he wasn't always cold but could be warm and generous.

I didn't mention how good he was in bed. Or what an amazing cuddler he was.

"Then what's the problem?" she asked.

"What problem? There's no problem," I lied. "He lives in New York, and I live here. Plus, he's a self-proclaimed commitment-phobe."

She waved a hand. "Clearly he cares about you."

"Pfft. Don't know what makes you say that." The sweet words written in his own hand floated in my mind's eye, but I shoved them away.

"Conor, he paid *full price*. In his world of corporate negotiation, that's equivalent to losing his shirt and his reputation. He hasn't paid full price for anything in his life. Add to that this ridiculous offer of health insurance they called about this morning. He's looking out for you. There's no other explanation."

Yeah, well. If he cared that much, he wouldn't have lied to me.

I shrugged. "Don't see how any of that matters now. I've got to get back to the shop. Poor Crystal is there by herself."

She hesitated only slightly but didn't press the issue of Wells. "Any luck hiring someone to replace Kyle?"

I stood up and cleared our lunch trash into the nearby can before making sure she had the remote and her water bottle close at hand.

"Haven't had time to even look at the applications on my desk, much less set up interviews. I'm going to go in early tomorrow to take a crack at it. I won't be able to take time off tonight to bring you dinner, but I should be able to take a lunch break around eleven tomorrow to drive you home."

"Bill can come get me. I'm sure he wouldn't mind."

I thought about Mom's next-door neighbor and how much we'd relied on him these past few months. I wanted to make sure he was able to have his own life now that I was back in town.

"I don't want to overburden him, Mom. Plus, I enjoy our time together. Maybe that makes me selfish." I smiled and leaned in to kiss her on the cheek. I recognized the mild scent of her favorite face lotion and mentally thanked Bill for the millionth time for being a lifesaver. I was sure having her special things from home helped soften the blow of being at the hospital. "Get some rest. I picked up a new puzzle from the shop for you to start on when you get home. It has famous women in science on it."

"Am I on it?" she teased as I walked out of the room.

"Not yet," I called over my shoulder. "But one day you will be."

Apparently fixing your life included swallowing your pride.

When I finally decided what I needed to do, I realized I needed James's help. Which would include asking him for a favor. Which required a level of humility from me that I wasn't sure existed.

Attempting to contact him at his office hadn't worked, so there I was, standing on the front step to his personal residence.

Like the desperate jackass I was.

I knocked on the door a second time and was about to go for a third when it swung open, revealing a man wearing a skimpy purple superhero costume. My eyes jumped from the helmet resting on the top of his normally neatly combed salt-and-pepper hair to the silver belt slung low around his sculpted, spandex-wrapped abs. It turned out that the lawyer was way more fit and trim than I'd expected.

"Hello, James. Or should I call you Jungle Fury?" I tried to hide my smirk but failed utterly.

His eyes narrowed with thinly veiled distaste. "What do you want, Grange?"

"I tried you at your office and your assistant said I could find you here," I lied. I took a deep breath and said something I hadn't said in years. "I... I need your help."

He stared at me for several long moments, my request apparently shocking him into silence. "For what?" he finally asked, clearly suspicious.

"It's a legal matter involving Conor."

He let out a snort of disgust and started to close the door. I threw myself against it, wedging my foot in the jamb to stop him from cutting me off. "I know I fucked up with him, and I hurt him and you must hate me for it. You should."

"Damn right," he growled. He pressed harder on the door.

"Please, James, just hear me out," I continued. "Then, if you don't believe me, I'll go, I swear." I wasn't someone who begged for anything in life, and James knew that. He eyed me through the crack in the door.

"My usual retainer is $20,000. For you it will be $50,000."

"Done."

If he was surprised at how quickly I accepted his terms, he didn't show it. Instead he swung the door open, admitting me to a marble-tiled entryway dominated by a sharp-cornered glass table topped with a steel vase overflowing with some kind of whip-thin silver stems that looked more like blades than any kind of floral arrangement. Without saying a word, he led me past a sweeping concrete staircase that dominated the center of the house and deeper into the brownstone. I caught glimpses of more rooms, all decorated with the same cold austerity as the front hall.

He stopped by a simple wooden door tucked in the back corner and pushed it open to reveal a cluttered but cozy study. "Wait here while I change. You can use the time to wire the money to my account." I stepped into the room, and he closed the door behind me without another word.

It took less than two minutes to give Deb the instructions about making the transfer. If she was curious about why I was suddenly paying Conor's lawyer a retainer, she didn't ask.

While I waited for James to return, I explored the room. It was small, and the rich mahogany bookshelves lining three of the walls made the space feel even smaller, but not claustrophobic. The fourth wall was dominated by a large fireplace flanked by french doors that led out into a courtyard nook featuring several dormant flowerbeds and a concrete statue of what appeared to be one of the Three Musketeers. If he'd been sculpted by Dali.

A solid wooden desk with a scarred top flanked one side of the fireplace, while two well-worn and comfortable leather chairs sat on the other side. The remaining space was filled with stacks of books of every subject and genre from a biography of Hamilton to a compendium of Stan Lee's comics over the years.

The shelves themselves were also crowded with books tucked behind framed photographs, souvenirs, and tchotchkes of every variety. One of the pictures in particular caught my eye, and I plucked it off the shelf. It was Conor and James, posed in some sort of convention hall, with their arms around each other and big grins on their faces. Both of them wore badges around their necks with Comic-Con written across them in bright yellow letters.

It was the first time I'd seen Conor's face since he'd left, and my heart ached looking at it. I missed that smile. Missed the familiar warmth of the laugh that I knew accompanied it. I squeezed my eyes closed, trying to refocus on what I was there to do.

The sound of James clearing his throat broke me from my thoughts. I snapped my eyes open to find him standing in the doorway, now dressed in a sharp navy blue suit, his brown wingtips shining with polish. He noticed the photograph in my hand and looked at me curiously. I said nothing, just slipped the picture back onto the shelf and took a seat in one of the leather chairs.

James settled into the one across from me. There was still hostility in his expression, but now it was tempered with the barest hint of sympathy.

I'd told myself I wouldn't ask, but I couldn't resist. "How is he?"

"It wouldn't be proper for me to discuss my other clients with you, Mr. Grange."

I hadn't expected him to tell me anything, but I was still disappointed. "Fair enough."

His eyebrow twitched, probably surprised that I wasn't pressing him on the issue. "What's this legal matter you'd like to discuss?"

"I would like to create a nonprofit foundation and transfer ownership of the printer and biological material patents to it. And I'd like Conor and his mother to be as involved in running it as they care to be."

Once again I seemed to have shocked James into silence. After a beat, he asked, "Why?"

"Because Conor was right, this technology is revolutionary and can save lives," I explained. "It isn't fair for it to only be available to those who are wealthy enough to afford it. Money shouldn't dictate who lives and who dies."

His jaw dropped. Before he could cover his surprise, his cell phone buzzed. He pulled it from his pocket and frowned at the screen. After a moment's hesitation, he sent it to voicemail. "And what will Grange BioMed get out of this?"

"Nothing. Well, it would technically count as a charitable donation but otherwise—" James's phone began buzzing again. The same man's face filled the screen. He ignored it.

"You can take that if you need to," I told him.

"It can wait," he said distractedly. "But what are you hoping to get out of this transaction, personally? You think you're going to be able to buy Conor back somehow?"

I let out a laugh. "It would be stupid of me to try to win him back that way. Conor doesn't care about my money."

James's phone buzzed again. With an exasperated sigh, he swiped his thumb across the screen to answer it. "Richard, honey, I'm with a client. Let me call you back?"

He listened for a moment, his expression morphing from annoyance to agitation. "You already booked the tickets to Hawaii? I thought we were going to discuss this first."

He ran his fingers across his forehead as Richard talked. "When?" he asked. At the answer, James's eyes flicked to me and then away again. He suddenly stood, pacing across the room and stepping into the hallway. The door didn't close completely behind him, and I could still hear his side of the conversation.

"You know that's the weekend I agreed to help Conor with ICECon," he hissed.

I stiffened at the mention of Conor and leaned forward to listen in.

"Trust me," James said, his tone growing more agitated. "I know how important this trip is to closing the deal, but Conor needs my help. I told you about this last night and—"

Another pause. "I know, Richard, but he's my friend; I can't just ditch him like that for work. I told you—"

Pause. "Richard. Richard, wait. Come on, that's not fair. Listen, can we discuss this tonight on the way to the benefit?"

Silence for a moment. "What do you mean you made other plans? We RSVP'd months ago. They're expecting us to be there," he said tightly.

I caught a glimpse of him through the crack in the door as he paced the hallway. He was running his fingertips over his forehead, a pained expression on his face. "Okay. Yeah. Fine. Bye." He hung up the phone and slipped it back into his pocket. He raised his hand to push back into the office but then hesitated.

"Fuck," he said under his breath, his head dropping. He stood for a moment, eyes closed as he took several deep breaths. A muscle twitched in his jaw.

Finally he arranged his features and strode back into the office to retake his seat. He tried to appear unruffled, but I could still see the strain around his eyes, the tension in his shoulders. "Everything okay?"

"Fine," he snapped.

I wasn't going to let it go. "I heard you mention Conor—"

"It's none of your concern."

I sighed and leaned forward, elbows on my knees. "Look, James. I know you don't like me. I know I was an asshole to Oscar, but I called things off because he was developing feelings for me that I could never return. It would have been cruel of me to continue seeing him."

He snorted.

I pressed on anyway. "But it's different with Conor. I fucked up, I have to own that. But that doesn't mean I can't still help him out when he needs it. And it sounds to me like he needs it now. We're on the same side here, James. Please, let me help."

"You think you're going to win him back that way?"

I shook my head. "I won't lie, I would love for that to happen. But no. I just want to help make his life easier if I can. He doesn't even need to know I'm involved."

He considered me for a long moment, but he still didn't seem convinced.

"I'm in love with him, James," I told him.

James's eyes widened in surprise. Before he could make a snarky remark, I continued.

"I swear I'll never hurt him again. Please."

Finally, a slow smile curled his lips. "Who'd have thought Glacial Grange would finally thaw. Okay, here's how you can help. But it's going to involve costumes."

Which is how I found myself getting fitted for a pair of black maternity pants two days later at some specialty cosplay shop James knew about in the Garment District.

"I don't... I don't remember Kylo Ren being topless in the movie," I said, twisting the stretchy material around my torso. It was not a whine. It was more of an observation.

"It's when he's talking to himself," James mumbled, squinting at the fit of the pants.

"You're looking way too closely at the cut of my jib," I warned. "Don't you have a Dick at home?"

"His name is Richard. And if you think I'd go anywhere near your disease-riddled—"

"Zip it," the tiny shop lady snapped. We both mumbled an apology. "No, zip pants. There, your ankle."

Before I could reach down, James yanked both ankle zips closed, catching my leg hair in one of them and bringing tears of pain to my eyes. I bit my tongue to keep from exposing any weakness to the predator.

"He needs a mask. At least a partial. No one wants to look at that face," James told the woman. I didn't even bother thanking him for his kindness. As it was, I was relieved I'd have something to hide behind for when thousands of strangers eyeballed me half-naked in this ridiculous getup.

"Why maternity pants?" I wondered aloud.

"They have to come up high around the torso. This is how cosplayers do it. Don't worry about it." He fussed a little more to get the waistband where he wanted it. The woman grabbed my crotch and began putting pins way too close to areas that definitely didn't want to be pinned. I pressed my lips tightly together to keep from telling them all to get the fuck away from me.

You're doing this for Conor. You're doing this for Conor.

"You'll need a spray tan." James wasn't even talking to anyone specific anymore. He was simply making mental notes under his breath. "And for god's sake stop the carbohydrates already. Oh, and we'll need to go back to my office so I can walk you through your speech."

Mental brakes squealed.

"My what?"

"Stop whining. You'll do fine. Surely you've given a presentation to a room full of people before," he challenged.

"Of course." My chest absolutely didn't puff up.

"Then it'll be a piece of cake. Only instead of biomedical bullshit, it'll be geekery bullshit. You can handle it."

I may or may not have completely unpuffed. "But I'm not a geek. There's not a geeky bone in my body. I thought *Star Trek* and *Star Wars* were the same thing until I went to college."

The woman and James both sucked in shocked gasps, each of them clasping their chests as if synchronized swimmers.

"Pipe down. It's not like I confused uranium and plutonium," I muttered. "Keep your pants on."

They continued fussing around me until I wore the eye mask and carried the light saber.

"Fine. It'll do. Thanks, Mika," James said, giving air kisses to the woman who'd fussed me into the getup. "Wells will pay for it."

Of course. It wasn't enough I was going to make a fool out of myself dressed as some half-naked junior Jedi. I had to pay for the privilege on top of it.

29

CONOR

Three more letters from Wells arrived before it was time to leave for Mom's trip to Chicago. Each one was handwritten just like the first, and two of the three contained another story about something light and embarrassing from his childhood.

In the most recent one, though, the story was still personal, but it wasn't light. He told me the story of Mark.

Dear Conor,

I hope you and your mom are having a good day. Deb told me that you agreed to let me charter a plane for your trip to the clinic. Thank you. I hope being able to avoid the big commercial airport stress means the trip will be a little less taxing for her. If there is anything I can do to make her more comfortable or her trip more of a success, please let me know. Between you and me, I think she and Deb may have struck a kind of friendship through all of this because I overheard Deb laughing and calling her Liz on the phone this morning.

So... today's embarrassing Wells story...

I told you about Mark's betrayal and how it caused various kinds of fallout in my business and in my family. What I didn't tell you was that in addition to being best friends in college and business school, Mark and I were also lovers. I worshipped the ground he walked on and thought the two of us would be together forever. He wasn't out, and keeping our relationship secret from my friends and family was tough, but I thought at the time he was worth it.

When he and his family came to my family's house for that Christmas celebration, I finally thought he was going to come out to everyone, that our relationship would be part of the excitement. Instead, he flirted with my sister. At first, I thought it was a defense mechanism, some way of proving his heterosexuality. I gave up on him coming out after that. But then it became clear. The flirting was real.

He dropped me for Win.

The rest of it you know. But now you can see why his betrayal hit me so hard. And why I was so quick to trust him over my sister. I was in love with him. Even then. Until he put my entire family's livelihood in jeopardy and betrayed his marriage to my sister, I still loved him. When he left me for Win, I thought it was because he simply loved her more—that she was somehow more perfect for him. In a way, I was flattered. I thought it was his way of having me but just the socially acceptable version.

After all of that, it was impossible to even consider putting my heart back out there again.

Until you.

Please take care of yourself and have a safe trip to Chicago.

Yours,

Wells/Trace

MY HANDS WERE SHAKING by the time I finished reading it. The mail had been delivered right as we'd loaded up in the car for the drive to the airport. I'd shoved the letter in my backpack and finally pulled it out once we were settled on the small plane.

Mom snoozed next to me in a fully reclined seat with one of her favorite blankets wrapped around her. Her hair was clean and neatly styled from an early-morning visit to her favorite stylist, something she'd insisted on doing before leaving town.

I was thankful she was asleep since I couldn't keep the tears from leaking out of my damned eyes. I fucking hated Wells for telling me that story. My heart was too broken before learning about his past, and now it was utterly shattered. That poor man. No wonder he was such a stoic, cold asshole. He was terrified.

I wiped away the tears with the back of my hand without letting go of the letter and caught a whiff of Wells's expensive cologne on the paper. It was most likely all in my head, but it made something tighten even harder in my gut.

I missed him so fucking much. Which was insane. Why wasn't this any easier by now? I'd hardly known the guy a few days. I needed my heart back. It was his—he owned the fucking thing and had it with him in a swanky high-rise in Manhattan. And without it, my chest was a caved in shell.

"What's wrong, sweetheart?" Mom asked in a sleepy voice. "Those tears better not be for me. I'm feeling strong like Serena Williams. If only my tennis game was just as good."

I shook my head from side to side, afraid if I spoke, it would sound like a gasping sob.

She turned in her seat until she was fully facing me. Her eyes narrowed. "Hells bells. It's a boy."

I shook my head again and looked away from her.

"Don't bullshit a bullshitter," she muttered, reaching for the little travel pack of tissues she always kept in a pocket. "Here."

I took a couple out and did triage on my face without looking at her.

"I'm sorry," I whispered after a few moments.

Her fingers sifted through my hair. "Honey, you can't help how you feel. No reason to be sorry. If anything, I'm sorry for being sick when you need me."

The feel of her hand in my hair was comforting. I slouched down in my seat and closed my eyes, remembering all the times she'd rubbed my head like that when I was little.

"Is it That Asshole?" she asked. The smile in her voice alerted me that she wouldn't judge me so much if it was.

I nodded. "I l-l-*like* him. A lot."

She snorted softly. "I'm not sure 'like' was the word your mouth was tripping over," she teased. "What is holding you back?"

I blew a breath out between pursed lips, ignoring her comment about the l-word. After thinking through what I wanted to say, I finally opened my eyes and met hers. "He lied to me about something... well, he omitted something really damned important."

"Is he married?"

"No, nothing like that."

"Oh shit, HIV? Is he on PrEP? Did you two use—"

"*Mother.* God. It's not anything having to do with his health. Or mine."

"Did he keep this thing from you out of malice?"

I didn't even hesitate before shaking my head. "No. I'm pretty sure it was more out of fear."

"Fear of what? Fear of losing you? Of disappointing you?"

"Both. Of making things even more complicated than they already were."

"Why were things complicated?"

I widened my eyes at her as if that would be enough for her to understand. "Mom, the deal. The negotiation. The fact I arrived there thinking he was That Asshole. Complicated."

"The deal is over. You don't think he's an asshole anymore. What's complicated now?"

"He hasn't had a relationship since he was in school. And that was with a horrible person."

"Poor thing. Sounds like he's overdue for some lovin'."

"Ew. You make that sound... dirty."

The sound of her light chuckle made me so happy, I couldn't help but join her which set her off even more. When the laughter died down, she gave me the mom look. "Conor, what do you *want*?"

"For you to be healthy. For my game piece business to grow and thrive. For Broad River Board Games to become more self-sustaining so I can spend more time on the game piece business."

The flight attendant came by to bring us some bottles of water. After we thanked her, Mom turned to me again.

"Game pieces don't keep you warm at night, and neither do I."

"Jesus, Mom. You're on a roll today with the gross innuendo," I said, even though I got her point. "But one of the best pieces of advice you ever gave me is that there's a time for everything. This doesn't have to be the time for me to find my person."

"That's a crock of shit," she muttered, pulling the blanket up around her neck and snuggling down into it. "If not now, when? And if my illness hasn't reminded you that life is short, then you're not paying attention."

The words hit me like arrows to the gut.

"Mom..."

"Don't *Mom* me. You know I'm right."

I rubbed both hands over my face. Just because she was right, didn't mean trying to figure out how to move forward with Wells would be easy. But maybe after I returned to Asheville and our lives slowed down a little, I could at least think about it.

As it turned out, that day was going to come sooner rather than later. Once we landed at O'Hare, spent one night in a hotel, and got Mom all settled into her room at the clinic the following morning, she sat me down for another conversation about her knowing what was best for me.

"You need to go," she said matter-of-factly.

"I am. My flight home is in two days." Mom's treatment was scheduled to last two weeks with another two-week treatment a month later. As much as I'd hoped to stay nearby while she was going through it, I really couldn't afford to be away from my businesses that long, especially with Kyle gone.

"Not home. Minneapolis. The con."

My stomach twisted. I'd tried to stay in close contact with James so I could help answer any questions while he worked my booth, but he'd told me the booth was located in a part of the convention center with no cell service. Being out of touch with him had left me nervous about how my company's presence there was going.

"I trust James, Mom. I'm sure it's fine without me."

"I can't have you sitting here staring at me. I brought a Kindle packed with sci-fi novels and would much rather lose myself in them than worry about you being bored and antsy. Go."

She was right. If I wasn't going to pursue something with Wells, I could at least go see the fruits of my labor with the game piece business. ICECon was my big break. Even if I wasn't there to show it off to its full potential, just having the technology there getting exposure to the right audience was a boon.

"Okay," I said, standing up before leaning over and dropping a kiss on her head. "But you'd better keep your phone handy in case I need a status check."

"Make it so," she said in her pathetic attempt at Jean-Luc Picard's voice.

～

I LOOKED DOWN at the green and blue badge they'd given me at the registration table. *Interactive Comic Entertainment Convention.* I was here.

Even though I wasn't in costume and didn't even have anything better to wear other than a Settlers of Catan T-shirt, walking into ICECon still felt like coming home. There were colorful superheroes everywhere and even decked-out kids riding on parents' shoulders. Fans, vendors, and celebrities chatted enthusiastically everywhere I turned, and I took a moment just to breathe it in.

My mom had been chatting happily on the phone giving Bill updates when I left, and knowing she was in good hands at the clinic had helped ease the departure. I'd fly back up to bring her home in a couple of weeks. In the meantime, I planned to attend the final two days of the con here and then head back home to catch up on work.

And think of Wells.

Since I was back to being pathetic, I sighed and glanced down at the app on my phone that showed the convention schedule and map. The Hold Your Piece talk had already started in the Rosemount Ballroom, but if I hurried, I could still make it in time to join James on stage to answer any questions at the end.

The convention floor was full of people, the crush of bodies nearly impossible to navigate through quickly, and I barely reached the right room a few minutes before the end of the session. Cursing under my breath for having missed so much of the talk, I hauled open the ballroom doors and stopped dead in my tracks.

The first thing I noticed was that the room was huge. Much larger than I'd expected. The second thing was that it was packed. To the point that several folks had been forced to stand along the perimeter by the walls, and many more crowded in the back. A few by the door glanced my way, one woman in a Jessica Rabbit costume even placing a finger over her lips to motion for me to be quiet before tilting her head to the stage to indicate the presentation was still going on.

That's when I noticed the third thing: a topless Kylo Ren was on stage giving the presentation. Or at least someone dressed as Kylo Ren. I swallowed a surprised laugh. Why in the world had James chosen to dress as the Supreme Leader of the First Order when he was a Trekkie all the way. And since when did he have such a toned chest?

I squinted and stepped a little closer.

Holy hot kyber crystals, that wasn't James.

The door slammed behind me with a bang, earning me several annoyed glances. I ignored them. Instead, I snuck closer, nudging a few people to the side so I could get a better view of what the hell was going on. Had they switched the schedule around? Had I missed the presentation entirely? But no, that was one of my printers on the table in front of Kylo, which meant I was definitely at the right place and right time. But that was definitely not my friend in the black and silver eye mask.

Then I heard the voice coming over the loudspeaker.

Wells's voice.

Deep and rumbling and so familiar it made my knees weak. And not only did the bees in my belly get shaken up again, but the lid came off the jar, spilling them all out. My entire body jangled with a mix of confusion, nerves, excitement, and terror.

I didn't understand why he was here. And where was James? He'd texted me earlier that morning to say he had everything under control at the booth, but then where was he? A panic began to send my pulse soaring. This was a disaster. Everything I'd worked for, all of my plans and dreams and—

My thoughts were interrupted by my name on Wells's lips. Familiar and yet foreign at the same time that it froze me in my tracks.

"Conor Newell wasn't the first person to bring 3-D printing to the gaming world, but he was the first person to make customizing and printing your own affordable game pieces something accessible and affordable to people without their own 3-D printing equipment or advanced design skills."

I brought my hands to my mouth. How the hell did he know that? I'd never talked specifics with him about this part of the business, only that I printed 3-D game pieces for customers. I hadn't even told him about my custom design work.

"By relying on a large database of custom design components he designed before starting his business," he continued, "Conor can create most custom designs in a fraction of the time it would take other designers to create something from scratch. If you stop by booth #1207, you'll be able to show us a photo of any toy or structure and see how quickly we can replicate it in our program and get it printed for you."

I blinked, realization filtering in slowly. He was actually giving the presentation on my competitive advantage. And it seemed like he was doing a pretty good job of it. And if what he said was true, he was actually the one demonstrating the design software and printer in the booth. How in the world was that even possible?

I watched as he clicked a remote in his hand, the movement drawing my attention back to his body. He was bare-chested, tanned, and toned. His actual physique wasn't any different than it had been when I'd had the pleasure of running my hands and mouth over it several weeks before, but the way he wore that villain costume made my dick hard in my pants.

Since when had weaselly Kylo Ren ever done a damned thing for my libido?

Despite having a black cape across his shoulders and high-waisted pants, there was enough of him on display that I wondered if it explained the standing-room-only situation in the room. I was trapped between being proud as hell and wildly jealous.

Though even if his body was what had brought everyone to the presentation, the man had an undeniable presence in front of a room full of people. All of them watched him on stage, almost enraptured. It was obvious from looking at them that if they hadn't been interested in my printing services before the session, they certainly were now.

Wells gestured to the big projector screen over his shoulder. "In the meantime, here are some close-up photographs so you can see the level of detail and precision we're able to accomplish in such a short period of time. The production time is noted on each photo. What this means for you is quick turnaround from concept to holding your custom piece in your hand. And because it takes us so much less time to manufacture your piece, it's more affordable. We're able to create more of your ideas in less time and for less money."

My brain stuttered, like a car engine choking and stalling out, when I realized what he'd just said. *We. We're* able to do this.

He spoke the words so passionately, as if he were a part of this project. As if my game piece printing business was something he believed in and cared about.

As if all of this mattered to him as much as it mattered to me.

I stared at him as the reason for his presence sunk in. He was there to give my presentation in my stead. He was there to make sure my fledgling company had the strongest start it could—not by buying it out or investing money in it but by swallowing his Brioni-clad pride to don a Star Wars costume.

For me.

"The realistic effects you can achieve with this technology make your imaginary game pieces attainable in real life." He beamed, his eyes twinkling with enthusiasm. "If you can imagine it, Conor Newell can create it. And have it on your doorstep by Friday's game night."

Several people began to clap, but Wells held up a hand, quieting them. The room fell silent. "I've spent most of this presentation discussing the technology, but I'd like to end with a little bit more about the man behind the tech."

He paused, removing his eye mask and rubbing his hand over his face and through his hair. "Conor would have loved nothing more than to be here today talking to you, but an illness in the family called him away. I'm honored to take his place, if only because I know if he were here he'd never be willing to toot his own horn. That's not the kind of guy he is—he's Harry, not Hermione." He smiled and the audience chuckled.

I felt my cheeks burn. A part of me wished the ballroom floor would open up and swallow me whole, but a larger part of me held my breath, waiting to see what he would say next.

"Conor got started in gaming because of his grandfather. He owned an old chess set made out of carved bogwood that had been passed down to him by his own grandfather. It's not the most beautiful chess set in the world, nor is it the most perfect. Every piece was created by hand and imbued with meaning. And every Sunday night, Conor's grandfather would pull it out and they would sit down for a game or five."

My throat tightened. Not only at the mention of my grandfather, but at the fact that Wells remembered me talking about him during our carriage ride in the park. It had been such a small story, more a passing reference than anything else, but he'd remembered.

"Not only did that inspire Conor's love of gaming, it inspired his creation of Hold Your Piece because he understands that gaming can be personal—it can be a reflection of who you are or who you want to be, whether an Alliance Night Elf or a Druid Halfling. In this day and age, finding the time to carve your own game pieces from bogwood isn't realistic, but that doesn't mean you can't create something meaningful."

He grinned, relieving some of the emotional tension in the room. "Or something ridiculous. That's the point. *You* get to be the creator. *You* get to decide."

He clicked the remote and the screen flashed again to show a single game piece sitting alone on a white background. At first I thought it was just Kylo Ren, but then I noticed the wider shoulders and cut abs and realized it was actually Wells dressed as Kylo Ren. An exact replica of how he looked on stage. It was a perfect demonstration of just how accurate the Hold Your Piece printing process could be.

The audience laughed and began clapping enthusiastically, and I found myself buoyed by their enthusiastic response. And also already planning on printing out one of the Wells Kylo Rens for myself when I got home.

When the crowd died down, I assumed all that was left was a thank-you and a final invitation to stop by the booth.

I was wrong.

"If you don't mind indulging me a moment longer, I just want to say one last thing about Conor Newell. I know how much he would love to see so many kids here today with their families. And there are also many of you who seem to be just starting out, like he did with his grandfather. This love of gaming and fantasy is what has brought everyone together. For many of you, it's a side piece. You may, in your real lives, be a mechanic or a nurse, a student or a soccer player. Gaming and fandoms are maybe something you do late at night, in the privacy of your own web space. But I would encourage all of you, even those of you who are older villains like myself," he said with a chuckle and gesture at his costume. "I'd encourage all of you to look at Conor as an example of what your *real life* can be like if you're brave enough to follow your passions."

I sucked in a gasp at the words. They were so unexpected and so heartfelt and not at all how I'd ever thought of myself. My cheeks heated at the praise. A part of me wanted to shrink back, not used to being so publicly complimented. But a larger part of me basked in the warmth of Wells's praise. I held my breath as he continued speaking.

"Conor Newell was raised by two scientists. Teachers. They were professors at a small-town university and did what many of us consider to be dry research. Complex stuff. But they always encouraged Conor to follow his dreams and always reminded him that science and teaching were their own dreams, but they didn't need to be his."

The ballroom around me seemed to disappear, the crowd along with it. Until it was just Wells on the stage and me on the floor, watching. Listening. He didn't know I was there—couldn't have known. And yet it felt as though he were speaking just to me. Telling me how he saw me, what he thought of me.

It filled my heart, causing it to ache with wanting.

"So when Conor grew up and went to college, he didn't simply follow the path of least resistance. He set a goal and made it happen. Got a business degree, opened his game shop, and worked his tail off to grow the company until he could support expansion. And when it came time to expand, once again, he didn't simply make his shop bigger or open a second location—in other words, do the expected. He thought about what he *wanted* to do. And he began designing and working until," he said, laying his hand on the top of the printer, "until he determined what his unique offering was. And then he worked even harder to perfect it before bringing it to market."

The room was silent, rapt, listening to Wells. He stepped forward and held his hands out with his palms up. "When I got to know Conor and saw what was possible when you allow yourself to pursue your dreams, it's like... it's like I woke up, you know? I woke up and realized that we don't ever have to keep doing what we're doing if we aren't happy anymore. We can reach for the stars and try new things. So I encourage you to look to Conor and all the other entrepreneurs and dreamers here this week and realize that this life, this passion, can be your *real life* if you want it to be. You just have to imagine it. Dream it. Believe in it. Then make it happen."

And then Wells Grange smiled his boxer-dropping smile—that

probably would have impregnated half the room had he truly been a superhero—and told everyone exactly what booth to visit to order their very own custom game pieces as soon as they returned to the show floor the following day.

The crowd applauded again and then began talking animatedly among themselves as they started filing out the door. I stood still, like a rock in a river as they surged around me. I kept my hands pressed to my mouth, as though trying to hold everything inside. Tears. Questions. The insane need to shout Wells's name at the top of my lungs so that he would know I was here... that I'd heard.

That I loved him.

I shook my head at that, trying to pull my thoughts back together. Only in the movies did people fall in love as quickly as I had. Only in movies did they then profess their love across a crowded room.

I had to remind myself that this was the real world. And in this world happily ever after wasn't a guarantee. In this world New York and Asheville were too far apart. Our lives were too separate and distinct to merge.

In this world I was afraid that I wasn't the passionate man Wells had just described to a room full of dreamers.

And even if I was, that Wells wouldn't want me as desperately as I wanted him.

30

WELLS

I finished the presentation on a high, the sound of the crowd's enthusiasm causing my grin to widen. I was used to giving talks to stuffy conference rooms full of stone-faced business folks where applause wasn't the usual reaction. My world of boardrooms and business suits was cold and hard-edged—the complete opposite of the friendly excitement infusing the air at ICECon.

I could see why Conor loved it here. Why he felt at home. This was his world. These were his people.

This was where he belonged, and it made me realize even more how right I'd been that I could never ask him to leave this behind to join me in New York. Even if he'd been willing to do so, it wouldn't have been fair to him.

Giving this up would have been like leaving a piece of himself behind.

I felt a pang of regret that he hadn't been here to bask in the crowd's excitement about his company. I could tell from the reaction that this was the beginning of something big for him—I'd been involved in enough business deals to recognize when a product was going to be a hit. He'd worked hard for this success—he deserved it.

I just wished I could be by his side as it happened.

But I had to accept that I likely wouldn't be. That I'd hurt him too much.

Still, I wished Conor had been here to see the presentation. To hear what I'd said about him.

Which made me realize all the things I should have said to him before. Christ, I'd just made it plainly obvious to a room full of strangers how much I cared about Conor Newell. Why hadn't I ever told him that directly back when I had the chance? When I knew he was getting and reading my texts. Or when I could speak to him face-to-face.

Now the only way I could communicate with him was through letters, and I didn't even know if he was getting them, much less whether he was reading them or just throwing them away unopened. After I'd sent the first one, I'd been keyed up and anxious, constantly checking my phone as I waited for him to respond. I became short-tempered and surly at work, which had driven Deb crazy.

Finally after I'd snapped at her through the intercom one too many times, she'd stormed into my office, fisted her hands on her hips, and told me get my ass to Asheville or fuck off.

Then she'd demanded another raise.

As if thinking about him made him appear, I looked up and saw a guy who looked exactly like Conor. So much so it caused my breath to catch. He stood alone toward the back of the ballroom, staring at me as the crowd swarmed around him to the exit.

I blinked in hopes my vision would clear, but he still looked exactly like Conor.

Because it was Conor. He was here. In front of me.

Before I knew what I was doing, I'd jumped from the stage and started toward him. I had to fight the urge to run. To sprint. My entire body vibrated, desperate with the need to touch him. Hold him. Feel him.

I slowed as I approached, afraid he might turn away. Terrified he might not want to see me or talk to me. But he stood his ground, and when I finally reached him, I didn't know what to say. So many words crowded in my throat—apologies, explanations, declarations of how I felt about him.

But all of that felt like too much, too fast, so instead I asked, "What are you doing here? Is your mom okay?"

His face broke into a shy smile. "Yeah. Yeah she is. She kicked me out. Told me to come to the con and enjoy the fruits of my labor."

My hands itched to grab him, feel that he was actually here with me, and never let go. I clutched them into fists at my side. "That's good. I'm glad she's doing well. So... you got her settled and... everything there is okay? With... with the treatment and..."

Smooth.

Conor took two more steps and slipped into my embrace, wrapping his arms around my waist and holding me as tightly as he could. I didn't even hesitate to pull him closer. He felt incredible. He felt perfect. And for that moment everything was right in the world.

"Thank god," I breathed into his hair, holding the back of his head with one hand and wrapping the other around his shoulders. I was about to tell him how much I fucking missed him. How desperately I wanted him back. How much he mattered to me, but he spoke first before I could.

"Thank you," he said, his voice muffled by my shoulder. He pulled his head back and looked up at me. "For everything. What you said up there... I don't even know what to say."

Oh. Right. He was simply showing his gratitude for my work. My speech. That didn't mean he was there to suddenly profess his forgiveness and undying love to me. I felt like an idiot for falling right into silly assumptions. For believing that what I'd done was enough to convince him I was worthy of his heart.

I stepped back and cleared my throat. "Uh, no problem. It's... it's the least I could do for, ah... you and your mom after everything that's... happened."

Conor's forehead wrinkled in confusion. His arms still hung in the air as if he'd been surprised by my sudden departure from them. He dropped them to his sides. And then crossed them over his chest, his shoulders curling slightly. "Yeah, sure," he said. "Well. Thanks. Again."

The moment went from perfection to awkward in two seconds. And all I could think was that this might be my last chance to see him, to speak to him in person, and I was fucking it up.

Conor looked at his feet. "I should probably... go man the booth. So you can... take off, I guess. Head back home to New York."

My back teeth ground together. If he thought I was leaving him here to work the booth alone, he was mistaken. I started to reach for his arm when a small voice behind me chirped, "Um, excuse me? Sir? Supreme Leader Ren?"

I turned to find a young kid with his grandfather. He looked up at me expectantly. "Could I, uh, get a picture taken with you?"

I blinked in surprise, not sure how to respond. Thankfully Conor swooped in. "Sure, I'll take it."

Next thing I knew, the kid had his arm thrown around my waist and stood beaming next to me. Conor snapped the picture and handed the kid back his phone. Before I could blink, another group of fans had taken his place, this one a gaggle of older teens. A small crowd formed a line behind them, all wanting a photograph with me for some reason. I could have sworn one young woman muttered, "Lord, he's so hot," as she waited her turn.

I felt myself turning red as I tried pulling my cape closed around my chest. No dice. Mika, the cosplay mistress, had made it so it only appeared voluminous. In reality, it forced me to appear topless everywhere I went.

Conor stepped in as the photographer, taking their phones and snapping the pics. He seemed to revel in the job, his glee becoming more apparent as my discomfort grew. By the time we were done, my cheeks burned from smiling and Conor's eyes were wet with tears from laughing.

"What?" I asked.

He shook his head, giggling. "Seeing you participating in cosplay and getting mobbed by fans ogling your hot bod is quite the treat. By the way, what's with the Kylo Ren ensemble? You never mentioned being a *Star Wars* fan."

I blinked at him. "It was required."

He frowned. "By whom?"

"You. I thought?" A sneaking suspicion began gathering steam in my head. I was going to kill James. Fucking *kill* him.

Conor threw his head back and howled. "Oh my god he didn't."

I narrowed my eyes. "Who do you usually dress as at these things?"

"No one. I usually wear geeky T-shirts and jeans. At most, I might add a cape or mask."

"I'm going to murder James in his bed," I growled. "Slowly."

Conor stopped laughing long enough to look at me with glittering eyes. He reached out a hand to my bare chest and ran it up and across my shoulder, pushing the cape even more out of the way. His touch made me both hard and tender at the same time.

His pupils had grown dark and wide. I could see his pulse fluttering at the base of his neck. I wanted to press my mouth against it, feel his heartbeat through my lips.

"You look amazing," Conor said in a low voice. "I'd pay big money to see this. I might even need to get my picture taken with you."

I reached a hand out to grasp his hip, more to keep my trembling knees from buckling than anything else. Conor's hand continued moving across my bare skin. The sound of the crowd outside the room dimmed to the background while every breath Conor took grew louder.

I reached a hand up to his face but hesitated, afraid that if I touched him I would never let go.

Afraid he might leave me again and it would destroy me. "I'm sorry," I said softly. "I'm so sorry I hurt you."

I couldn't resist. I smoothed a wayward piece of hair at his temple. Conor's eyes closed briefly at the touch.

My brain warred with itself. I wanted to take control of the situation, to throw Conor over my shoulder and carry him out of here. Up to my room. Where I would throw him on the bed and—

I swallowed a groan, trying to rein in my thoughts before they ran too far.

Conor cleared his throat. "Can we go somewhere and talk?"

Thank god. "Yes." My voice came out in a rush, the breath I'd been holding finally releasing.

Standing so close to Conor, I could see how worn he looked around the edges. His cheeks seemed sharper than the last time I'd seen him, and I reminded myself that he'd likely just gotten off another flight after spending days caring for his mom as he got her settled.

I frowned, unable to stop my protective instincts from kicking in. "Have you eaten?"

At the mention of food, his stomach growled loud enough to be heard over the dwindling crowd. My lips twitched into a smile. "I take that as a no. Want to go grab a bite?"

He hesitated, breaking eye contact to look around. "Finding a place to eat without a reservation is going to be a nightmare."

My stomach clenched, wondering if it was an excuse—a polite way of declining my invitation. Maybe he didn't want to spend any more time with me than he had to. "Oh. Okay. Well."

Conor blinked back up at me, unsure. "There's, um... always room service. And it's technically your room anyway. That way you can change... I mean, if you want... and we won't have to worry about the crowds..."

"That sounds perfect," I said, trying not to let my sigh of relief escape.

Conor grabbed a backpack from the floor by his feet and slung it over his shoulder. As we made our way out of the ballroom and into the crush of the large hall, I wanted to reach for his hand to keep him close among all the other people around us. But I didn't. The closest I came was putting my hand on his lower back when a hotel elevator opened up.

Once we entered the hotel room, I noticed how much quieter it was. Conor let out a breath and set his backpack down in the corner. I went straight to the desk and found the menu. I handed it to him and started for the bathroom. "You figure out what you want to eat while I change."

"Wait." There was an authority to Conor's voice that caused me to stop in my tracks. I turned to face him.

Whatever courage had possessed him a moment ago seemed to have fled. He now appeared awkward, his eyes flitting everywhere but at me. He took turns sitting at the desk chair and popping back up again to fiddle with different items like the curtains, the notepad and pen set, and the little coffee maker caddy.

He looked untethered. Like he needed something, or *someone*, to anchor him.

Finally I pointed to the bed. "Sit."

Conor's nostrils flared in defiance, but he sank onto the king-sized bed facing me.

I crossed my arms but kept my expression soft. "Good. Now tell me what you're thinking and don't hold anything back."

His jaw tightened before he spoke. "I'm thinking I want to get you naked."

It wasn't the answer I'd been expecting. Heat shot to my dick, and I swallowed a groan. Mentally I'd already begun to undress him when he added, "But I'm also thinking I shouldn't want that."

The mental image I'd been enjoying disintegrated. "Because?"

"Because I feel like an idiot, Wells!" He popped up from the bed and started pacing. "You knew. All that time when I was... when I was making myself vulnerable to you, you knew it was me," he said, waving his arms for emphasis. "You knew about my mom. I told you things I never would have told you if I'd known you weren't some random stranger. I told you what turned me on and what I wanted in bed and I told you—"

He'd begun speaking so frantically, I was afraid he'd hyperventilate. In one swift move, I reached out and snagged his wrist, pulling him until he was flush against me. Then I cupped his cheeks and forced him to meet my eyes. His hands came up to hold my wrists and I noticed them trembling slightly.

"I did know it was you," I told him. "I'm so sorry, baby. Please..."

please believe me. I'm so, so sorry I hurt you. I never want to hurt you. I never want to make you feel more vulnerable or have regrets. I want you to be happy, to thrive. And if I could do it all over again, I... hell, Conor."

I swallowed, wishing I could tell him what he wanted to hear, but knowing I had to tell him the truth. "I don't know what to say. I know I should have told you I was Trace, and I regret that more than anything. But I can't apologize for those moments we shared. I loved every second of my interactions with NotSam. It's so hard to say I'd give it up if I could. Because I'm not sure I would."

I ran a thumb down his cheek, brushing the corner of his lip. "I learned things about you as Trace that I'm not sure I would have learned otherwise. That I'm not sure you would have ever told me if it had just been us face-to-face."

"I miss you," Conor said so softly I almost didn't hear it. "I miss you so much, it hurts." He shook his head, his words brimming with pain. "But I know you don't do relationships, so I don't know what to wish for."

"Oh, Conor." I breathed his name like it was precious treasure and I was its keeper. I closed my eyes and leaned my forehead into his. "I am in this, Conor. If you'll have me."

I swallowed, needing to share it all with him. My deepest fears. My most vulnerable places. "I was scared," I told him. "Stupidly scared of being hurt again. But I'm already hurt. Don't you see? I'm hurting *now*. My biggest fear in putting myself out there was falling for someone who would leave me. But I already fell. And you already left. And now nothing is okay. I don't want to move forward without you."

The words came out of me trembling and desperate. I'd laid myself utterly bare before him in a way I'd never done for another person. It was all I knew how to do—to show him I was his and hope that he would want me.

He moved until the soft whiskers of his several-day stubble brushed my cheek a split second before his gentle lips followed. They trailed a whisper line across my face almost as if he didn't realize he was doing it.

I ran my fingers into his hair and held on. My other arm slid around his waist to pull him in tighter. His cock pressed under my balls, and I grumbled low in my throat.

"Please, Conor," I breathed into his skin. "Please."

31

CONOR

Honestly, his words didn't even matter. I could see the truth in his eyes, hear the commitment in his voice, taste the apology on his lips, and feel the affection in his touch. It was all I needed.

Even though I was terrified, I finally released the words I'd kept pinned inside.

"I love you."

I fought the urge to immediately apologize. It was fast—I knew it was fast. And we still barely knew each other. But I also knew my heart. And my heart belonged to Wells whether he wanted it or not.

"Say it again," he growled low. "Please." We were both talking so softly, I was almost surprised we could hear each other. It was so new, so fragile, we were both afraid of fucking it up.

I brushed my lips across his and smiled when his body shuddered. "I love you. Trace."

"Baby," Wells whimpered into my mouth. "I love you so much." He crushed his lips to mine and held me tightly to his body. I felt the hard press of his bulge against my lower belly and ground mine into his upper thigh. The resulting groan from him set my skin on fire, and I wanted more more *more*.

A bubble of happiness turned into a laugh in my throat. "Say it again," I teased.

He stepped forward, crowding close against me and forcing me to step back until my ass hit the side of the bed. He kept pressing, pushing me onto the bed and climbing on top of me. He thrust a thick thigh between mine, nudging my legs apart. His hard cock pushed against my own, making me suck in a breath. It felt amazing.

"Naughty boy," he rumbled. His grin turned wicked and promising. With the tip of his tongue, he trailed a line down my throat and along the collar of my shirt. "What should I do with a naughty boy?" His eyes were deep pools of desire and dominance.

"Anything you want," I croaked. "As long as it includes your dick in my mouth or ass."

With a gruff grunt of approval, his mouth sucked a mark into my neck while his hands shoved under my shirt in search of my nipples. The man had magic hands. And a magic mouth. And, if I recalled correctly, which I did, a magic dick.

In the haze of desire that clouded my brain, a thought rose to the surface. As much as I wanted him to fuck me, as much as I'd forgiven him, we still hadn't resolved anything. Yes he might be willing to give a relationship a try, but he still lived in New York. He was still married to his job.

This was all still temporary. And I wasn't sure I could handle that.

I wasn't sure I could take him walking out the door to fly home to New York.

"Stay," I blurted, suddenly panicked. "I don't want you to leave."

He pulled back, his eyes dark as they searched mine. "I'm not leaving."

I frowned, unsure if maybe I'd lost enough blood flow to my brain to confuse things. "But New York. Your flight…"

The look on his face was downright adoring. It flooded me with warmth. "Con, I'm not leaving you." He ran a hand through my hair, cupping the back of my head. "I was never leaving you. We'll work the rest of the show together and fly back to Asheville when it's over."

I pushed him off me and sat up. "Wait. What?"

Wells pushed up next to me, the skin between his eyebrows furrowing. "Unless you don't want—"

I didn't even let him finish that ridiculous sentence. "Of course I want! But your job, you have to..."

His frown was replaced by his easy smile again. "As it turns out, my company is transferring me to a small town in the Blue Ridge Mountains of North Carolina."

My stomach swooped with nerves and excitement. But it seemed too good to be true. Too perfect. "What do you mean?"

His eyes twinkled. "The CEO decided I needed a more balanced lifestyle. He thought the mountains would be good for me." He reached for me, his hand closing around mine. "The people too."

I shook my head. "But... wait, really?"

He laughed. "Yes. In fact, studies show that almost 100 percent of humans in love prefer living in the same city and state as their partner. That's true. You can look it up."

As he spoke, his hand ran up my arm, leaving a trail of chill bumps in its wake. It was like he couldn't keep himself from touching me, which was really very fine with me.

Still, I needed to make sure I understood. He spoke so casually, like he was discussing what he might like for dinner, not where he might live. "But what about Deb? What about Win? What about your management team?"

"I have an incredible team, and Deb pretty much runs the place anyway." He lifted a shoulder. "If something important comes up, I'll fly up there. I can stay in a hotel or, if you prefer, we can keep my apartment to use for trips to the city."

I thought about just how many zeros were in the price of his apartment. For him to offer to keep it for random visits reminded me just how filthy rich he was. The thought of all that money suddenly made me nervous.

"I don't want your money," I began. "I don't ever want you to think—"

He laughed. "I couldn't think that about you. Ever. Are you

kidding? Karen from Life Support told me you've been trying to slip her cash when she wasn't looking."

"Shut up," I said, playfully pushing at his shoulder. "You shouldn't be paying for someone to help me do my job."

He placed his hands on my shoulders, turning me to face him on the bed. "Conor Newell, listen to me." Jesus, he sounded like my mother. "You're working your ass off. Don't you think you deserve a little help? Do you have any idea how good it makes me feel that I somehow lifted your burdens even a little bit when you weren't talking to me?"

Well, when he put it that way, maybe it was different.

"Still," I said.

"Don't pout. Even though you're sexy as fuck when you do it." He reached up to tug my bottom lip with his thumb. I took his entire digit into my mouth and sucked on it, which caused him to make an obscene sound that went straight to my cock.

I tried to picture Wells Grange in Asheville. It was weird. Like imagining Taylor Swift scanning six-packs and cigarettes behind the counter at the quickie-mart.

But it also felt good. Giddiness began to bubble inside me at the thought of sharing my town with him.

Sharing my life.

"Maybe I could show you that hiking trail I told you about behind my mom's house," I said around his thumb. "And we could go camping under the stars when the weather gets warmer."

His voice pitched low and gravelly. "You're sending me mixed messages, beautiful. Your voice is making long-term plans while your mouth is making short-term promises. Dirty ones."

He rocked his stiff cock against mine again, and I brought my legs around him to lock him against me.

"What about dinner?" I teased. "Didn't you say I was looking gaunt and needed to eat something?"

"Oh, I have something I can feed you."

I threw my head back and laughed. Wells watched, a grin on his lips and a promise in his eyes. I reached out to run my hands through his hair. "You're really going to consider moving to Asheville?"

"Not consider. Do. Deb has found several places for me to look at when we get back there after the conference. I'd love your opinion on them."

I stupidly felt a little disappointed. When I pictured him in my town, I pictured him with me.

"Hmm," Wells said with a teasing smile again. He pressed his thumb against the spot between my eyes, smoothing it. "Interesting. You frowned just now when I mentioned finding my own place."

"Mmpfh."

"A little bird told me you moved into an apartment over your mom's garage since she got diagnosed. I figured I could buy some-place you and I both like not too far away from your mom's place, and... well, you could still be there when you felt like she needed you, but when she's doing well..."

My heart thumped happily against my ribs when I realized what he was saying. I put my hand on my chest and batted my eyelashes. "Why, Wells Grange, are you suggesting what I think you're suggest-ing?" My Southern drawl poured out like honey.

He grabbed my hand and pulled it to his lips, drawing his mouth across my knuckles. "I'd rather demand it if we're being honest. This implying shit is for the birds."

I let my mouth curl into a teasing smirk. Then I very slowly and very deliberately ran my tongue along my lower lip, sucking it into my teeth. "Then demand it."

Before I knew what happened, I was on my back on the bed. Wells had my wrists in one of his hands, pinning them over my head. He straddled me, the strain of his cock against his pants painfully obvious. I ground my dick up into his ass, and he let his weight settle more fully on me, pinning me to the bed.

I loved the power coiled through his body, the way he held it in check so that he wouldn't overwhelm me. The way every fiber of his being was focused on me in that moment as if I was the most precious thing in the world to him. As if nothing else mattered to him than me.

"Do you want to know what I demand?" he growled.

God yes. I nodded vigorously.

He leaned forward so that his face hovered just over mine. "I demand that you let me share my life with you." He dropped his head, pressing a kiss to the base of my throat, at the hollow of my collarbones. Then he lifted up again so he could look me in the eyes.

I nodded again. "Yes," I told him, breathless.

His hands tightened around my wrists. "Yes, what?"

I groaned, my eyes practically rolling back in my head at the gravelly command of his voice. "Yes, sir."

He smiled and a fierce pleasure stole through me. He dropped his head to the side of my jaw, tracing his mouth along it until he reached my ear. "I demand that you allow me to pleasure you," he whispered, taking the lobe between his teeth.

I couldn't help it—I ground my hips against his ass again. "Yes, sir."

His lips trailed up to my temple, brushing against my eyelids as soft as breath. "I demand that you let me worship you."

I arched, wanting to feel more of him against me. Needing more of him. "Yes... *sir*."

He took my other earlobe in his mouth, running his hot tongue across the sensitive flesh. "I demand more. I demand everything."

His words set me on fire from the inside out. I was having a hard time remembering what I was supposed to say. "Yes, it's yours," I told him through gasping breaths.

He pulled back slightly, putting a sliver of space between us, and the absence of his heat and weight against me seemed almost cruel. I wanted to reach for him, to pull him back against me again, but he kept my hands pinned over my head. He cocked an expectant eyebrow, waiting.

Oh, right. "Yes, sir," I amended with a grin.

But he didn't allow himself to fall back against me. Instead he held himself like that, hovering just above me. He released my wrists, bringing his fingers to brush against my temple, whisper down my cheek. "I demand that you let me love you, Conor Newell. Forever."

My heart swelled so large I wasn't sure I would ever be able to breathe around it, much less speak. "On one condition," I told him.

He quirked an eyebrow at the unexpected response.

Smiling, I reached up, tangling my fingers through his hair and pulling him toward me so that his lips were little more than a breath away. "You let me love you forever as well."

EPILOGUE

WELLS - THE FOLLOWING SUMMER

"Babe, it's fine. Crystal doesn't need you hovering. She can handle the shop while we're gone. Plus, your mom and Bill are waiting for us at the festival."

I walked up behind Conor and slid my arms around his waist, pressing a kiss to the back of his neck. He tilted his head to the side to give me better access when I noticed Crystal mouth the words *thank you* to me from where she was cleaning up stock in one of the board game aisles.

"That's not it. I'm finishing up a few notes for Roya about the foundation. One of Bill's old law partners knows a woman who needs help paying for her treatment. I just want to make a note of her contact information so Roya can get in touch."

I waved goodbye to Crystal with a wink and steered Conor out the shop entrance to the storefront right beside it. The crisp, clean sign above the door still caught my eye every time I saw it. Conor himself had designed the logo and branding for the Newell Foundation, and on the redbrick building next to it was the familiar logo of Grange BioMed. We now owned half the block between Broad River Board Games, Hold Your Piece, the foundation, and Grange. Liz teased Conor all the time by saying she had a "real estate baron" for a son.

Conor continued scribbling furiously on his notepad.

"Con, she'll be at Downtown After 5—you're going to see her in like five minutes."

He waved a hand. "I know, but I didn't want her to have to worry about keeping track of it. Just give me a sec."

I opened the door and nudged him into the cool, quiet office. Everyone had already left for the day, most of them heading to the music festival Asheville held downtown every third Friday of the month. It was where we were supposed to be as well if Conor would tear himself away from work for the weekend.

But as I watched him rest his notepad on the high counter of the reception desk and continue scribbling, I couldn't get that mad. After all, the Newell Foundation was a passion of his, and he loved it dearly. Eventually it would be able to run itself without too much direct involvement from him or his mother, but while it was getting started Conor sunk as much of his extra time into it as possible.

Well, except for the time he spent with me. Which was a considerable amount seeing as how we lived together and worked next door to each other.

I glanced out the glass doors at the crowds making their way toward the festival. "What are the odds James and his man leave the hotel long enough to join us?"

Conor snorted but didn't say anything more.

"Think they'd be down for a foursome? Ever since we invited them hiking I've been imagining—"

Conor dropped his pen and slapped his hand over my mouth. I grinned and pressed a kiss against his palm. "I guess you were paying attention after all."

"I was," he said, grabbing his pen again. "Just give me one more second."

I glanced at the notepad, assured myself that all the relevant information was there, and then took it out of his hands and chucked it in front of Roya's monitor. Then I grabbed my man and slung him over my shoulders.

"You are so getting your ass reddened this weekend. And if we pick the right campsite tomorrow, no one will be able to hear you screaming for more," I warned, smacking his tight butt over his shorts.

I felt his dick jerk against my shoulder and laughed. He was so predictable, and it never got old.

"Don't make promises your hand can't keep," Conor grumbled from the area of my ass. His arms had gone around my waist to help keep him from falling, and I noticed one sneak its way under the waistband of my own shorts.

"Oh, I can keep my promises," I told him. "You know that better than anyone."

He found his way into my boxers and groaned appreciatively when he realized how hard I already was for him.

"Let's have a quickie in your office like last time," he suggested, his voice filled with mischief.

As tempted as I was to turn and take us deeper into the building, I forced myself to continue toward the door, pushing out into the warm summer evening. "Nope. Your mom's waiting for us, and after we were late to your birthday dinner because *somebody* lost the key to the handcuffs, I'm not inclined for a repeat."

His cool hand slid over my hip to the bare skin of my ass and toyed lightly in the crease. "You sure about that? We don't have to use cuffs. In fact—"

I smacked his ass again. "Behave. If you want to fuck me later tonight, that's fine. You know I'm happy to bottom for you."

He went quiet for a minute, and I was sure he was debating whether he wanted the pleasure of fucking me, which he enjoyed on occasion, or his usual preference for having me take him and own his body completely.

"Uhhh," he finally answered. "Can we do both? Or..."

I set him down so I could lock the office door. "Or?"

And my sweetheart suddenly blushed to the tips of his ears. "Or, could maybe I ride—*oof!*"

I clapped a hand over his mouth as soon as I spotted his mom and her neighbor Bill turn the corner right in front of us. "Ponies!" I blurted. "Hi, guys. Conor wanted to know if there were pony rides at the festival." I pulled Conor's face into my chest and wrapped my arms around him to hide his mortification.

Liz wrinkled her brow. "I think you're confusing Downtown After 5 with Saturday Night Lights, honey. I'm pretty sure there won't be pony rides tonight. But they do have dancing. We were just coming by to show you where our crew is sitting."

I stepped away from Conor long enough to kiss Liz on the cheek and shake Bill's hand.

"You all set for your camping trip tomorrow?" Bill asked as we made our way up the street in the direction of the music.

"Yes, but still no word from James about whether they plan to join us," Conor huffed. "I still don't get why he'd fly all the way here just to spend the weekend in a hotel room."

"Really?" I asked him, reaching for his hand and giving it a squeeze. "You can't think of *any* reason?"

He swatted at me.

I took his fingers and brought them to my lips. "Like I said, hon, there's no way he's joining us. I'm not sure James is the outdoor type. When he met us at Comic-Con last month, I swear he even got itchy when he stood too close to Groot."

Conor's eyes got big. "Did you just make a correct Marvel reference? Oh my god. You leveled up."

Liz snorted. "So proud of you, Wells. You'll be full geek by Christmas."

When she almost lost her step over the edge of a curb, Bill quickly reached out to steady her with an arm around her waist. Once she regained her footing, he kept his arm there.

I met Conor's eye and raised a brow. Thankfully, Conor was smiling. I knew he respected and appreciated Bill, and he seemed happy that the two of them might have something special going on.

When we reached the festival, we wove our way through the crowd to join our group of friends sitting at a big round table by the dance floor. Everyone cheered our arrival and handed us drinks they'd been saving. Roya was there, along with Conor's employees from the shop and two of my coworkers from the foundation. A few minutes after we sat down, our new neighbors John and Andros waved to us from one of the drink stalls. We gestured for them to join us so we could introduce them around.

As I sat and watched Conor chat animatedly with the incredible community we called home, I thought about how much richer my life was. I remembered Saturday afternoons this time last year. I would work in the office by myself until it was time to take a long run in the park and get dinner. Then I'd most likely work some more from home.

Now, my Saturdays were filled with fun and family. Conor and I would sleep in and make a lazy breakfast or walk to a nearby bagel shop. Then we'd go for a hike or a long drive down the Blue Ridge Parkway before making our way back to grill something over at Liz's house. Usually, her big backyard would be full of her old students or other faculty friends from the university. When she was having a bad day, we'd have the party at our house or do all of the work for her at hers. But she loved the company, even on her weaker days.

Thankfully the treatments had resulted in far fewer weak days, which put a light in Conor's face I hadn't seen there before. Our foundation funneled as much money as possible into research for the disease, and we all had high hopes it would help make a difference. In the meantime, she was already pestering us to make our relationship official and start a family. While both of us wanted kids one day, we were in no hurry. And since the doctors were optimistic about Liz's prognosis, we had time to enjoy our lives together before adding another family member.

Conor loved going to work every day at his printshop, and I felt the same about my work at the foundation. Most of the Grange business was managed smoothly by Deb and my management team, and I was able to handle the rest of it just fine thanks to the great people we'd hired at the foundation.

I smiled, enjoying the moment surrounded by so much love and support, content for the first time in my life.

Conor leaned over and put his head on my shoulder. "What're you cogitating about so hard over there?"

I turned and placed a kiss on his head. "What a difference a year makes, yeah?"

He snuggled against me. "I think you mean what a difference love makes." Before I could respond, he suddenly sat up and gasped. "Oh my god, I can't believe I forgot to tell you!" he said, grabbing my arm. "Scotty is coming to visit and then going to Dragon Con with us."

Roya leaned over and deposited her leftover curly fries in front of Conor. "Who's Scotty?"

Conor grinned. "Remember the story in the news a few months ago about the carriage driver from New York and I told you the guy was a friend of mine?"

"Wait, the crazy story—with the cop and the high-speed carriage chase?"

Conor nodded with a grin. It was a great story and still managed to make him chuckle. "That's the one. Scotty the carriage driver. You'll meet him. He's a good guy."

I thought back to the young man who'd been so chatty with Conor. A streak of latent jealousy shot through me, despite knowing Scotty was zero threat to my relationship. "You mean the one who wouldn't stop flirting with you?"

He rolled his eyes. "No, I mean the one who seemed interested in dating your ex-boyfriend Oscar."

Now it was Conor's turn to sound a tiny bit jealous. I pressed a kiss to his nose. "Oscar was never my boyfriend," I corrected him.

He waved a hand. "Close enough."

"And besides," I added, "don't forget that James dated him as well. In fact, I think that's who he was with when he met Richard."

Conor tilted his head to the side, thinking. "So you dated Oscar, and then broke up with him and fell in love with me. And James dated Oscar, and now he's madly in love as well."

"As evidenced by his reluctance to leave the hotel room," I pointed out.

"Exactly. He's a good-luck charm of sorts."

I ran my thumb over his knuckles, before bringing them to my lips, enjoying the shiver that passed through him. "You're such a romantic."

Conor's eyes twinkled and he leaned forward to give me a lingering kiss. "Romantic for believing your ex had something to do with bringing us together?"

I threaded a hand into his hair, cupping the back of his neck and pressing my forehead to his. "If he's the reason I ended up with you, then he's the best thing that ever happened to me."

Liz let out a dramatic sigh. "Cut out the kissyface nonsense, or I'll regret slipping that phone number into your coat pocket."

"What phone number?" Conor asked with a smile, pulling away from me but clasping my hand to make up for it.

"Wells's cell number. The one I gave you before that first New York trip."

It took a second for her words to process, but then Conor and I both whipped our heads around to stare at her. "Mom!" Conor gasped. "What the hell are you talking about?"

She rolled her eyes while Bill started laughing. "Honey, you were so nervous to take my place in the negotiations. 'Mom, what if I forget how the printer works?' 'Mom, what if the hotel lost my reservation?' 'Did you write down the address for the office?' Conor, I told you if all else fails, call Mr. Grange himself. And then I gave you his number. You almost left it on the kitchen counter for goodness' sake. Don't you remember?"

The look on Conor's face was hilarious. "Mom, *no*. I do *not* remember that. Not at all."

I felt the same shock evident on his face. He and I had wondered for ages how he'd gotten the wrong number that night. It had become a running joke between the two of us.

Liz waved a hand like it was nothing but added a wink. "Well. All's well that ends well. Right, Wells?"

I looked at Conor's incredulous, beautiful face.

And felt like maybe, just maybe, I owed Dr. Elizabeth Newell another foundation.

Before I could agree with her, Conor threw himself in my arms again and most definitely did *not* cut out the kissyface nonsense.

Want more After Oscar love? Hop right into Scotty's story in *LOL: Laugh Out Loud* available now on Amazon!

LETTER FROM LUCY & MOLLY

Dear Reader,

Thank you so much for reading *IRL: In Real Life*, book one in the brand new "After Oscar" series! We would love it if you would take a few minutes to review this book on Amazon. Reader reviews really do make a difference and we appreciate every single one of them.

Lucy and Molly are pen names of a real pair of sisters who are excited to collaborate on our first ever joint project. While Molly has been a full-time author for a decade, this is her debut novel in the gay romance genre.

There are five stories planned in the After Oscar series, so please stay tuned. Up next is the story of what happens when a cop hops into Scotty's horse carriage and yells *Go!* What happens next will hopefully have you *Laughing Out Loud. LOL is available now on Amazon.*

Be sure to follow us on Amazon to be notified of new releases, and look for us on Facebook for sneak peeks of upcoming stories.

Feel free to sign up for our newsletters, stop by www.LucyLennox.com, www.MollyMaddox.com, or visit Lucy's Lair on Facebook to stay in touch.

To see fun inspiration photos for this book, check out the Pinterest page for IRL.

Happy reading!

Lucy & Molly

ABOUT MOLLY MADDOX

Molly Maddox is the romance pen name for a New York Times bestselling author who started writing at an early age because her older sister, Lucy Lennox, was a writer and Molly wanted to be like Lucy in all ways (she still does).

When she's not writing, Molly likes to cook, read, take pictures of her dog and cat cuddling, and finds an odd satisfaction in folding sheets so that the top sheet is indistinguishable from the bottom sheet.

She loves all things romance and is grateful every day she gets to write for a living.

Connect with Molly on social media:
www.MollyMaddox.com
AuthorMollyMaddox@gmail.com

ALSO BY MOLLY MADDOX

After Oscar Series (with Lucy Lennox):

IRL: In Real Life

LOL: Laugh Out Loud

BTW: By The Way

Also be sure to check out audio versions here.

ABOUT LUCY LENNOX

Lucy Lennox is the creator of the bestselling Made Marian series, the Forever Wilde series, and co-creator of the Twist of Fate Series with Sloane Kennedy and the After Oscar series with Molly Maddox. Born and raised in the southeast, she is finally putting good use to that English Lit degree.

Lucy enjoys naps, pizza, and procrastinating. She is married to someone who is better at math than romance but who makes her laugh every single day and is the best dancer in the history of ever.

She stays up way too late each night reading M/M romance because that stuff is impossible to put down.

For more information and to stay updated about future releases, please sign up for Lucy's author newsletter on her website.

Connect with Lucy on social media:
www.LucyLennox.com
Lucy@LucyLennox.com

ALSO BY LUCY LENNOX

Made Marian Series:
  Borrowing Blue
  Taming Teddy
  Jumping Jude
  Grounding Griffin
  Moving Maverick
  Delivering Dante
  A Very Marian Christmas
  Made Marian Shorts
  Made Mine - Crossover with Sloane Kennedy's Protectors series
  Hay: A Made Marian Short
  Made Marian Mixtape

FOREVER WILDE SERIES:
  Facing West
  Felix and the Prince
  Wilde Fire
  Hudson's Luck
  Flirt: A Forever Wilde Short

His Saint
Wilde Love
King Me

Twist of Fate Series (with Sloane Kennedy):
Lost and Found
Safe and Sound
Body and Soul
Above and Beyond

After Oscar Series (with Molly Maddox):
IRL: In Real Life
LOL: Laugh Out Loud
BTW: By The Way

Standalones:
Hot Ride (short story)
Inn Love (novella)
Virgin Flyer (novel)

Free Short Stories available at www.LucyLennox.com.

Also be sure to check out audio versions on iTunes, Amazon, or Audible here.

Made in the USA
Monee, IL
30 October 2020